ALONE

Praise for Simon Kernick

'Simon Kernick writes with his foot pressed hard on
the pedal. Hang on tight!'
Harlan Coben

'More twists and turns than a boa-constrictor on speed'
The Times

'A potent cocktail of thrills'
Guardian

'Keeps the action breakneck'
Time Out

'Doesn't let up till the very last'
Daily Mirror

'Thrilling and twisty, it never lets up'
Daily Mail

'Breathless'
Sunday Times

'An addictive thriller full of gritty details and fast
frenetic action'
Sunday Mirror

Also available by Simon Kernick

Simon Kernick

DIE ALONE

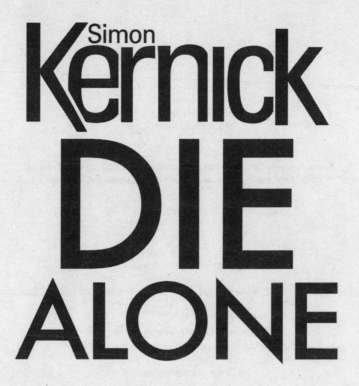

arrow books

1 3 5 7 9 10 8 6 4 2

Arrow Books
20 Vauxhall Bridge Road
London SW1V 2SA

Arrow Books is part of the Penguin Random House group of companies
whose addresses can be found at global.penguinrandomhouse.com.

Copyright © Simon Kernick 2019

Simon Kernick has asserted his right to be identified as the author of this Work in
accordance with the Copyright, Designs and Patents Act 1988.

First published in Great Britain by Century in 2019
First published in paperback by Arrow Books in 2020

www.penguin.co.uk

A CIP catalogue record for this book is available from the British Library.

ISBN 9781784752309

Typeset in 11.04/16.2 pt Times New Roman
by Integra Software Services Pvt. Ltd, Pondicherry

Printed and bound in Great Britain by Clays Ltd, Elcograf S.p.A.

DIE
ALONE

Prologue

Hugh Manning awoke from his dream screaming into the silence.

His eyes shot open. He couldn't breathe, his scream suddenly a muffled whine. Panic shot through him as he realized there was a hand covering his mouth and nose. He tried to struggle in the darkness and then a face he recognized loomed into view, leaning in close to him.

'Don't speak. Don't breathe. Stay absolutely still,' hissed DC Liane Patrick.

Manning knew instantly that his enemies were here for him. Deep down, he'd always known they'd come. In the end, they were simply too powerful, and had too much to lose ever to let him tell the world what he knew. What terrified him so much now, though, was the speed with which it had happened. He'd barely been in the police safehouse three days, had yet to be officially questioned by officers from the National Crime Agency, and already his cover was blown.

'Get up very quietly, and do everything I say,' continued Patrick.

Manning nodded. He was dressed in a sweatshirt and tracksuit bottoms. They'd told him to wear clothes in bed, just in case he had to be moved fast. His babysitters, DC Patrick and her colleague DC Lomu, were both hard and professional, and, most importantly, armed the whole time. There were always at least two other armed officers on duty as well, one at the back of the house, one at the front, and security cameras covered every floor, as well as the perimeter. These were administered 24/7 by staff at the headquarters of the National Crime Agency, supposedly Britain's answer to the FBI.

And yet, it seemed that somehow the defences had been breached.

Patrick removed her gloved hand from Manning's mouth and stepped away to give him room to get out of the bed. He moved as silently as he could, noticing that she had her gun drawn and was looking towards the bedroom door, as if someone might come through it at any moment. But there was no noise in the house. Nothing.

Outside, somewhere in the night, an owl hooted in the woods. Manning looked at his watch. 3.10 a.m.

He pulled on the pair of trainers next to the bed and stood up quickly.

Patrick put a hand on his shoulder and came in close. 'There's someone in the house,' she whispered, her voice barely audible in the silence. 'We need to get you out of here. Do everything I say, and you'll be fine. Understood?'

'Where are the others?' Manning hissed, feeling his heart hammering in his chest.

There was a pause. 'I don't know. No more speaking. Follow me.'

Why weren't the alarms going off? Manning wondered. And why was there no sound of sirens? Apparently, there were also sensors lining the perimeter that would pick up any sign of an intruder and automatically set off alarms in the house, as well as at NCA HQ, and Northampton police station, five miles away, where a dedicated armed response unit was on call.

But he knew better than to ask any more questions. He trusted DC Patrick. She'd given him her full background when she'd first arrived. Five years in military intelligence, followed by ten years' service in the police, seven of them as an armed protection officer. She had three commendations for bravery, was a champion sharp shooter, and even had a karate black belt. If anyone was going to get him out of here, it was her.

Manning's bedroom was at the top of the house. The window had been boarded up to prevent entry from the outside. It made the room stuffy on a warm summer night. It also meant you couldn't go out that way. Instead, they would have to take the official escape route, which meant going outside into the hallway.

DC Patrick crept over to the door, put her ear to it, then very slowly turned the handle, motioning for him to get behind her.

Manning pressed himself against the wall, his heart continuing to pound as DC Patrick pulled the door open and put her head round it. It was hard to believe that once again his life was in danger. For years, he'd lived the upper-middle-class dream. A beautiful Georgian townhouse in fashionable Bayswater; long-haul holidays with first-class flights and boutique hotels; a loyal wife and plenty of girlfriends. He might have been doing work for some extremely insalubrious characters, but it had been easy enough to justify it to himself while sipping a pina colada on a beach in the Seychelles, and anyway, he'd just been providing a service, and as long as he didn't think about it too much, everything would be all right.

Except it hadn't been, because a few weeks ago it had all gone very, very wrong. His wife was now dead. He'd almost died himself. And now it looked like his enemies might finish the job and silence him before he could talk to the police and bring them down.

DC Patrick turned to him, put a finger to her lips and crept quietly out into the hallway, gesturing for Manning to follow.

It was dark and silent out there, with just the faint glow of the landing light on the floor below coming up the stairs.

That was when Manning heard it. A scraping sound followed by a low animal moan, coming from DC Lomu's bedroom next door. And then words that chilled his bones.

'Help me ...'

DC Patrick heard it too, and even in the gloom, Manning could see the pain on her face. He knew that she and Lomu got on well, and Lomu had told him that they'd worked together for several years.

4

Manning looked towards Lomu's bedroom door, knowing they couldn't leave him there. Lomu was whimpering now, and the sound made Manning nauseous. It was awful to think of a big strong guy like him sounding so helpless.

Manning turned towards Patrick, his expression imploring her to do something, but she shook her head emphatically, mouthing the word 'sorry', then steered him away.

As he looked back over his shoulder, expecting at any moment the killer to come into view at the top of the stairs, a thought nagged him. Surely the killer must have already been up here. So how had he missed him the first time? His door locked from the inside, although both DCs had keys, so it was possible that the killer had tried the door and couldn't get in, in which case he would be waiting somewhere close by in ambush. Except there was no obvious place to hide.

So where the hell was he?

The hallway came to a dead end at what looked like a blank wall, but when Patrick moved in front of Manning and pushed her palm hard against the surface at waist height, a door in the panel slid quietly open. They'd rehearsed going out this way every day since he'd got here, and Manning recalled that each time, either DC Lomu or Patrick would reassure him that the chances of them ever having to use it were next to nothing. And Manning had almost convinced himself that they were right. Now Patrick pushed him inside, following close behind, and, as the door closed behind her, a set of overhead lights came on, revealing a curving flight of steps that wound all the way to the ground floor.

They moved downstairs quickly, coming to another door that led directly into a storage shed at the side of the house. Patrick moved in front of him and opened the door and the two of them crept inside. A single window at head height looked out over the back garden and Patrick peered through it before turning to him in the darkness.

'It looks clear out there. Are you ready?'

'Why's no one coming?' he whispered. 'If someone's broken in and done ... done that to DC Lomu, then why aren't the alarms going off? And where are the other guards?'

Patrick looked at him, her face silhouetted in the pale moonlight so he was unable to read her expression. 'I don't know,' she whispered, sounding scared. 'All I know is we're on our own, and we've got to get as far away as possible.'

'Isn't it best just to stay put? Wait for help? You could call for help on your mobile.' Manning felt safer inside the house than outside it.

'It's not working,' she said, without checking it.

'What do you mean it's not working? You said we had reception.'

'We've lost it. Someone's jamming it somehow. Just like they've managed to disconnect the alarm.'

'Jesus,' hissed Manning, shaking his head. He wanted to rant and rave about the incompetence of those charged with protecting him, but it was way too late for that. Right now, all he cared about was staying alive. 'What are we going to do about DC Lomu?' he asked.

'As soon as we're away from here, I'll call for help. But we've got to move, Hugh. OK?' She grabbed him by the arm, and for the first time he could see the fear in her eyes. She was just as scared as he was.

He nodded weakly and followed her as she unbolted the shed door and stepped out into the night.

The silence was oppressive as they moved slowly through the garden, keeping tight to the fence. The lawn was perfectly manicured and bordered by flowering shrubs that provided basic cover but, even so, Manning felt terribly exposed. Someone might be watching them from the house right now, aiming a gun at him, ready to pull the trigger. He didn't dare look back, but just kept going, each step seeming to last far too long. He vowed that if he ever got out of this then he wasn't going to say another word to the police, whatever the consequences. They could build their case without him – even though he knew that without him, there was no case. And that was the problem. Whichever way he cared to look at it – and he'd looked at it plenty of different ways these past few days – his life was ruined.

It was when he and Liane Patrick came to the high, ivy-covered wall at the end of the garden that they both saw the black-clad figure lying on the grass next to the back gate. Manning immediately recognized the body as one of the armed officers whose job it was to secure the perimeters. The machine gun the officer usually carried was nowhere to be seen.

Patrick stopped dead and crouched down, and Manning followed suit. She held that position for what felt like a long time, then looked round and listened.

The silence was all-consuming.

'Follow me,' she whispered, and they hurried over to the back gate. The gate itself was made of heavy oak and could only be opened from the inside by punching a four-digit code onto a keypad. The house and garden were near enough impregnable. The wall was twelve feet high and topped with a thick thatch of tangled ivy. Anyone climbing into the garden, even if they didn't set off the alarm, would have made a lot of noise and been spotted by the officer on the ground, the man who was now dead.

So how did the killer get in?

Patrick punched in the code and flung open the gate, immediately taking up a firing stance in case there was anyone on the other side.

But there was no one. The narrow footpath that ran across the back of the property was empty. Rather than turn and head back to the main road, Patrick climbed over a stile opposite and ran through the empty paddock on the other side of the road towards a small stable building about thirty yards away. Manning ran after her, watching as she pulled out her phone and checked it, still holding her service pistol.

'Have you got a signal?' he asked, struggling to get alongside her.

She was punching something into the phone, ignoring him. It was clear she was sending a text.

'Give me a moment,' she hissed, shoving the phone back into her pocket.

By this time they'd passed through a gate into the deserted yard in front of the stable block.

'What the fuck's going on?' Manning demanded, experiencing a growing sense of dread. 'Tell me.'

And then, in the next second, he got his answer as a masked figure stepped out from behind the stable block, only a few yards in front of them, holding a pistol with a suppressor attached.

Manning stopped dead. Patrick still had her own gun in her hand and he expected her to fire.

But she didn't. Instead, she stopped too, keeping her gun lowered.

Manning swallowed and his legs felt weak. He'd run straight into a trap. He turned to DC Patrick. 'Why?'

But Liane Patrick was ignoring him. 'Is my son safe?' she asked the gunman. 'I need proof. Right now.'

'He's unharmed,' said the gunman. Except it wasn't a man. It was a woman, and she had an accent. Was it South African? 'He's sleeping like a baby.'

'Prove it. Now. Or I'll kill you.' Patrick raised the gun.

'Here,' the woman said, reaching into the pocket of her jeans and pulling out a phone. 'Call him.'

She threw the phone to Patrick, who caught it one-handed. In that same moment, the masked woman shot her twice in the face, the bullets making a popping sound as they left the gun.

Both the phone and Patrick's own gun clattered onto the cobblestones. She stumbled, made a noise like a sigh, and then fell to her knees.

The masked woman stepped forward and shot her a third time, then turned the gun on Manning. So, that was how they'd got to her, he thought. By using her son as collateral. It was typical of them. Find a weakness. Exploit it. Then clean up the mess.

And he was the final bit of that mess. Remove him from the equation and their problems went away.

He looked imploringly at the gunwoman. Her eyes were dark and hard behind the mask. 'Please don't do this,' he said, knowing that his words wouldn't change a thing, but knowing too that this was his last shot of the dice. He'd been on the wrong end of a gun twice in the last ten days. On the first occasion, they'd killed his wife. But he'd escaped. That wasn't going to happen this time. His luck had run out. He knew it.

The sheer, wrenching terror he'd felt last time was gone. Now he was filled with a deep resignation and regret that his life had turned out this way. At least this time it would be quick. DC Patrick was already dead. Soon he would be too. And yet, in those last few seconds, time seemed to slow right down, stretching out interminably as the woman in the mask kept her gun trained on him.

Beside him, he could see DC Patrick's blood pooling on the cobblestones, the sight making him want to retch. He took a deep breath, and in a final act of defiance said, 'Tell Alastair Sheridan, I hope he rots—'

But he never finished the sentence as the woman in the mask pulled the trigger and ended another life.

As the first sirens started somewhere on the horizon, she turned and melted away into the darkness.

Part One

A Year Later

1

One of the saddest stories I ever heard took place on a sunny summer's day in 1989. A thirteen-year-old girl called Dana Brennan had planned to bake cakes with her mother and younger sister, but they were short of ingredients. The family lived in a cottage in an especially pretty part of north Hampshire, less than a mile outside Frampton, one of those bucolic picture-postcard English villages with a church, a pub and, in those days, a shop. Traffic was quieter then, and when Dana offered to cycle to the shop to buy the ingredients, her mum had been happy to let her go.

Dana cycled away and never came back. Her bike was found abandoned next to some trees at the side of the road, with the shopping bag containing the cake-making ingredients lying a few feet away. A huge police search for her was launched that same evening. But the spot where her bike had been found was on a quiet back road and, aside from the shopkeeper who'd sold her the produce, no one else had seen her on her journey. It was as if she'd disappeared off the face of the earth.

What followed was one of the biggest investigations in British policing history, assisted by blanket media coverage. Every sex offender within a twenty-mile radius was picked up and questioned, but to no avail. There were no obvious suspects, no witnesses and no body. No reliable sighting of Dana was ever reported, and no trace of her was found. Eventually the investigation had been wound down and, finally, closed altogether, while the media moved on to other stories with more likelihood of an ending.

And then, nearly three decades later, Dana's remains were unearthed in a small patch of woodland close to the River Thames, which had once been part of the grounds of a private boarding school but which had since been sold off for development. The remains of a second body, that of a young woman called Kitty Sinn who'd gone missing in 1990, were discovered nearby, and suddenly the case was open again.

I'd been twelve years old when Dana had gone missing, a year younger than she was. And yet it was her murder that had destroyed my own life and meant that I'd ended up in here, awaiting trial for double murder, having already survived two attempts on my life in the past year, and knowing that another one could be coming at any moment.

Like now.

It had been going for hours. A slow-motion riot, steadily gathering pace. Getting closer and closer.

Let me tell you one thing. There's nothing much worse than being trapped in the Vulnerable Prisoners wing of a huge Category A prison while all around you the other wings burn as the prisoners seize control of it from an outgunned and outnumbered staff. I've been in some very bad situations in my life, and have come close to death on more occasions than I'd like to admit, but I had an especially bad feeling about this one.

The VP wing is the worst, most claustrophobic place to be in any prison. It contains the lowest of the low in the prison hierarchy. The rapists and the child molesters; the informants who've either betrayed or are about to betray their criminal brethren; and then, of course, men like me – former police officers. We were supposedly safe here, although I could testify to the fact that there was no such thing as safety in a prison when there was a price on your head as large as the one on mine. And the atmosphere in here now was the tensest I'd known it in the year I'd been here.

It had all begun just after six p.m., during recreation time when the cell doors are unlocked and the inmates have the freedom of the wing. The alarms had gone off. There'd been four guards on duty in our wing at the time and they'd disappeared en masse, almost without a word, locking the single exit door behind them. That had been more than three hours ago now and none of them had come back, which was pretty much unheard of. We were on our own in here, and what made it worse was that we could see everything that was happening on TV. Every cell had one, and there were a further two, with wide screens, in the main communal area. Prison life might be claustrophobic but it wasn't without its comforts.

I was standing on the first-floor balcony while my cell mate Luke, a thin, nervous twenty-five-year-old with bad skin, gave me a running commentary on what was happening from inside our cell. And it was bad. The inmates had completely taken over two of the other wings, and on B wing they'd taken three guards hostage.

The speed and scale of the riot was a shock, but the fact that it had happened wasn't. This prison was built to hold twelve hundred and now it housed two thousand. According to a report I'd read, there was also a 30 per cent shortage in staff. Add to that a heatwave that had sent temperatures soaring in recent days, as well as riots in two other prisons in the past week, and it made for a combustible mix.

'The Tornado Teams are coming in,' called out Luke, referring to the specialist squads of officers deployed whenever there was a major prison disturbance. 'Hundreds of 'em. And riot police too,' he added, sounding mightily relieved at the prospect of the outbreak soon being brought under control. But then he would do. This was his first time in prison, and he was on remand for unspecified sexual offences. I didn't want to know the details, but I was pretty certain it involved a minor, which just made me feel sick. He'd always claimed he was innocent but I didn't believe it. I doubted anyone in here was, and that included me. I knew too that if the other prisoners got in here, they weren't going to be spending too long establishing guilt or innocence. They'd tear the place apart and everyone in it.

I was glad the Tornado Teams were coming but they were going to have to move fast. Even over the sound of the alarms coming from the other wings, I could hear the rampaging mob. They made a kind of ecstatic howling noise. It was the pure joy of destruction and violence. The release of all the frustrations that build up when you're locked away for years on end, unloved and forgotten by everyone outside. It was a rage against their powerlessness.

I knew that feeling. I had it every day in here.

The problem was that there was no way out for these prisoners. The first thing the staff always do is secure the perimeters, lock all the outside gates, so that no one can get out and everything can be contained away from the public eye. Which meant their violence was going to be directed at something else. I'd been hoping it would be against property, or even the staff. But now I knew they were coming for us.

They were getting closer. I could hear them. Inside the walkway that separated us from the rest of the prison. They must have stolen keys.

Which meant there was nothing between them and us.

Everyone else in here knew it too. Some of the inmates were grouped round the two full-sized pool tables in the centre of the wing, talking quietly in frightened huddles. I recognized almost all of them. There was the grossly fat Roger Munn, who raped and murdered his stepdaughter, then cut up her body and hid it in the loft where, incredibly, the police missed it twice during their searches. He was slouched on the sofa in his wifebeater vest, watching the news footage of raging flames on the big-screen TV. Then there was Ricardo Webster, the night caller, who liked to rape old ladies in their homes, and who was now standing watching the doors, armed with a pool cue, while a group of prisoners huddled behind him for protection.

And there, standing at the back of the communal area, partially hidden behind a larger group so he wouldn't get spotted if someone came through the door, was the worst of them all. Wallace Burke, the infamous child killer, who'd abducted and murdered two ten-year-old boys more than twenty years ago and who was also suspected of at least two similar murders, for which there'd never been enough evidence to prosecute.

These were the lowlifes I now lived with. Men who I'd gladly put in the ground myself. As a former soldier and police officer I was a long way above them, but I had a feeling that this wasn't going to help me. Because I was a bigger target than anyone in here.

The bounty on my head was half a million pounds. Now, half a million isn't much use to you when you're in jail, but most of these guys were planning to get out at some point, and even if that wasn't a possibility, that amount of money can do a hell of a lot to help a family on the outside. And it wasn't just the prisoners I had to watch either, it was the guards. As a general rule they were honest and hard-working but, even so, the average prison officer's wage is £27,000 per year, and that's before the taxman gets his hands on it, so it was a big temptation for them too.

All of which meant I had to watch my back. A month after I got here, I found ground glass in my food. A month after that, my cell mate at the time, a bent cop called Pryce who was on remand, put smuggled sleeping pills in my water and tried to smother me in my sleep with a pillow. I'd liked him too. He was good fun to be around with a raconteur's love of tales. Unfortunately for him, he'd got the dose wrong, and I'd only drunk half the water, so I woke up and broke his arm, and after that he'd been transferred.

From then on I was constantly alert. I was in the gym every day for my allotted hour. I did weights. I did cardio. I practised my self-defence moves. Right now, I was as fit as I'd been in a long time.

But even so, I'll be honest, I was scared. I could almost smell the closeness of the mob.

Then I heard it. An unintelligible howl just beyond the reinforced door – and a couple of seconds later it flew open and two guards rushed inside. One was bleeding from the head, but they were moving fast. As I watched, they tried to shut the door only for it to be forced open from the other side, and they were flung to one side as a crowd of screaming and yelling prisoners streamed in.

I stepped back inside the cell, watching the vulnerable prisoners scatter in all directions as the invading inmates ran among them, throwing punches and howling insults. Meanwhile a separate group, their faces masked, ran into the nearest cell, grabbed hold of its occupant – Fanning, who'd killed his own baby – and dragged him outside. It looked like they were interrogating him.

A second later, I saw him turn and point up towards my cell.

So they had come for me.

'What's going on?' asked Luke, in a whimpering voice. 'What are they doing?' He was crouched in a foetal position in the far corner of the cell, shaking like a leaf.

'Stay put and you'll be OK,' I said, watching as the masked group, close to a dozen strong, turned as one in my direction.

Another alarm had gone off now, this time in the wing itself, and it would now be clear to the authorities that lives were in imminent danger. But there was still no sign of the cavalry and, even if they'd already entered the prison, it was going to take them a few minutes at least to get here. And I didn't have a few minutes, because already the group – their faces covered with a mixture of scarves and rags, several of them carrying makeshift weapons – were racing up the steps towards the first floor, and my cell.

A primal fear rose up from somewhere in my gut. Like I said, I've been in frightening positions before. I've faced down guns, both as a soldier and a police officer, and I've even been caught up in a full-scale street riot, with hundreds of people baying for my blood, but at least then I'd always had colleagues not far away. Here, I was on my own, and trapped. The only two guards who could have helped me were backed up in a corner surrounded by jeering inmates, several of whom were throwing missiles at them.

I made a fast decision. There was no point trying to hide in the cell. I'd be finished. I had to go out and meet them.

The group coming up the steps caught sight of me as I came out onto the landing. One of them howled my name like some kind of mocking battle cry.

'May-suun!'

One thing I've learned is that, channelled correctly, fear is good. It concentrates the mind, makes you physically stronger, and gives you new reserves of energy. The key is not to let it overcome you.

Pulsing with adrenalin, I ran to the top of the steps. The masked gang could only come up one at a time and the front guy was wielding a bloodied chair leg so, putting a hand on each of the rails, I launched a snap-kick at him as he came into range, putting all my force into it.

The kick was a good one. It caught him full in the chest before he could strike me with the chair leg, and he fell backwards into the guy behind him, dropping his weapon in the process.

But the guy behind pushed him out of the way and kept coming. He was ripped, hard, and a lot younger than me. Worse, he was carrying a homemade shiv with a short but wicked-looking blade, which was already bloodied. His face was partially concealed behind a mask made from a torn shirtsleeve but I could see the thick black beard poking up above it, the short curly hair and the dark eyes and, though we'd never met, I recognized him as a convicted gangland thug called Troy Ramone who was serving a life sentence for the murder of two rivals, one of whom he'd burned alive. I've got a good memory for killers, even ones I haven't put away myself, and Ramone was one of the worst. He was serving a minimum term of at least thirty-five years, and he hadn't been in here that long, so he had very little to lose if he killed a third time, and a lot to gain in terms of prestige and power.

I launched another kick as he came into range, but he was expecting it and retreated a step, so my foot fell short. He then threw himself at me, bringing up the shiv in an upward stabbing motion.

I jumped backwards out of the way, then swung my body forward into a bowing motion with arms crossed over the top of each other in front of me, slamming them down onto his forearm to block the blow. It's an old martial arts trick that I'd practised plenty of times before, and if you do it right, it's incredibly painful for the guy holding the knife.

It worked this time and Ramone yelped and dropped the knife as I twisted out of the way, elbowing him in the side of the head, before taking off down the corridor.

'You fucker!' he roared, picking up the blade and setting off after me.

I knew I hadn't hurt him badly, not even dazed him, and had bought myself only a couple of seconds at best.

In front of me I could see two more inmates in makeshift masks racing up the wing's central flight of steps, cutting off my escape. If there'd just been the two of them, I'd have risked taking them out, but I knew I'd never manage to get past them before Ramone and his friends caught up with me.

That only left me with one option.

I jumped over the guardrail and onto the safety netting that stretched between the balconies. As I half ran, half stumbled across it, I heard Ramone leap onto it behind me, the force of his landing causing a shockwave in the netting that sent me sprawling.

As I scrambled to my feet, I felt his presence only feet away and turned just in time to see his shiv arm sailing through the air. Instinctively I put an arm up to protect myself, and felt the searing white-hot pain as the knife cut through the flesh of my forearm. I stumbled backwards on the netting, trying to keep my balance. I could see some inmates watching from their cells – some of them cheering, as if this were a tussle in school rather than a life-and-death struggle – while the other masked inmates who were with Ramone climbed over the guardrail and came towards me like a pack of wolves.

I knew that Ramone was smiling at me behind the mask. His eyes gleamed. He had the advantage and he knew it. Blood seeped through my torn sweatshirt, dripping down onto the floor below.

Ramone lunged again and I stepped backwards out of range, conscious that the others were only feet away now, and lost my balance on the netting. I went down on my back and Ramone was on me like a puma, pinning me down. I managed to free my injured arm and grab him by the wrist of his knife arm as the shiv bore down towards my face, using all my strength to hold it at bay.

But he was stronger. He had the momentum too, and slowly the blade bore down until it was taking up my entire field of vision, although I was conscious of the other inmates gathered round in a tight circle so that no cameras could film what was happening. Someone stamped on my leg hard but I barely felt it. All I could think about was the blade.

It continued its descent bit by bit, the tip now through my skin, drawing blood. In a moment it would all be over.

And then I heard it. The sound of something ripping.

Ramone realized what was happening and hesitated, and I drove myself upwards, grabbing him round the neck and yanking him round, just as the net gave way and split. And then suddenly we were all hurtling through the air towards the next floor, except this time I was on top of Ramone.

We slammed straight into the communal area pool table which collapsed under our weight and we ended up entwined in each other's arms on the floor while all around the bodies of the others on the net came crashing down, one missing me by inches.

The force of the landing had taken the wind out of me but Ramone had come off a lot worse, and his features were contorted with pain. I pulled out of his grip and climbed to my feet but he wasn't giving up that easily, and with a roar he sat up and made a grab for me.

I jumped back out of the way, grabbed a pool ball and threw it at him as hard as I could, catching him square on the forehead. At the same time I retreated across the floor, counting five other inmates lying there, most of them writhing around in pain, none of them offering an immediate threat. Two other guys, their faces covered, both holding broken pool cues, stared at me. At their feet, next to the overturned TV, lay a bleeding paedophile called Jones, whom they'd clearly just been beating.

The two guys started towards me, moving warily, knowing that, as the only man still standing, I was obviously no pushover. I was bleeding from the arm, and from the cut to my face where the blade had made contact, but I could feel my confidence returning as I grabbed one of the pool table's broken legs and turned to meet them.

'Leave him, he's mine!' came a shout from my right. It was Ramone. Even after the punishment he'd taken, he was getting to his feet, the shiv still in his hand, a huge lump already appearing on his forehead. I knew he had a reputation as a hard man, and unfortunately for me, he was excelling himself tonight.

The two inmates paused, and once again it felt like the whole place was watching us. I risked a look over my shoulder, but there was no one behind me, just a wall.

'You're going to fucking die, Mason,' snarled Ramone, his muscles rippling under his T-shirt.

'Well, come and kill me then,' I said, dropping the table leg, and throwing my arms wide.

It might have seemed like a suicidal gesture, but it was a calculated move. A pool table leg was more of a hindrance than a help in this situation, and I wanted Ramone to lose his wariness and charge me.

And he did. He came straight at me, leading with his free arm so he could grab me by the shirt, pull me in close, and then drive the knife in. It's the classic knife attacker's move.

Except it didn't happen like that. I tensed, waiting, and then launched a snap-kick with my back leg. Ramone might have been younger and stronger than me, but I was six feet two and he was a good six inches shorter and, in this case, height counted, because my foot connected with his groin before he had enough reach to strike me, and it connected perfectly. There are many injuries a man can withstand in a fight without it affecting his performance and, to be fair, Ramone had withstood quite a few of them, but a kick in the groin, particularly when delivered with real force (and mine was), isn't one of them.

As Ramone bent double, I delivered a second kick, this time straight to the face, and he took an unsteady step backwards, lost his balance, and fell over on his back, dropping the shiv in the process.

The rage took me then and, grabbing a pool ball from the floor, I leapt onto his chest, pinning down his arms, and, before he could recover, I drove the ball into his face again and again, turning it into pulp, unable to stop myself. No longer caring about anyone or anything else as all the frustrations of a year of incarceration came tearing to the surface.

I could hear shouting, a commotion behind me, and then suddenly hands were grabbing my arms and I was being dragged off him.

Still consumed with rage, I struggled furiously, determined now to fight until the end, but a baton came out of nowhere, striking me on the shoulder, and suddenly my vision was filled with the black boots and flameproof trousers of the Tornado Teams, the riot-trained prison officers always brought in to quell jail disturbances.

I let go of the cue ball as I was forced round onto my front with a knee pushing my face into the floor and, as I watched more and more of the riot officers pour in, some of them lashing out with batons and sending the inmates scurrying in all directions, I'd never felt so relieved in my life to be handcuffed.

2

Adrenalin's an incredible thing. When your body pumps you full of it, you feel no pain at all. Consequently, I hadn't noticed that when we were falling through the netting, Ramone had managed to slash my belly, leaving a nasty wound about four inches long that had bled all over my prison-issue sweatshirt.

Fifteen minutes had passed and I was in the holding area at the front of the prison where inmates are placed when they're being transferred or released. The place was bedlam. At least twenty injured staff and inmates were either being examined or waiting their turn, while the three flustered prison doctors on duty tried to calculate who was the most seriously injured. Meanwhile, the two senior managers on duty were trying to organize secure transport vehicles to take prisoners to the nearest hospital, as the prison's own hospital had been looted and set on fire. One guard looked very bad. He was unconscious and covered in blood, and they were placing him on a gurney with a drip attached. Wallace Burke, the child killer, was sitting nearby, holding a wet towel to his head and complaining loudly that he needed help. Unfortunately, his injuries looked largely superficial. It seemed the men who'd invaded our wing couldn't get anything right.

A young female doctor in a headscarf approached me, and my handcuffs were taken off while she examined my injuries and did a quick, and remarkably efficient, job of dressing them. The adrenalin was fading now that I was comparatively safe, and the pain was kicking in. I winced as she applied the antibiotic cream. Ramone had hurt me pretty bad, although I was still standing, which was more than could be said for him. He was at the other end of the room, sitting in a chair, his face a complete mess where I'd beaten him with the pool ball, but still conscious as a doctor examined him. After bad blood like this, one of us would have to be evacuated to another prison. It would also go on both our records. That wouldn't matter so much for Ramone who was in here for the best part of the rest of his life anyway, but for me, with my trial coming up in a month's time, it was an added complication.

Not that I had much chance of smelling the fresh, sweet air of freedom any time soon. I'd been charged with the murders of two people, a man and a woman. I'd shot them dead, then set fire to the house where I'd killed them, burning it to the ground. There was little point in me denying I'd done it. I was the only suspect.

A gun had been recovered from the ruins of the scene with my DNA on it. The man I'd killed had been armed but the woman hadn't. She was sixty-four years old and I'd shot her in cold blood.

In my defence, both of them were brutal killers in their own right, and the world was a better place without them in it, but that wasn't going to help me, since I was one of only a handful of people who knew their history. As far as everyone else was concerned they were innocent of any crime, and there were people out there – very powerful people – who wanted to make sure no one found out the real truth. Hence the half-a-million-pound bounty on my head.

My lawyer had told me I had next to no chance of being released. According to her, my best defence was diminished responsibility, which seemed to be the only sure way of avoiding a life sentence. I'd probably be successful too. As well as being a decorated soldier and police officer who'd been at the centre of plenty of incidents which could have caused severe PTSD, my trump card (my lawyer's words, not mine) was the fact that, at only seven years old, I was orphaned in an incident that made the front pages of every national newspaper in the country. One night my father, a drunk and a philanderer, murdered my mother in a booze-induced rage, a killing I witnessed. He then stabbed to death my two young brothers, before stalking the house hunting for me. I'd escaped by jumping from a first-floor window after he'd set the house on fire. I survived; he'd perished in the flames. At the time the press had called me 'the boy from the burning house' and, as my lawyer pointed out, anyone who'd been through that was going to get a sympathetic hearing from a jury. It had taken me a long time to come round to her way of thinking but ultimately anything was better than rotting in a place like this for the rest of my days.

'This inmate's going to have to be evacuated,' the doctor said over my shoulder to one of the prison managers, referring to me. 'He's lost quite a lot of blood and needs stitching up.'

'All right, he can go on the next van, along with Ramone and Burke. You're not going to give us any trouble are you, Ray?' The manager put a hand on my shoulder. His name was Stevenson and he was one of those guys who'd been around for ever and preferred quiet diplomacy to playing the tough guy. I got on with him well enough. I think he liked the fact we were both ex-army although, like most people, he was still wary of me, as if I was a friendly but unpredictable dog, and one with an especially nasty bite.

'Of course not, sir,' I told him. 'But can I travel without the cuffs? My arm's killing me.'

He gave me a sympathetic look. 'Afraid not, Ray. Regulations.'

He nodded to the guard, who replaced the cuffs and then led me through the gates to the main entrance where a prison transport van was waiting on the forecourt with its double doors open, amid an army of roughly parked emergency service vehicles, their flashing lights illuminating the night sky.

It was the first time I'd been outside the main prison building in a year, and it was a strange feeling. My immediate impulse was to make a run for it, but there were riot police everywhere and, in the end, where the hell was I going to go anyway, on foot, injured, and with my hands cuffed behind my back? I looked behind me and saw thick clouds of toxic smoke, glowing pink from the flames at the rear of the building, disappearing into the night sky. A helicopter was circling noisily overhead. The air out here was humid and unpleasant, and I could smell burning plastic.

Two other guards led me inside the back of the van, which was divided into three individual cubicles on each side so that the prisoners couldn't have any physical contact with each other. I was put inside the one nearest the driver's cab. As the guard leaned down to do up my seatbelt, he whispered in my ear in a soft Geordie accent, 'Keep fighting, Ray. You'll get through it.'

It was a rare but welcome show of support and I nodded a thanks. I'd always had a high profile as a cop, not just because of what had happened to me as a kid, but also because five years earlier, while working in counter terrorism, I'd survived a kidnap attempt by a gang of Islamic radicals who'd planned to behead me on camera. I'd managed to shoot two of them dead, and arrest the third, which had gained me a lot of airtime, and yet more enemies. But it had also earned me a grudging respect from some of those on the right side of the law. And that had undoubtedly helped me in prison.

Unfortunately, right now I needed a lot more than sympathy.

The guard locked the cubicle door, and I heard Burke being led in behind me, still complaining about the way he hadn't been protected by the authorities, as was his right. Then, after him, came Ramone, who was still compos mentis enough to yell threats at me, and even managed to land a kick on my door before being manhandled into his own cubicle.

Two minutes later, the van pulled away, drove out of the main gates of the prison, and accelerated quickly as it took us on the two-mile route to hospital.

'You're a dead man, Mason!' yelled Ramone. 'I will tear you into little pieces and gnaw on the bones.'

Full marks to him. As threats went it was one of the more imaginative ones.

'Yeah, whatever, Ramone,' I said, sitting back in the hard metal chair and closing my eyes, wondering how different life could have been if I'd played the cards I'd been handed better.

The thing was, before I'd ended up in here, I was a wealthy man. With the death of my family I'd inherited a sizeable amount of cash, and through shrewd investments over the years it had turned into several million. Not enough to put me in the super rich league, but financially speaking I'd been very comfortable. I hadn't needed to be a soldier or a cop. I could have got a different job entirely, something outdoors, like a tour guide or a diving instructor, lived an uneventful life of contentment, maybe with a wife and kids. Sometimes when I was lying in my cell at night, listening to the shouts and sobs of my fellow prisoners from across the landing, I fantasized about this alternative life.

It never did me any good, but at least it was a useful escape from a grim reality.

The van did a sudden emergency stop and I was flung forward then backwards in the seat. I could hear the two guards in the front cursing, but then their tones changed.

'Reverse! Reverse!' yelled one of them.

The driver put the van into reverse but not before I heard the distinctive blast of a shotgun, and the vehicle immediately dropped on one side as a tyre was shot out.

We were being hijacked, which could only be because of one of us in the back. No one was interested in Wallace Burke. He'd been inside twenty years and was largely forgotten. And Ramone might have been a brutal killer but ultimately he was still small-time with no major organization to back him up.

Which only left me.

There were at least two hijackers and they were yelling orders to the guards as they came round the side of the van, passing directly below my window.

'Open the fucking doors, or you're dead! Now! Move! Move!'

The guards' voices were muffled but I knew they'd be complying. Like all prison guards, they were unarmed, and therefore an easy target, although to attempt a hijacking in the middle of London like this, and less than a five-minute drive from hundreds of armed police, you had to be either highly reckless or highly professional. Either way, it didn't bode well for me.

My hands were cuffed behind my back, palms outward in the 'back to back' position, which made it pretty much impossible for me to get out of them, but I tried anyway, scouring the floor for a pin, a paper clip, anything that could be used to pick the lock, knowing I had to do something, anything, that made me feel less helpless.

The back doors opened. My adrenalin flooded back as I wriggled in the cuffs.

'Which one's Ray Mason in?' demanded one of the gunmen, close now.

'The left cubicle at the end,' replied the guard who'd spoken to me earlier.

'Unlock it. Now. Move!'

I could hear the guard put his key in the lock, and I knew I had only seconds to live, that this had been their plan all along. Stage the riot, make sure I was transferred, and then take me down en route. It showed the power of the people who wanted me dead.

But I wasn't going to die quietly.

The cubicle door opened. I braced myself for the inevitable shot, but it didn't come. I couldn't quite see the gunman but his arms and the shotgun were just in view, pointed at the guard. Smoke was still coming from the barrel from when he'd shot out the tyre.

'Get him out of there,' the gunman ordered. 'Fast, or I'll kneecap you.'

The accent was local, my guess belonging to a white man in his forties, and from the way he was holding the gun he definitely had a firearms background. A pro. I knew that if they'd wanted to kill me here they'd have done it already. Which meant they were taking me somewhere, and that was an even worse prospect.

The guard didn't look at me as he came into the cubicle, unclipped my seatbelt and pulled me to my feet. 'Sorry, mate,' he whispered. 'I can't help.'

'It's OK,' I told him as he pushed me out into the corridor and I saw the gunman for the first time. He was wearing jeans, trainers and a bomber jacket, his face covered by a balaclava, and he held a Remington automatic shotgun in his gloved hands.

'All right, bring him out fast,' demanded the gunman, retreating out of the van while still keeping his weapon trained on me.

Behind him, I could see the second gunman. He had a pistol pressed into the back of the other guard.

The lead gunman got out of the way as I climbed down the steps at the back of the van. We were on a one-way residential street, and there were already three or four cars backed up behind us. One of them even beeped his horn, and it looked like the driver of the car in front was filming the scene on his mobile. There was a convenience store with its light on and door open barely ten yards away, and it felt strange to be so close to normality and freedom, and not to be able to do a thing about it.

The second gunman swiftly bundled the other guard into the back of the prison van and slammed the doors shut, automatically activating the locking system. I was now on my own. He grabbed my arm, shoved the gun against the wound on my belly, and manoeuvred me round the front of the van, with the lead gunman following close behind. I could see several people looking out of windows, and another person filming the scene, but no one seemed to be calling the cops or making any move to intervene.

I could see their car now: a white Toyota saloon parked at a right angle to the flow of traffic, blocking the road. The boot was open and they were manhandling me towards it.

It's hard to make the decision to make a run for it when you've got two guns trained on you, especially when one of them's pressed against your gut, and if I'd been living the life of a free man I don't think I'd have done it. But as it was, I didn't have a lot left to live for, and if I had to die, then at least it would be on my terms.

As we reached the boot and the second gunman's grip on my arm momentarily eased, I slammed my body into his and twisted away from him, bolting up the street, almost losing my balance but somehow managing to right myself just in time, waiting for the inevitable bullet to slam into me and end it all. But in that handful of seconds I felt a real sense of elation. I was a free man.

And then my back spasmed uncontrollably, followed a split second later by every muscle in my body. My legs went from under me and I toppled over, unable to break my fall as the concrete raced upwards, slamming into the side of my face. I tried to lift my head and move my legs, but nothing seemed to work, and I lay there utterly helpless as a car wheel roared into my field of vision, stopping inches away. The gunmen were shouting at each other but I couldn't make out what they were saying, and their voices sounded far away.

And then I was being lifted up and forced into the darkness of the car boot, and I knew then that I hadn't been shot, but tasered, and already the effects were beginning to wear off.

The boot slammed shut and, as I regained feeling in my body, the Toyota accelerated away in a screech of tyres, making continual sharp turns and hardly braking as my abductors tried to get as far away from the crime scene as possible. I was forced to brace myself against the side to stop myself from being flung all over the place.

A few minutes later, the car screeched to a halt. I made a promise to myself that I was going to resist as I heard the gunmen come round the back, but as the boot flew open and I found myself staring at the barrel of the shotgun, I felt my will fading, and I hardly moved as the second gunman reached in with a hypodermic needle and jabbed me quickly in the arm.

I remember being taken out and led unsteadily over to a bigger car, then bundled into the back of that, thinking that, having gone to this much trouble to take me alive, whatever they had planned for me was going to be very, very bad indeed, before mercifully I lost consciousness.

3

For Alastair Sheridan, being born without a conscience had always been a boon. It had enabled him to achieve what weaker, less ruthless people had never been able to, and it had propelled him to the position he was in now: a self-made businessman with a reported net worth of £60 million (it was actually a few million less than that, but who was quibbling?), a beautiful trophy wife ten years his junior, an even more beautiful six-year-old son, and now, out of the blue, a career in politics which was threatening to go stratospheric thanks to the squabbling that was tearing his party apart. Having been parachuted into a safe government seat barely nine months earlier, things had moved rapidly and now the prize at the very top was his to win. He was good-looking and in the best shape he'd been for years, thanks to the recent diet and exercise regime that had knocked a stone off his six-foot-three frame. And most importantly of all, the public loved him. Even the very few in the party who'd got wind of some of the suspicion that surrounded him were no problem. Especially when he had someone as powerful as George Bannister in his pocket.

Sheridan and George were old friends from school, although George probably didn't see it that way any more. In fact, Sheridan was fairly certain the other man secretly hated him, but that didn't matter. The most important thing was that when Sheridan whistled, George came running. As he'd done so this evening, bringing his singularly unattractive second wife and their rather wimpish ten-year-old son, the atrociously named Rafferty, for an early evening barbecue at the Sheridan family home deep in the Hampshire countryside where Sheridan had grown up, and where he had his constituency.

'So where are we at on my leadership bid, George?' demanded Sheridan as the two of them walked alone through the woodland at the end of the house's immaculately tiered gardens.

'We've definitely got the forty-eight MPs in place to trigger the election,' said George, 'and from the private polling I've done, you've got the support of at least a hundred MPs if you stand.'

'That's a long way short of a majority.'

'It's more than any other candidate. And there are going to be at least five standing. In a second ballot, I think the bulk of the parliamentary party would get behind you.'

Sheridan looked down at George, enjoying the fact that he had six inches in height over the other man. '"Think" isn't enough,' he said. 'I need more certainty.'

'I can't give you any more certainty than that, Alastair. You're a fresh, exciting face in the party, a very popular candidate, and you've certainly got the charisma to appeal to a wide spectrum of voters, but there's no denying you're also controversial. There are rumours about your links to organized crime, and Cem Kalaman in particular. You know that.'

'I have nothing to do with him,' said Sheridan, irritated to have Kalaman's name brought up. 'We knew each other once. We did some business through the hedge fund, but that was a long time ago. And it was all above board. I haven't seen him for several years.'

'That's good. Because I know of at least two ongoing investigations into his criminal enterprise, and there's a very good chance he'll be arrested and charged in the near future. If any links, however tenuous, between you and he are discovered, it'll do immense damage to any leadership bid.'

'But if I'm already Prime Minister, it'll be hard to push me out. Therefore, now is going to be my best chance.' Sheridan didn't like the idea of running for leadership and being defeated, but he knew that, given his background, and the balancing act he'd performed for so long to keep his dark secrets out of the public domain, it was also too risky to wait to make his move. And, in truth, he'd never felt readier for the highest role in British politics. He had some excellent, if vague, policy ideas to free up the economy and drive it forward. He had the common touch. He could reach areas the other candidates couldn't hope to reach. He was, in short, a winner.

'We'll make the move in September,' said George, 'when we're back from the summer recess. We just need the PM to keep floundering over these next few weeks, a few more prison riots to add to the general impression of chaos and disorder, and then all the momentum will be with us. I think we can definitely do it, Alastair.'

George looked up at him with a good attempt at enthusiasm on his chubby, middle-aged face, but Sheridan didn't buy it. George wasn't nearly enthusiastic enough – which, Sheridan had to admit, was unsurprising given that he more than virtually anyone knew the truth about the man he was helping to become Prime Minister. Sheridan was definitely going to have to bring him into line.

'Are there are any criminal investigations aimed at me at the moment, George?' he asked, revealing the real reason why he'd brought him here tonight.

'I don't believe so.'

'I need a yes or no. You're the Home Office minister for the police. You ought to know.'

'I keep my ear to the ground, Alastair, and I do everything I can to make sure I'm made aware if there's anything serious going on.'

It was a typical mealy-mouthed politician's response, evasive and unsatisfying. It was no wonder MPs were so despised. Sheridan stopped and put a firm hand on George's shoulder, looking down at him like a headmaster addressing an errant pupil.

'I need to know exactly who is after me, and how they're doing it, George. I don't trust my new colleagues in the government. And you're my inside man, aren't you, George? Because if I go down, old friend, you might find yourself answering some rather unpleasant questions yourself. I've still got the evidence of your little indiscretion, you know.'

And there it was. Out there. Sheridan's secret weapon.

'I know,' said George, wilting under his old friend's gaze.

'I don't want any nasty surprises, and I'm sure you don't either. You just need to do one thing for me, George. Get me into power. After that, I'll do the rest.' Sheridan patted him on the shoulder and grinned. 'Come on, let's head back to the ladies.'

4

My eyes opened and I sat up fast, expecting to find myself in some kind of restraints.

Instead, I was in a comfortable double bed with what smelled like the first truly clean sheets I'd had in a year. And I was naked, my prison sweatshirt and tracksuit bottoms nowhere to be seen. I pulled down the covers and examined the wounds on my arm and belly. The dressings had been changed, and the area around the injuries cleaned up. They throbbed dully.

I looked around. The room was small. The bed and an old-fashioned wardrobe at the end of it took up most of the space. There was also a bedside table with a lamp, along with a clean glass and a full jug of water. It was daylight, and sunshine was poking round the edges of the blackout blinds.

Some time had clearly passed.

I drank two glasses of water in quick succession before climbing out of the bed. My head ached angrily, and for a couple of seconds my vision blurred before clearing again. I opened the blinds and saw that I was on the first floor of a house that looked out onto a leylandii hedge that must have been a good twenty feet high, and was separated from the window by a short stretch of well-kept grass. I tried the window handles and wasn't surprised to find them locked. Next, I tried the bedroom door. It too was locked, and there was a camera above it I hadn't noticed before, pointing towards the bed.

Where the hell was I?

The bedroom had an en suite with a power shower. It was all very clean. I took a leak and examined myself in the mirror. I looked how I felt. Washed out and exhausted. The dressing that had been applied to my right cheek by the doctor back at the prison was no longer there. Instead, the wound now had two old-fashioned, but effective-looking, string stitches. It was the same, I discovered, on my belly and forearm wounds, which had six and ten new stitches respectively.

This was strange. I'd assumed my kidnappers, or the people they were working for, would only keep me alive if they wanted to torture me, which meant they wouldn't be bothering to stitch my wounds or let me sleep in a comfortable bed. I'd be in some kind of basement cell somewhere chained to the wall.

So who had abducted me? And more importantly, why had they done so?

I was intrigued, but whatever the answer it could wait until after I'd had a decent shower. Showering in prison is no fun. Firstly, you can't do it alone. In our wing, more than a hundred prisoners shared the same small shower block, and there were only certain times of the day you could use it, so it was always busy. Second, you were rationed only three tiny sachets of shower gel a week, and it was expensive to buy more, so a lot of the time you were just rinsing yourself.

But this place was different. Inside the shower unit was a full, unused bottle of some nice-looking stuff on a tray. Whoever had taken me had clearly prepared for my visit, and stitches or no stitches, I was going to take full advantage of their generosity.

Ten minutes later, warm, refreshed and a lot less groggy, I emerged into the bedroom, towelling myself, just as a voice came over an unseen intercom:

'There are clothes in the wardrobe. Put them on.'

The voice belonged to a well-educated woman, middle-aged, with a soft Scottish burr.

Feeling suddenly self-conscious, I wrapped the towel round my waist and checked the wardrobe. There were a number of tops and jeans hanging up, and in the drawers were clean under-wear and socks. There was even a pair of new trainers at the bottom. Everything fitted me too. My captor seemed to know a lot about me.

I'd barely got the last of the clothes on when there was a knock on the door. I told whoever it was to come in, but it had already opened, and in walked a man of medium height and build, dressed in casual clothes, but wearing a similar balaclava to the gunmen the previous night. Unlike them, however, he was carrying a tray containing bacon, fried eggs and beans on toast, along with cutlery and a mini-cafetière of coffee. He also didn't appear to be armed but, even though the door was open, I didn't contemplate making a break for it. I was too interested in the food for that. I suddenly realized I was starving, having missed the previous night's meal, and not eaten a thing since the crap we'd been fed at lunchtime the day before. Prison food, as you'd imagine, is uniformly awful. I'd had bacon only twice in the whole time I'd been inside. The meat had been a weird grey colour, and had tasted like rubber. This stuff looked like it had been carved off the pig that very morning.

The guy put the tray down on the bed.

'I'm assuming that means you don't want to kill me,' I said, unable to resist picking up a rasher with my fingers and shoving it straight in my mouth. Believe it or not, before I ended up in prison, I had good table manners.

'Miss Lane will tell you everything,' he said. 'I'll be back in ten minutes to take you to her.'

'Who's Miss Lane?'

'The woman you work for now.'

Miss Lane was sitting at the end of the table in a dining room on the ground floor of what was a fairly spacious older house of character, the kind that costs a lot of money, when I walked in. She was dressed somewhat incongruously in a suit and not quite matching balaclava, and black leather gloves, and she had a cup of something on a saucer in front of her.

'Miss Lane, I presume,' I said as the guy who'd shown me in slipped back out, shutting the door behind him.

'That's right,' she said in the same Scottish burr as the voice on the intercom, gesturing for me to take a seat.

I sat down at the opposite end of the table and looked round the room. It was sparsely but expensively furnished, and the dining table was a beautiful mahogany. 'Well, you've gone to considerable effort and risk to get me out of prison, Miss Lane, and it doesn't look like you want to kill me, so what is it you do want?'

'You know who Alastair Sheridan is, don't you?'

Alastair Sheridan was a murderer, and one I'd been hunting, and getting close to, when I was arrested. Now just turned fifty, he'd been killing young women for close to thirty years. But Sheridan was a clever man and he'd been so good at covering his tracks that he'd remained undetected. Few people in the world who weren't involved in his crimes knew his secret. One of them had been a friend who'd worked as his lawyer, and also witnessed one of his killings, called Hugh Manning. I'd arranged for Manning to be handed over to the police after he'd gone on the run, and he'd subsequently been murdered along with four police officers at a supposedly secure location, before he could tell the world what he knew.

'You know I know who he is,' I said.

'Alastair Sheridan is a threat to national security,' said Lane.

'I could have told you that. In fact, I tried very hard to tell plenty of people, but no one seemed to want to listen.'

Lane shifted in her seat and sighed. 'That's because there's no evidence linking him to any of the crimes he's suspected of. And now, as you're probably aware, he's made a move into politics.'

I'd read in the papers that Alastair Sheridan had been shoehorned into a safe government seat and was now an MP, and that the hedge fund he managed was doing incredibly well, which just shows you how much justice there is in the world. 'I'm aware,' I said.

'Well, what you're probably not aware of is how popular he is within his parliamentary party,' continued Lane. 'The government have lost control, the opposition are a complete mess, and Alastair Sheridan is looking increasingly like a potential leader, someone who can turn things around. The public know nothing of what he's suspected of, neither do most MPs. He's even being talked about as our next Prime Minister. We can't let that happen.'

'Who's "we"?'

'I work for the security services, Mr Mason. I'm not going to give you any more detail than that. Only a handful of people in the world even know I'm here talking to you, but they include individuals at the very top of government.'

I've learned over the years that corruption and a complete disregard for the law go right to the very top in both business and government, and it wouldn't have surprised me if senior politicians had sanctioned last night's hijack.

'Did you set up the prison riot? Because if so, it almost went very, very wrong. If it hadn't been for some cheap netting, I'd be in the morgue now.'

Lane shook her head. 'Your enemies did that. Mr Sheridan, and of course his close friend Mr Kalaman, who I believe you're also acquainted with.'

Cem Kalaman. There are three things you need to know about him. One: he's a violent underworld figure who runs a criminal empire worth at least a billion pounds. Two: nearly twenty years ago he murdered his own father so that he could take over the business. And three: he has been Alastair Sheridan's partner in crime since the very beginning. Two very different men but the backbone, and last surviving members, of a cabal of killers who'd murdered possibly dozens of young women over three decades.

'We were planning on getting you transferred and taking you then,' continued Lane, 'but things had to be brought forward very fast. We had intelligence that there was going to be an attempt on your life, but we didn't know how or when. When we got word you'd been injured in the riot and were being transferred to the hospital, we moved fast.'

I sat back in the chair and thought about this. It made some sense, but it also left a lot of unanswered questions, like how did they get there so fast? And of course, the most important question of all.

'So what do you want me for now?'

Lane sipped her drink before replacing the cup carefully on the saucer. 'I think you already know,' she said. 'We want you to kill Alastair Sheridan.'

She'd delivered the request so coldly that it made me snort in disbelief. 'Don't you think that's a little extreme? You know, for a democracy where the law is supposedly sacrosanct? There must be an easier way. Why not try gathering evidence against him, like I was trying to do before I was arrested? He's committed enough crimes.'

'We've tried,' said Lane. 'But he's got good security, he's savvy, and he has friends in high places.'

'Even though they know what he's done?'

'What it's *alleged* he's done. Remember, there's no actual evidence. And he doesn't look like a killer, does he? He looks and sounds like a charming, handsome and charismatic man. And looks count. Most people would never believe it. Unfortunately for Mr Sheridan, the people who count do. So they've decided on a course of action, and the reason we've chosen you to take him down rather than anyone else is—'

'You don't have to tell me,' I said. 'I'm expendable.'

'That's not quite how I'd have put it. But yes, if you fail and you're caught, it wouldn't be that difficult to concoct a motive for you as a damaged man suffering from PTSD, with an irrational grudge against Alastair Sheridan. And if you succeed and you're caught, everything about Sheridan will come out anyway. Either way, you'll be on your own, and no one will believe you if you try to blame it on the security services.'

'You're not exactly selling it to me.'

Lane smiled behind the balaclava. 'That's the advantage for us. We don't have to. You're a man awaiting trial for double murder with a half-a-million-pound price tag on his head. You're not exactly operating from a position of strength. And if you decide you don't want to take the job, we'll put a needle in your arm again, drop you off somewhere, and let the police take you back in, where you're almost certain to be murdered on Alastair Sheridan and Cem Kalaman's orders at some point in the next few months.' She paused, leaning forward in her chair and resting her gloved hands on the table. 'But if you succeed in killing Sheridan, you'll receive a new passport, a new identity, a new face, and you can start a new life somewhere a long, long way from here.'

'What about Cem Kalaman?' I asked her.

'He's not in our remit,' said Lane. 'But without Sheridan's help, he'll fall soon enough. There are a number of investigations into his affairs at the moment.'

I thought about what was being offered to me. Lane was right. I wasn't negotiating from a position of strength. They held all the cards. But there was something else too. A little over a year ago I'd personally promised Steve and Karen Brennan, the parents of Sheridan and Kalaman's first and youngest victim, thirteen-year-old Dana, that I wouldn't rest until I'd brought her killers to justice, and the fact that I hadn't done so had played on my mind throughout my time in prison. Now I was being offered the opportunity to make good on at least half that promise.

'So, if Sheridan's got such excellent security that you people can't get to him, how the hell am I meant to?' I said.

Lane smiled again. 'You'll be pleased to know we've got a perfect way in.'

5

Tina Boyd's life should have been easy. She'd enjoyed a safe, comfortable, middle-class upbringing in the Home Counties, with parents who were still together and who'd shown her and each other the kind of love and compassion that was in short supply in so many families. She'd had a great time at university, left with a pretty decent degree, and had spent an adventurous and hugely satisfying gap year travelling through Asia (still the best year of her life by far, although in truth, the competition had been limited). Happy days, and they could have continued that way: a decent job, maybe marriage, a comfortable if slightly boring life like her brother and his family.

But of course it hadn't happened like that. She'd made one bad decision from which all other bad decisions had sprung like weeds: she'd joined the police. A chequered and highly eventful career had followed in which she'd been taken hostage twice, shot, had witnessed close colleagues being killed, and had killed several suspects herself; and been fired from the job on two separate occasions. There'd been no third chance, and now she was a single forty-something private detective working mainly divorce cases.

At least she had her own house, she told herself as she poured a lime cordial and walked out into her small garden, sitting down at the table at the end. It was a beautiful evening, with birds singing in the trees, and light jazz music playing in the background. It was funny how your musical tastes changed. A few years back she would never have even countenanced jazz, now she found it soothing. She sat back in the chair and looked up at the rapidly darkening sky, lighting a cigarette and taking a sip from the drink, wishing it could have been red wine, but knowing that that ship had long ago sailed. She knew she should be happy now that her life was calmer, but it hadn't worked out like that. Instead, it was dull and empty, and there was still a nagging feeling that she had unfinished business.

The previous year Tina had found herself working on a case alongside a Met detective, Ray Mason, whose career had been almost as controversial as hers. The case had pitted the two of them against some very powerful people who were responsible for some horrific crimes. One of those powerful people included the man who was now being talked of as the next Prime Minister, Alastair Sheridan.

And that was the problem. She and Ray had failed in their task, with Ray ending up in prison, awaiting trial for double murder. Tina had thought about continuing the investigation alone but she knew that the forces she was up against were too strong. She also had no doubt that, after his abduction from the prison van a few days earlier, Ray was dead. Sheridan and his associate Cem Kalaman would have made sure of that. The thought hurt her terribly because she'd fallen in love with him, and for the few short weeks they'd worked together she'd been genuinely happy.

The Tina Boyd of ten years ago would have been planning revenge on the men she was certain were behind this. The Tina Boyd of ten years ago would also have reached for the bottle and drunk herself into a stupor. Now she did neither of those things. Instead she tried to forget about Ray, the past, the myriad injustices of the world (which, however hard she tried, she knew she would never be able to expunge), and for once just get on with her life. She'd even started online dating for Christ's sake, although the jury was still out on its effectiveness. But she had a date the following week with a decent-sounding (and decent-looking, if his pictures were to be believed) guy called Matt who, unlike a lot of the men out there, hadn't been immediately fixated on her past. They'd spoken once on the phone and he'd been chatty and funny, and there was a lightness about him that Tina had missed, and felt like she needed right now.

She sat back in her seat and took a long drag on her cigarette, concluding that it might just be possible that things were looking up for her.

6

The days I spent in the care of Lane and her associates were some of the strangest of my life, and also the most relaxing. I was still effectively a prisoner. I didn't have access to a mobile phone or the internet, but they did give me a selection of second-hand paperbacks to read, and brought in a small TV that they put on a stand at the end of the bed, so I could watch the usual junk, or see the news on the prison van snatch.

I was on the news a lot. The fact that I'd been quite a high-profile cop in my time, coupled with the embarrassment and drama of my abduction, meant the media were playing it for all it was worth, even more so as the days passed and there was still no sign of me.

I was also allowed out into the garden for fifteen minutes twice a day, under the watchful eye of one of Lane's two male colleagues, who I was now certain had been the duo who'd freed me from the prison van. They were hard men but professional, and I guessed they were ex-army. They never spoke except to give instructions and they didn't appear to be armed.

The garden was sheltered from the outside world by the leylandii hedge that surrounded the whole property, and high wooden gates at the front. I either walked round and round the house followed by whichever guard was on duty that day, or simply sat in the sunshine, looking up at the sky and enjoying the feeling of the sun on my face after so much time inside. There was a back gate built into the leylandii. I wasn't sure if it was locked or not but it never occurred to me to make a break for it. There really wasn't a lot of point, even if I did manage to get away.

It was a lot easier to stay put as I was being fed really well too. Three meals a day, simple but tasty fare like steak and chips and roast chicken, always brought to my room by one of the guards.

After that first meeting with Lane I didn't see her again for a while, and I got the feeling she wasn't staying in the house. During that time I followed her instructions to grow a beard and, with only limited exercise, and plenty of hearty food, I put on a fair amount of weight, which was no bad thing. Prison, and the stress of always being on my guard, had kept me thin and given me a gaunt, haunted look I was happy to lose.

When she did finally reappear, I was actually quite nervous to see her, having settled into my new life of incarceration pretty well, and having no desire to end it.

'We need to get you ready for your new passport photo,' she told me, coming into my bedroom while one of the guards stood in the doorway behind her. As before, she was wearing a bala-clava and gloves, on top of a navy trouser suit and flat work shoes.

It was late afternoon and I'd been sitting in my pyjamas reading a book on medieval history.

She was carrying a holdall, and she dropped it on the bed. 'There are scissors in there as well as an electric shaver. You need to shave your head. There's also black dye for the beard. Get everything done and I'll be back in fifteen minutes.'

I'm one of those vain forty-year-old men who's far too proud of his full head of hair, and the thought of getting rid of it filled me with horror, but I knew there was no point arguing.

Twenty minutes later I was sitting in a chair against the wall in the downstairs dining room, with a bald head and a dark beard. I didn't look pretty, but I looked different, and clearly this was the point. Lane took some headshots on a Lumix camera and told me that my new passport would be ready in three days. 'When we've got that, you'll be ready to go out into the world. The hunt for you's already scaling down.'

This didn't surprise me. The prison rioting had now spread to almost a dozen institutions, and there was constant footage of burning buildings on the TV news as the inmates vented their frustrations. I was still mentioned as a footnote but the rioting itself was sucking up most of the airtime, which suited me fine. It was strange really. I'd spent so much of my adult life putting criminals behind bars but I'd never given any real thought to what it was like for them in there. Now, having spent a year inside myself, I had a lot more sympathy with them. Prison was an over-crowded, debilitating hell, and it wasn't peopled entirely by monsters, even on the VP ward. With the exception of child killers like Wallace Burke, they were just men who'd fucked up, made bad decisions, who'd been unable to control their emotions and had acted rashly. Some of them were mentally ill, including plenty of services veterans who'd spent years serving their country only to be deserted by the powers-that-be when they'd returned home with PTSD. They were the dregs of society and they knew it, locked away and forgotten by the outside world, only noticed when they finally fought back in a furious, desperate and ultimately futile way.

I wouldn't say I was rooting for them. But I wasn't exactly rooting against them either.

Three days after she'd taken the photos, Lane returned as promised.

It was early afternoon and I was told to get dressed, pack my bags, and be ready to go. My rest and recuperation was over. It was time for the real work to begin.

When I was done, I was led downstairs to the dining room by both guards. Lane was standing there, in the same tailored suit she'd had on last time, a number of items next to her on the table.

'Good afternoon, Mr Mason. Are you ready to check out?'

I guessed this was her idea of a joke, and I have to say, even with the balaclava on she looked in a jaunty mood. Perhaps she was just glad to be seeing the back of me and this whole operation, which was clearly both secretive and very risky. 'I've been sat on my arse in here for the last fortnight, stuffing my face and putting on weight, and I was sat on my arse in jail for the year before that. Of course I'm not ready.'

'You're a pro, Mr Mason, and you're ex-army,' she countered. 'You also managed to fight your way out of a murder attempt by a number of assailants. I'd say you were ready.'

'So, what's the plan?'

'It's a very simple one, as the best usually are. As you know, Alastair Sheridan is fond of young women.'

'That's one way of putting it.'

'There's a very discreet establishment in a townhouse in Bayswater where the tastes of certain wealthy businessmen are taken care of. Alastair visits it quite regularly, and always likes to be entertained in the penthouse, where he won't run into anyone else. He only stays for an hour or two at a time and then he's gone. We've rented a top-floor flat in a townhouse on the same block, six houses down, where there's access to the roof.' Lane unrolled a set of detailed drawings of the buildings, and beckoned me closer. 'We have a trusted insider among Alastair's team who will let us know when he's going to be there. Our insider doesn't get much notice so you'll have to be ready, and when you get the call, you will make your way across the roof to this building.' She tapped the drawings with a gloved finger. 'A flight of steps leads down to a black fire door, which is usually locked.' She pulled something out of her jacket pocket. 'Here's the key,' she said, putting it on the table. 'The door leads straight into the hallway. There are three rooms on the penthouse floor. The jacuzzi room, the main bedroom, and a separate bathroom.' She pointed them out on the drawings. 'So, as you can see, there's not much chance of getting lost, and the only people up there will be Sheridan himself and whichever woman he's with. The security stay downstairs. All you have to do is find him and effect the termination with minimal fuss, restrain any witnesses using the gags and ties you'll be supplied with, then leave the way you came in.'

I nodded, and she stepped away from the paperwork and opened up a backpack on one of the chairs, removing a wooden display case containing a pistol, a separate magazine and a six-inch detachable suppressor that would help muffle the sound of the bullets discharging. As she opened it, her sleeve rode up and I saw she was wearing a simple silver bracelet. She had a tiny, very dark mole on her wrist, and her skin was mottled with sunspots. I'd never been this close to her before, and I guessed her age to be late fifties.

'The gun's a SIG Sauer,' continued Lane. 'It's new, and as you'll see, the serial number's been removed. There's no way it can be traced back to us, or you. The magazine's been pre-loaded with ten nine-millimetre rounds, which should be more than enough for you.'

I went to take out the gun but she closed the case and put it back in the backpack. 'There'll be plenty of time to examine it later.'

'So what happens after I "effect the termination"? How are you going to extract me from the area?'

'You leave the gun at, or near, the scene. Then head straight back to the rental flat. If all goes well, no one will have seen you, and it will take several minutes for anyone to raise the alarm. You should already be packed and ready to leave. Go out the front door and get to the pick-up point, which is approximately six hundred metres away at the intersection of Seymour Place and Upper Berkeley Street.'

I frowned. 'So you're not providing me with a car.'

'No, the traffic around there can be a problem. It'll be far quicker for you to get to the pick-up point on foot. There's a map in the backpack with it marked. Then you'll be brought back here, and then you can have this.' She handed me a brand-new British passport.

I opened it at the photo page and saw a shaven-headed man with a dark, closely cropped beard. This apparently was Mr Neil Bennett. If you looked close enough you'd see it was me, but I had to admit, the photo looked a lot different to the police-issue one of me they'd been posting on the nightly news, so unless I was very unlucky it wasn't going to get anyone's attention. Nor was the passport itself, which was impossible to tell apart from a genuine one.

Lane took the passport back. 'That's yours if you carry out the task. Along with the ten thousand euros in cash I promised. We'll then drop you at one of the quieter ferry ports, furnish you with a ticket, and after that, you're on your own. But I'm sure you've also got money stashed away, haven't you?'

'Why should I trust you? Surely it's a lot easier for you to leave me out there rather than take the risk of being caught extracting me?'

'If you're caught, it's far more complicated,' said Lane. 'You know very little about us, but what little you do know could provide leads, and it's obvious that you've been sheltered and well fed somewhere. Even if you're killed, it throws up some very unwelcome questions. But if you simply disappear, people will eventually forget about you.'

I shook my head. 'I'm always going to be better off dead to you.'

Lane sighed. 'Listen, I know you probably don't believe it, but we're actually trying to do the right thing. The prospect of Alastair Sheridan becoming Prime Minister is unthinkable, not least because he could potentially be subject to blackmail by enemy states. We want him dead because it's the only way of being absolutely certain he's stopped. We don't want anyone else hurt. And that includes you, Mr Mason.'

'We'll see,' I said, giving her the kind of look that said I was going to be no pushover if they were planning on killing me.

'And please don't try to do anything foolish like disappear on us,' Lane said, meeting my look. 'I'm sure you think you've got a good chance of escape but let me tell you something, you haven't. There's an in-built alarm in a chip somewhere in your body. It was put in while you were unconscious on the night we took you. If you tamper with it, we'll be alerted immediately and the deal's off. If that happens, we'll inform the police of your whereabouts, and you'll be caught in hours, however resourceful you are. Don't try to contact anyone else either. There's a burner phone in the backpack but that's just so you can receive calls from us. We'll know immediately if you use it. You're to stay inside at the rental address 24/7, waiting for the call to move. It could come at any time. It may take a day. It may take a week. It's unlikely to be much longer. There's enough food and drink on site to last you at least a month, so you won't starve. And you're used to being cooped up, so it shouldn't be too much of a chore. Is that all understood?'

I nodded. 'Understood.'

'OK, meeting over. I'll see you again when this is all over and done with. In the meantime, good luck.'

I picked up the backpack and was led out by the two guards, thinking I was going to need a lot more than luck to get out of this one.

7

A few hours later, Lane's two associates dropped me at the safe-house, a spacious penthouse apartment that must have cost a fortune to rent, set in one of those attractive Georgian squares with a tree lined private garden running through the middle of it. They didn't hang around, just threw me the keys and told me to get inside immediately, then drove away, although not before I'd managed to steal a glance at the number plate of their Range Rover.

That was one thing I'd learned as a detective. However well laid a plan, its perpetrators will always make at least one mistake, and that was theirs. They'd been very careful to hide anything that would have helped me identify them, or the place where they were holding me, even going so far as to make me wear a hood for the duration of the journey here. Unfortunately, they'd had no choice but to remove it when they dropped me off.

As soon as I was upstairs and inside the apartment, I pulled out the burner phone they'd given me, found the notes section, and keyed in the number plate details. I had no idea how long I was going to be here for but I was operating on the basis that it could be as little as a few hours, which meant I needed to move fast if I was to turn the odds of survival in my favour.

After spending the best part of an hour scouring the apartment for cameras and finding none, I threw off my clothes and searched for the microchip they were using to track my movements. Now I'm no expert, but I was sure that Lane had been bluffing when she stated that they'd know if I tampered with it. I was also fairly certain they wouldn't have had the expertise or resources to put it in too far beneath the surface of the skin – and I was proved right when I located a barely perceptible splinter-shaped bump in the small of my back which was still tender to the touch.

Removing the chip turned out to be something of a rigmarole involving a small chopping knife from the kitchen drawer, a lot of manoeuvring in front of the bathroom mirror, and a fair amount of blood, but eventually I got it out intact and left it on the kitchen table, while I pressed the wound with damp toilet paper.

But I wasn't going to get out of this on my own. I needed help, and I knew the one place where I could get it, which meant making a phone call. The burner phone was no use to me, as it was being monitored by Lane, but I wasn't deterred. On the way up the stairs I hadn't heard any noises coming from inside any of the other apartments and guessed that they were probably empty. It was late July after all, and the beginning of the school holidays. Also, in the last ten years huge numbers of apartments and houses in central London had been bought up by overseas investors, often with dirty money, and left empty. All I needed was a working landline.

I picked up a butter knife from the cutlery drawer in the kitchen and went down to the apartment on the floor below. I listened at the door for a good minute, then, satisfied there was no one in there, I wedged the end of the knife into the old-fashioned seventies-style lock and wriggled it from side to side like a key until the door opened, which took all of about twenty seconds.

The apartment was fusty and decorated in an unpleasant style that befitted the lock, but it was clear it was still being lived in, and I was pleased to see a landline phone in the kitchen.

I took a deep breath before I made the call. Involving someone else meant exposing them to danger, and I cared deeply for Tina Boyd, the woman I was falling in love with when I was arrested a year ago. But I also knew she'd want to help if she could.

The two of us had kept burner phones that we used to contact each other on to avoid having our conversations monitored. Clearly I no longer had mine but I was hoping she still had hers. I'd memorized the number long ago but, even so, my hand hovered above the handset for a long moment before I finally picked it up and punched in the numbers.

The phone rang. And rang. Finally it kicked into voicemail.

'It's me,' I said. 'I'll call back.' Then I hung up.

I stood there in this stranger's apartment for another five minutes, contemplating my next move. The dishwasher was open and half full and there were two empty cups with dregs of tea in the bottom on the sideboard, so I knew that the occupants could be back soon.

I tried the number one more time and waited.

It must have been the tenth ring when she picked up.

'Is it you?' she asked, and I felt a pang of something powerful as I heard her voice.

'It's me.'

'I didn't expect this. Are you OK? What happened?'

I sighed. 'It's a long story, and I can't tell you about it right now, but I need you to do something for me.'

She didn't argue. I knew she wouldn't.

'Start talking,' was all she said.

8

Tina put the burner phone back on top of the bathroom cabinet, out of sight.

It had been up in her loft for most of the past year but when she'd heard that Ray had been broken out of the prison van, she'd taken it down and recharged it in case he attempted to make contact. She'd checked it repeatedly in the first forty-eight hours but gradually, as hope had faded that he was even alive, let alone in a position to call her, she'd started checking it less and less, and she hadn't looked at it for a couple of days before today. She wasn't even sure she wanted to hear from him. In the end, Ray represented the danger and violence of the past. In the few weeks they'd been together, she'd almost been killed twice.

Tina had ridden her luck too many times over the years and she knew with certainty that at some point, and probably soon, it would run out.

And yet she couldn't help feeling a frisson of excitement at hearing his voice again. Her date with Matt had been OK. He was a nice guy, and funny too, and he looked like he did in his photos, but she couldn't help feeling he was just a little bit lightweight. There were no rough edges to him. He would, she knew, be a pushover, and halfway through the date when he leaned forward and said 'I can't believe I'm sitting here having a drink with *the* Tina Boyd', she knew that there was no future for the two of them.

Because that was the problem. For most men she'd always be *the* Tina Boyd. The killer cop; the Black Widow who'd lost two of her close colleagues in the line of duty; the one who'd been fired from the job twice, shot twice, and involved in some of the biggest cases in UK criminal history.

But Ray had never seen her like that. To him, she was a woman; an equal; a partner. He wasn't in awe of her, because he'd been through the same things. And for the past year she'd thought she'd lost him for ever.

And then, just like that, he'd reappeared.

If she helped him, Tina was taking a huge risk. The maximum sentence for assisting an offender was ten years, and if she got caught they'd throw the book at her, so she'd definitely be looking at the upper end of that. It was a prospect that filled her with dread.

She went back downstairs and out into the garden, lighting a cigarette and pondering her next move. She knew Ray wouldn't hold it against her if she didn't help him. He'd said as much on the phone.

But the problem with Tina was that she'd never been able to turn her back on someone in trouble, even if it meant getting into a whole load of trouble of her own. And she owed Ray, there was no question about it. He'd only been arrested on that fateful night because at the time he'd been in the process of rescuing Tina from two people who would have killed her given half the chance. Ray had killed them, and been charged with double murder as a result, taking the rap so Tina didn't have to.

It was for that reason more than any other that she made the fateful decision to get involved.

9

It was just before 10.30 p.m. on my first night in the apartment when I slipped out the front door of the building. I'd been watching the street below for the previous hour and was certain there was no one down there watching me. Very few cars came past and those that did all seemed to stop further down the road at the brothel, disgorging their passengers before driving off again. There were no pedestrians and, as far as I could make out, no one in any of the nearby parked cars, which were all in Residents Only bays. It would be almost impossible for Lane and her associates to keep me under surveillance 24/7, especially with only three of them, and I suspected they were relying on the chip they'd planted in me to monitor my whereabouts.

It was a warm evening and I headed off to Connaught Street where the pubs and restaurants were busy enough that there were a fair few pedestrians about. None of them gave me a second glance. My new look of shaved head and full-face beard was clearly working, helped by the fact that it was now more than two weeks after I'd gone on the run, and my face was only now rarely appearing in the media.

I turned off onto a residential road after about a hundred yards, taking up a position in a doorway out of sight.

Three minutes later, as I waited, a black Ford Focus turned into the street. I recognized it and the driver immediately. As Tina slowed the car, I stepped out of the doorway and raised an arm to show it was safe for her to stop. Our eyes met, and I experienced something I hadn't felt in a year. It took me a second to realize it was excitement.

I jumped inside and she pulled away.

'Jesus, Ray, you look different,' she said, glancing over at me. 'The bald look really doesn't suit you.'

I smiled. 'It's temporary, I promise. It's good to see you, Tina.' I wanted to lean over and touch her but held back. She looked beautiful. Her skin was pale and flawless beneath a jaunty-looking bob cut I hadn't seen before, and she could have passed for close to a decade younger than her forty-one years which, given some of the things she'd been through over the years, was pretty impressive.

I glanced over my shoulder to check that the street behind us was empty.

'Don't worry,' she said, 'I wasn't followed. The police were in touch with me just after you got broken out of prison, but they've left me alone since then. I'd know if I was under surveillance.'

'I know. I guess I'm just paranoid.'

We came to the end of the street and she pulled into a parking bay in the shade of an oak tree and looked at me properly for the first time. There was concern in her expression but also a certain wariness. 'So what happened, Ray? Did you organize the escape? It looks like the men who sprung you must be good cooks. You've put on weight.'

'They were,' I said. 'But I didn't ask them to spring me.' I told her briefly what had happened from beginning to end.

She didn't interrupt me, or look sceptical, and I knew she believed my story.

'Do you think they're really security services?' she asked when I'd finished. 'I know they do some dodgy things, but springing you from jail and getting you to murder one of the most prominent politicians in the country is a pretty big thing.'

'They may not be working for the security services but they've gone to a lot of trouble, and they definitely want Sheridan dead. Whether they want me walking away from the hit afterwards, well, that's another matter.'

'But how do they know you're actually going to carry out the hit? They're not exactly keeping strong tabs on you, and relying on a bug that you've managed to remove on your own seems a bit weak.'

I thought about this. 'They know I hate Sheridan for what he's done, so they figure I've got the incentive to kill him anyway, and that the prospect of money and a new passport will be enough to seal the deal. You've got to remember, they've treated me well these past two weeks, and their argument for letting me go is a sound one. So why wouldn't I trust them?'

'But you don't.'

'No. I don't.'

'So why don't you run then? You must be able to access some money somewhere. You've always been a resourceful guy.'

'I can probably make it. But I'm going to kill Sheridan first. He deserves it. And don't forget, I made a promise to the Brennans that I'd bring their daughter's killer to justice.'

The promise. It would forever be a millstone round my neck. When thirteen-year-old Dana's remains had been found in the school grounds the previous year, almost three decades after she'd gone missing, I'd been the detective sent to tell her parents what had happened. To my dying day, I will never forget the terrible pain they were still experiencing as they spoke to me of their long-gone daughter. And somehow, in that room, I'd taken on some of their pain and had made the biggest mistake any detective can make: I'd become emotionally involved in one of my cases. And it had come close to killing me.

Yet strangely, even after all that had happened to me, I didn't regret making that promise. In fact it hardened my resolve to kill Alastair Sheridan.

'You're a man of your word, Ray,' said Tina. 'Most of the time that's a good thing.'

'But not now?'

Tina sighed. 'The thought of a man like Sheridan in power scares the hell out of me.' She looked at me, and I could see concern in her expression. 'But no, I don't think you should try to kill him. You've suffered enough. And you're right not to trust these people. Killing Sheridan is a major assassination. They can't let you survive that. So save yourself, Ray. Go off grid, lie low for a bit longer, then disappear, start a new life somewhere. I've seen it done before.'

I smiled. It was good to talk to her again. She knew how our world worked.

'Did you manage to bring the stuff I asked for?'

'Yup. It's all in the glove compartment. A big wedge of currency and a burner phone. It's a cheap Huawei but it's got smartphone capabilities, and a pre-paid sim with fifty megs' worth of data on it, so you can get limited internet access. It's untraceable back to me but try not to get caught with it.'

I reached inside and pulled them both out. I'd given the money – €10,000 and £5,000 in cash – to Tina for safekeeping not long after we'd started seeing each other over a year ago. I'd stashed even more cash in my old flat in Fulham as well as a storage unit in Clapham, but I couldn't access any of that now. There was a good reason for my hoarding large quantities of mixed currency. Believe it or not, the current half-a-million-pound bounty on my head wasn't the first time a price had been put on my life. Two years earlier, a wealthy Arab businessman, whose brother had died during an operation I'd been part of during my army days, had hired a freelance operative to kill everyone involved in the op, including me. The killer had failed, but the experience had left me paranoid that I might one day have to disappear in a hurry.

'I didn't spend any of it,' said Tina as I opened the envelope and peeked inside before putting it in my jacket pocket along with the smartphone.

I sighed. 'I'm sorry. I didn't want to involve you in any of this.'

'I've been involved from the start, Ray. Remember?' There was an edge to her voice, and she seemed agitated. 'Why did you stop me from visiting you when you got sent down? You know I wanted to.'

'I couldn't face seeing you when I was behind bars. I thought a clean break would be best for both of us. I was facing life in prison. I still am. But that doesn't mean I didn't care, Tina. I've always cared. And I've always missed you.'

She stared out of the window into the night. 'I don't know what to say.'

'Then don't say anything. I shouldn't have asked you to come.'

'No, it's a relief to see you. I'm glad you made it. I thought it was Kalaman's or Sheridan's people who'd kidnapped you, and that you were dead, or being tortured somewhere.'

I could hear the pain in her voice, and the car fell silent for a few moments.

'Look,' I said eventually, 'there's something else I need. It's something that's not going to arouse any suspicion or put you in any danger, I promise. But if you don't want to do it, I'd understand.'

'What is it?'

'Lane and her people made a real effort to avoid any kind of identification, or give me any clue as to where I was being held for the last two weeks. They even made me wear a hood and lie under a blanket on the way into London. But they made one mistake. When they dropped me off here, I managed to get the car registration. You're a private detective. Do you know anyone who can get access to the ANPR database and find out the route their car took yesterday afternoon?'

She thought about that for a moment. 'I know someone who might be able to help, but what use is that information to you?'

'I know exactly what the house I was kept in looked like from the outside. I walked round it enough times. If there's an ANPR camera within a mile or so of it, I might be able to get its exact location, and the more I know about these people the better, especially if they do decide not to play ball.'

She wrote the registration number down. 'Leave it with me. If I find anything I'll message you on your new phone.'

'Thanks,' I said, feeling awkward. 'For everything. I wish it hadn't ended like it did. I really do.'

'I'm used to it,' Tina said with a small shake of the head. 'I've always been unlucky in love.'

We looked at each other for a long second, and I knew the spark was still there for both of us. Instinctively I went to kiss her on the lips, but she turned her cheek, and my lips brushed against it. Her skin smelled soft and sweet and I longed for just one more night. I'd been so long without human affection that I suddenly yearned for it.

'You broke my heart, Ray,' she said as I moved back in my seat. 'I know you didn't mean to. But that's what you did.'

I took a deep breath. 'I know. And I can't tell you how much I regret that.'

'I have to go. Good luck, and I'll see what I can do about that registration.'

I got out of the car, keeping my head low as I walked down the street, and Tina drove past me, quickly disappearing from view, and leaving me feeling more empty than ever.

Part Two

10

The next morning I rose early and made myself instant coffee from the store cupboard. It tasted like crap after the good stuff I'd had for the past couple of weeks, but it woke me up, which was useful as I had a busy day ahead. Whatever happened, I was determined not to go back to prison, and since I couldn't trust Lane and her associates to come through with their promises, I was going to have to make my own plans.

Contrary to what some might think, it's not easy being on the run. To stay hidden you need money, and lots of it – more than the handy spending cash Tina had passed to me the previous night. I no longer had access to my savings and pensions, but one of my luckier investment decisions had been buying up bitcoin when it was still relatively cheap, and I had it stored in a wallet hidden away on the net a long way from the prying eyes of the authorities. I wasn't sure how much it was worth right now and didn't want to waste my data finding out, but figured it must be in the region of a quarter of a million pounds, all of it untraceable.

But money's no good without a whole new identity. Fake passports and driving licences can be bought over the net but a lot of the sites offering the services are scammers and the finished products often shoddy and easily identifiable as fakes. If you're buying from criminals, it's always better to do it face to face. They're less likely to scam you that way.

Unfortunately, and not surprisingly, there's no list of reliable providers of high-quality fake IDs for me to access. However, being a former detective has its advantages, and I knew immediately who could help me find the right person.

For a number of years I worked for the Met's Counter Terrorism Command, or CT as it was better known. Although technology plays an increasingly large part in catching would-be terrorists before they can carry out their attacks, one of the most reliable methods of disrupting terrorist activity is still the use of informants. These people aren't necessarily right on the inside of plots; often they're petty criminals on the fringes who keep their ears to the ground, and come up with the occasional titbit of information in exchange for being left alone by the police. It's not officially like that of course, but that's how it tends to work, and the best informants are those who provide a steady stream of information over a long period of time without ever falling under suspicion.

Zafir Rasaq was one of those. A thief, minor drug dealer and occasional fraudster, he seemed to know everything that was going on in his area of west London, and information he'd provided about possible radicals had led to us breaking up two potentially very dangerous terrorist cells, long before they could properly get going.

I'd left CT two years earlier, and hadn't seen Zafir for a year prior to that, but he wasn't the type of man who would have travelled far, and during the time I'd known him – a period of close to four years – he'd lived in the same Hounslow flat. I was hoping he still lived there now.

I knew I was taking a big risk by leaving the safehouse for an extended period of time. I couldn't take the phone they'd supplied me with in case Lane had placed a tracker in it, and if she called to check up on me and I didn't answer, she might call the whole thing off. I didn't think I'd miss Sheridan turning up at the brothel, though. I had a feeling he'd turn up at night when he could relax rather than on a working day, especially as today was the last day before Parliament broke up for summer. Either way, I figured it worth the risk.

I left by the front door and just over an hour and a half later, after a mix of walking and a ride in a minicab with a supremely disinterested driver, I arrived at my destination.

Hounslow's not the most attractive London borough, and where Zafir had lived in the old days was in one of the crappier parts, not far north of the Mogden Sewage Treatment Works where, if the wind was blowing in the wrong direction, it was best to hold your breath. Today, with the air temperature already in the mid-twenties, it was certainly best to hold your breath. It was also right beneath the flight path into nearby Heathrow and the planes were passing only a few hundred feet overhead with a deafening roar as I made my way up to a group of five tower blocks formed in a rough semi-circle around a litter-strewn green with a kids' playground in the middle. A couple of mums were watching their toddlers but otherwise the place was deserted.

Zafir's flat was on the fifth floor of the central block. Number 27, set right back in the south-western corner. I remembered all this because I'd helped kick the door in on my one and only visit. That had been on a raid, and we'd led him out in handcuffs, one of six men arrested as part of a major anti-terrorist operation his information had initiated in the first place. The raid had been a sham to deflect attention away from him and he'd been expecting us, but had played the part perfectly, being dragged yelling and cursing from the building as neighbours looked on, and the plan had worked. Three of the six had gone down for a total of twenty-two years, whereas Zafir had been released without charge after four days, and had received a payment of £5,000 a few weeks later for his services, courtesy of the taxpayer, which I have to say was money well spent.

I climbed the concrete staircase, sweating under my jacket, found number 27 and knocked hard on the door, hoping I hadn't had a wasted journey.

There was no answer, but that wasn't unexpected. Zafir was a career criminal and, like many of that ilk, wasn't an especially early riser.

I knocked again, harder this time, and put my ear to the door. I could definitely hear movement. I knocked a third time, keeping it going for a good ten seconds, then waited until I heard footfalls.

'Who is it?' came a voice slurred with sleep that I recognized immediately as belonging to Zafir.

'Police. Open up.'

'What the fuck?' he said wearily, opening the door a few inches on a heavy chain. His face appeared in the gap, staring at me. There was no immediate sign of recognition, which meant that either he hadn't been watching the news much or that my new disguise, which I'd added to on the way here by buying a baseball cap and sunglasses, was working. 'You're not the police.'

I took off the glasses and gave him a smile. 'Hello, Zafir. Aren't you going to invite me in?'

He frowned, still not entirely sure, then it dawned on him. 'Shit. Ray Mason?'

I put a finger to my lips. 'Keep it down.'

He didn't look happy to see me but removed the chain and moved aside to let me in.

His flat was tidier than I remembered but there was still a stale food smell in the air.

'Are you on your own?' I asked, following him into his sitting room.

'Yeah, I am,' he said, pulling on a pair of sweat pants that were conveniently lying in the middle of the floor. 'Luckily for you.' He turned to face me. 'What do you want? You're taking a big risk coming here.'

'Am I? No one's given me a second glance so far. Even you didn't recognize me. I'm here because I need a new passport and preferably a driving licence fast. I've got the cash to pay for it.'

'I've never been in that game,' said Zafir.

'But you know who is, and you're going to take me to him.'

'No way,' he said, shaking his head. 'I've got a girlfriend now. I don't need to take risks helping you.'

'Look, I don't want to involve you either, but I've got no choice. Help me and I'll be out of your hair. But if you don't, I'll make sure the whole world knows you're an informant, and that you've been putting your friends and associates away for years. You won't last five minutes.'

Zafir sat down hard on his sofa, and it made a squeaking noise. He wasn't a big man but he was running to fat, no doubt courtesy of spending his life idling in this place. He ran a hand through his unkempt hair and looked up at me.

'You got the money to pay for it, right?' he said.

'I told you I did.'

'I know a brother who might be able to help. But he'll charge top dollar.'

'As long as it's top quality, I don't care. But I need it done fast.'

He nodded, and fished a brand-new smartphone from somewhere in his sweat pants.

I listened while he made a call to his guy. It was clear they knew each other well and they had some quick banter before Zafir got down to business, asking about the service and vouching for me as a good friend. He'd recovered his poise and I remembered that he'd always been a smooth liar, which was why he'd lasted as long as he had.

He looked up from the phone. 'It'll cost you two grand cash for a perfect UK passport, and he can have that done within three days of getting the photo. If you want it done faster, it'll cost more.'

'I want it done faster. How much for twenty-four hours?'

Zafir asked him and they had a further to and fro on the phone, eventually settling on a figure of £3,000 for a passport and full UK driving licence, with half payable up front, which I agreed to without complaint.

This is the modern criminal world. If you want something, know where to look, and have the money to pay, there's very little you can't buy, be it a new ID, a kilo of coke, or even an AK-47 and a belt of ammunition. The reason most criminals don't have access to these things is because in general they're not very forward-thinking and consequently no good at covering their tracks, which is why professional criminals – the ones who make the real money – tend to avoid selling to them. I knew that the person Zafir had called would be a pro, which was good on the one hand, but also meant I was going to have to be careful, because if he got wind of who I was, there'd be trouble. As well as the half-million bounty on my head from the Kalaman crime gang, there was now a further £50,000 put up by the Met Police. Unfortunately, I'd become a very valuable commodity in my own right.

*

Less than half an hour later, Zafir and I were standing outside a curry house just off Hounslow High Street. This area was almost exclusively non-white but, with my shaved head and black beard, I could quite easily pass off as a local Muslim man, and once again no one bothered giving me a second look.

Zafir pulled out his phone and made a call, telling the person on the other end that we were outside, and a minute later, a stocky Asian man with a much thicker beard than mine appeared and unlocked the door, letting us in. Zafir seemed to know him and they performed an elaborate handshake.

The big guy looked at me suspiciously but didn't ask any questions as he locked the door again and led us through the empty restaurant and up a narrow flight of stairs at the back. I could hear clattering about and talking coming from the kitchen beyond, and the smell of cooking was already in the air, making me feel hungry.

The big guy knocked on a door at the top and we were led into a surprisingly large but very cluttered office with a desk at the end, behind which sat a rotund Asian man in his fifties with a face like a toad, wearing a three-piece suit that looked like it hadn't been dry-cleaned in a while. Two large fans on either side of him blasted cool air round the room. The window behind looked out onto a brick wall.

'Hey Faz,' said Zafir, approaching the man behind the desk, who stood up.

The two of them embraced, and the man called Faz looked my way.

'This is a bro of mine, Bobby,' explained Zafir by way of introduction, using the name we'd agreed for me. 'He's the one I was telling you about on the phone.'

Faz nodded and put out a hand, giving me a long, lingering look up and down.

I shook hands quickly, keen to get on with this. 'I need a passport and driving licence very quickly, and it's got to be the best quality.'

Faz nodded slowly and sat back down, picking up a pen and tapping it steadily on the desk. 'How do you know Zafir?' he asked.

'We were in prison together a few years back, and kept in touch,' I said, using the cover story we'd rehearsed on the way down here. 'Sometimes we do a bit of business. But now I've got a problem, and I've got to get out of the country fast.'

Faz didn't look convinced, probably because he hadn't been expecting a white man. Almost all of Zafir's associates were Muslim Asians, and it's often the case that criminals tend to stick within their own ethnic groups.

'I can vouch for him,' said Zafir confidently. 'We've known each other a long time. He can be trusted.'

Faz glared up at him suspiciously. 'I haven't seen you around much, not since the Ramses brothers got jail time over that drug stuff.'

'I've been around,' said Zafir, but there was an edge to his voice and I had no doubt that information he'd sold had been responsible for putting them away.

Faz turned his attention back to me. 'How do I know you're not the police?'

'Because I'm vouching for him,' Zafir insisted.

I didn't like the way this conversation was going, although it was some consolation that he hadn't recognized me. 'Because undercover police in this country don't carry guns and point them at people,' I said, pulling out the SIG Sauer Lane had supplied me with from underneath my jacket. In one quick movement I turned and pointed it at the big bearded guy who immediately took a step backwards with his hands high in the air. I then shoved it back in the front of my jeans where it remained visible.

Having deployed the stick to good effect, I now opted for the carrot. I pulled a wad containing £1,500 in cash that I'd counted out in Zafir's flat earlier from the back pocket of my jeans, and threw it on the desk in front of a flustered Faz. 'I just want the ID then I'll be gone. OK?'

Faz's eyes darted from the money to the gun sticking out of my waistband, then to my face, and finally back to the money, because in the end, like all criminals, he was greedy. And all the time I could see he was making a steady stream of calculations as he tried to work out whether or not a real police officer would behave like this. I can tell you with hand on heart that there is no way an undercover cop would bring a gun on an op to nail a fraudster, still less wave it around at everyone in the room. He'd be out of a job in minutes.

Evidently Faz had come to the same conclusion because he picked up the wad and counted out the notes with a practised yet shaky hand, while I stepped away from the desk so I could keep my eye on Beardie, who'd dropped his hands now and was scowling at me from behind the beard. I gave him a long look back and he was the one who turned away first.

'OK, OK,' said Faz, pocketing the money. 'I can do this for you.' He got to his feet and walked over to an adjoining door. 'This way please. We need to take some photos.'

I pushed past Zafir who looked away fast, like he didn't want to be seen with me – which to be fair to him he didn't – and followed Faz into what looked like a tiny stock cupboard containing nothing more than office stationery; but then he knocked three times on the far wall, and it was suddenly opened from the other side, revealing a larger room much of which was taken up with high-end computer equipment, including a bank of fridge-sized printers. A group of three men sat working at adjoining desks. One of them was hunched over, painstakingly modifying a UK residence card, while another had a pile of passports on the desk next to him as he typed away on a keyboard. It was an impressive set-up but, unlike next door, the room was stiflingly hot with only one window, opening onto a flight of fire escape steps, letting in any air.

I wiped sweat from my brow and moved the gun so it was hidden by my jacket before going inside. A chair had been placed against the wall at the other end of the room facing a camera on a tripod, next to a photographer's umbrella, and Faz invited me to sit down. None of the three young men paid me any heed as I took a seat but I did notice that Faz spent a long time looking through the camera as he took the photos, as if he was inspecting me from behind the lens. He was obviously curious to know more about me but had the good sense not to ask questions. I knew he'd speak to Zafir afterwards though, and that was a concern.

We finished up quickly and he showed me the photos. I wasn't sure if it was paranoia or not but the images of the bearded bald man staring blankly at the camera suddenly seemed to look a lot more like me than I'd been expecting.

I told him the photos looked fine.

He nodded. 'Good. You come here with Zafir tomorrow evening at six o'clock and the documents will be ready for you. The passport will even fool airport scanners.'

'It'd better do for three grand.'

'You're getting a bargain, my friend, I can promise you that. Six p.m. tomorrow, OK?'

I didn't like the way he looked at me as he spoke. He was smiling but there was something reptilian in his expression, as if somewhere behind his eyes he was sizing me up as prey.

I gave him a hard look. 'Just don't try to fuck me about.'

The smile disappeared and his eyes narrowed. 'I'm a businessman. I don't fuck anyone about.'

Which was almost certainly not the first lie he'd told today but I let it go.

However, when I was outside with Zafir I laid my cards on the table. 'You come with me tomorrow to get the stuff,' I said, leaning in close to him, 'and make sure he doesn't try anything stupid or I'll kill you both. You got me?'

'Yeah, yeah, yeah,' he said, leaning backwards. 'Chill out.'

'Give me your phone number.'

Die Alone

He reeled it out and I keyed it into the phone Tina had given me, then immediately called it. It started ringing in his pocket.

'You really don't trust me, do you?' said Zafir, looking genuinely put out.

'I don't think I need to answer that,' I told him, then turned and left him there.

11

Alastair Sheridan loved his Chelsea mews house, tucked away behind the King's Road, an oasis of calm amid the bustle of the city. He spent as much time as possible here, away from his wife and child back in their constituency home. His wife bored him. He'd only married her for appearances' sake. She was attractive – ten years his junior and a former model – and adequate in bed, but she had no real sense of adventure, of excitement. She'd never push any boundaries. She was a good breeder, but that was it. They'd produced a fine-looking boy whom Alastair supposed he loved, although he still wasn't entirely sure since he had very little concept of what love actually was. When people talked seriously and passionately about how they'd die for their children,

Alastair smiled and nodded and agreed with them, but inside he wondered what on earth they were talking about. He wouldn't die for anyone. Why would you? The most important person in Alastair's world was Alastair, and this was never going to change.

It always amused him to think that his wife didn't know him at all, yet thought she knew him perfectly. He'd enjoyed manipulating her in the early days, making her believe what a kind, generous man he was, and remembered getting a huge kick from proposing to her during a candlelit dinner at Le Gavroche in Paris, barely forty-eight hours after he and Cem had tortured to death an eighteen-year-old Estonian girl with the most exquisite skin Alastair had ever seen, slices of which they'd carefully removed while she'd still been alive.

He and his wife lived near enough separate lives these days. Even so, Alastair knew he'd chosen well. His wife hadn't come from money so she was content to live the life of a wealthy yummy mummy, lunching and playing tennis and keeping well out of Alastair's hair, and leaving him to enjoy life's pleasures.

Alastair had seen things that others could only dream about. He'd wielded the ultimate power – that of life and death – and it was a pleasure so intense as to make all others pale in comparison. The downside was that such pleasure could only be shared with a handful of people.

One of those people was Cem. Alastair had known him since childhood. They'd grown up together. They'd carried out their first kill together, snatching that Brennan girl from her bike as she cycled down a country lane and taking her out to Cem's old school by the Thames. There the two of them had dispatched her and buried the remains in the grounds, where they would have stayed for ever if it hadn't been for the greedy bastards on the school board selling a plot of land for development.

That was the moment it had all started to go wrong for Alastair and Cem. A new murder investigation had been launched, the house in Wales where they'd been killing illegally trafficked young women for years had been discovered, and a witness who could testify about Alastair's involvement in one of the murders had come forward. Thankfully, Cem had managed to get rid of Hugh Manning before he could give a statement to the police, but even so, the authorities had come far too close to Alastair for comfort.

Which was when he'd decided that the time was right to get rid of the last person who could link him to any of the murders.

12

The first thing I did when I got back to the apartment was check
the phone Lane had given to me to see if I'd missed any calls.

I had. Two. Both from an unknown number. One at 11.38, the
next at 11.49. These could only have been from Lane, and I'd
broken rule number one by not answering either of them. I stared
at the phone, wondering what her next move would be. I didn't
think she'd throw me to the wolves. Not yet. Not after investing
so much in me. But if she had, it meant that armed police were
probably on their way here right now.

I opened the French windows onto the roof terrace and poked
my head outside. There was no one around. The temperature by
now was in the late twenties, but the cloud cover made it feel

even hotter. From where I stood I could see both far entrances to the square, and all was quiet. No one, it seemed, was coming just yet.

The phone in my hand rang. The same unknown number.

I retreated inside. 'Yeah?'

It was Lane. 'Where the hell were you?' she demanded. 'You were instructed not to leave the safehouse.'

'I had to,' I said. 'I pulled a calf muscle doing some exercises and I needed some Ibuprofen. You didn't supply any.'

The lie seemed to calm her somewhat. She might have forbidden me to leave this place but she didn't want me injured. 'How's the calf now?' she asked.

I told her it was settling down, then asked, 'Any news on when our man might be turning up?'

'Not yet, but you'll hear as soon as I do. Do not leave the safehouse again. If you miss this chance, I will make sure the police have your current location as well as your brand-new passport photo. Don't mess it up, Ray.'

She ended the call and I went into the kitchen and for lunch chose a plastic tub of instant seafood noodles from the selection of unappetizing long-life food. It actually tasted quite good, and I was just working out which tinned fruit to have for dessert when the burner phone Tina had given me started ringing.

'I've got information about the car that took you to the safehouse,' she said.

'That was quick. Do I owe you any money?'

'Call it a favour.'

'I don't know when I'm ever going to pay it back.'

'Me neither,' she said. 'But that's not why I did it. Anyway, the car began and ended its journey at some point within a few square miles of a speed camera on the Epping Road in Essex, close to a village called Toot Hill. If you know the shape of the house and the garden you were in you may be able to find it on Google Maps.'

'Thanks, Tina. I really appreciate it.'

'Why don't you just leave, Ray? Run while you can. Don't try to be a hero. You've done it before and look where it's got you.'

'I could say the same thing to you, Tina.'

There was a pause down the other end of the line. I could hear kids shouting in the background and the sound of traffic. She was outside somewhere.

'Good luck, Ray. Whatever you choose to do.'

There was so much I wanted to say to her. That I missed her every day. That I loved her. That I wished it could all have been so different. But there was no point. Instead I just said thanks, took the postcode of the speed camera, and that was it. The conversation was over, and I was back on my own.

Using the data on the smartphone, I pulled up Google Maps, found the speed camera and homed in on the satellite images of a largely rural area of west Essex, about thirty miles northeast of central London, with a scattering of hamlets set in farmland.

It took me a good ten minutes but eventually I found it – a white, detached house set in the middle of a plot surrounded by high hedges and backing onto woodland. It was definitely the place, on its own at the end of a track with a handful of houses and a farm in a hamlet a couple of hundred metres away. A perfect spot if you didn't want to attract attention.

I made a note of the coordinates and shut off the phone before I ran entirely out of data, and for the first time I seriously considered doing what Tina was suggesting. I had options. I could get hold of a car, drive up to where Lane and her friends had held me, and neutralize them. Then I'd collect my passport and make a break for France, where I could cash in some of my bitcoin, set up a new bank account, and fade from view. Hell, I didn't even have to kill Lane. I could just run.

I don't know if it was my promise to the Brennans to bring their daughter's killers to justice; my instinct that Alastair Sheridan not only deserved to die but had to, in order to stop him becoming the most powerful person in the country; or simply pure revenge over his part in sending me to prison and destroying my life. Whatever it was, for the moment at least it made me stay put and, as the afternoon wore into the evening, I paced the stifling confines of the apartment, working out my next move, unable to settle. Unable, it seemed, to make a decision, as day turned into night, and the air began to cool as the predicted heavy showers approached from the west.

And then at 9.30 p.m., the decision was made for me when Lane's burner phone rang again.

It was on the side in the kitchen, and as I picked up on the fourth ring, Lane's voice came down the line, calm but tense.

'The target is en route. Be ready to strike in twenty minutes.'

13

Fifteen minutes later, I stood in the darkness of the apartment dressed all in black, a pack containing my belongings on my back, and the pistol with suppressor already attached pushed into the back of my waistband. My breathing was steady and I was tense but not afraid. The gun gave me confidence. I've used one plenty of times before, which almost certainly put me at an advantage over anyone I was going to come up against tonight. And best of all, I had surprise on my side.

My only doubt was whether I'd be able to pull the trigger when it came to it. I've been a soldier, and I've been a police officer. But I've never been a contract killer. I've killed in cold blood once before but the evidence of my victim's crimes was all around her, and she was revelling in it as I faced her down. I'd acted in anger then, and had felt physically sick afterwards. Did I regret it? I honestly don't know, but the act itself ripped away a part of my humanity that I would never get back.

When I confronted Alastair Sheridan, it would be different. He wouldn't be revelling in his crimes. He would be naked, probably helpless, almost certainly begging for his life.

Could I do it?

I shut my eyes and pictured Dana Brennan. Her mum had given me a photo of her, aged eleven, posing with her pet dog, taken about a year and a half before she was abducted and murdered by Sheridan and his friend, Cem Kalaman. I no longer had that photo. It had been taken from me, along with my wallet, when I'd been arrested, but I'd stared at it long enough to have Dana's face etched on my memory.

I had to do it for her, and for the ghosts of all the other young women he'd destroyed.

I went through the open French windows and onto the roof, shutting them behind me. A welcome breeze caught me full in the face as I stood there looking out across the lights of the city, spreading as far as the eye could see. The night was just about as dark as it ever got in London at this time of year and an angry swirl of clouds was racing overhead.

I looked round. There was no one else out on any of the other roof terraces tonight, but a few doors down I could see the lights on in one of the apartments, and the French windows were open. I walked to the edge of the roof and looked down at the square, an oasis in the heart of the city, the one-way traffic system and speed bumps discouraging any cut-through drivers – and I could see why the wealthy would enjoy living behind its grand facades, although I suspected few of them actually did, preferring to leave them empty as investment vehicles for dirty money. I guess if you were going to open a high-end brothel anywhere, here wouldn't be a bad spot since it was unlikely there'd be many people around to complain about it.

Whoever Lane's insider was, he or she was bang on the money because, as I stood there, two black SUVs with blacked-out windows turned into the far side of the square and drove in convoy round the central gardens, coming to a halt outside one of the neighbouring buildings. I heard rather than saw them disgorge their occupants as they were outside my field of vision, but I knew who they were.

Being dressed in black was always going to make me conspicuous on a night like this, so I crouched down behind the waist-high wall that separated my terrace from the one next door and pulled on a black balaclava, counting down the seconds until it was time to move. I knew to give Sheridan five minutes from arrival to get into the room, but I'd already decided to give him ten. I wanted him vulnerable, and hopefully in flagrante, when I made my move.

I stared at my watch, emptying my head of all wasteful thoughts, concentrating on what I was about to do, slowing my breathing even as the adrenalin pumped through my system, remembering my long-ago army training.

And then, just like that, it was time.

I'd memorized the map of the building and knew that I had to cross five separate roof terraces to get to the entrance to the brothel's penthouse area. The distance was thirty-five metres, and I made it in less than thirty seconds, keeping low so I couldn't be seen by anyone down on the street.

A flight of steps led down to the heavy fire door and I descended slowly, placed my ear to the wood, and listened. Silence – but I was aware the area could be soundproofed. The nightmare for me was running into one of the girls before I located my target. It would be hard enough putting a bullet in Alastair Sheridan. There was no way I was going to put one in an innocent bystander.

I placed the key Lane had given me in the door and, as I did so, wondered how on earth she'd managed to get a key to this place. Still listening hard, I pushed the door open and stepped inside, closing it carefully behind me.

I was in an empty hallway, decorated in a rich burgundy. My footfalls were muffled by the thick, expensive-looking carpet as I moved through it, remembering the plans Lane had given me. To my left was the jacuzzi room. The door was half open, and I poked my head inside. The raised, round jacuzzi took up most of the available floor space, and was full of foam-topped water bubbling silently. The interior was lit by strategically placed candles and smelled like the perfume section of an airport duty-free, and I guessed it had all been got ready for Alastair Sheridan to enjoy with the lady of his choice, if indeed she was still in a position to enjoy any of it. I wasn't sure how it worked in this place. The way Lane had explained it, it sounded like it was the kind of establishment where the clients could be rough with the girls without them making a complaint. But I knew Sheridan would have to work very hard to keep his self-control and not get too carried away. I'd heard from an impeccable source that he'd killed a prostitute by mistake once while doing whatever it was he liked to do with them.

At the end of the hallway was a flight of stairs leading down to the next floor. Just before it, there were two doors, one on the left, one on the right. The left-hand one was the main bedroom where Sheridan would be. As I stopped outside, it struck me that the insider had almost pinpoint-perfect information of Sheridan's movements, as well as his use of the prostitutes. It therefore had to be someone he'd trust absolutely, and with someone so careful of his reputation there could only be a handful of these, and they almost certainly wouldn't include members of his security detail.

So who was it?

I was just about to put my ear to the door when I heard the sound of a door opening downstairs followed by footsteps, and people talking as they came up the stairs.

I opened the bathroom door opposite and took a quick glance in. Ambient chill music was playing from an unseen speaker, but the room was empty and I darted inside, closing the door behind me, and stood there in the darkness, the gun in my hand, hoping like hell no one decided to come in here and take a leak.

The voices grew louder, and their owners were now directly outside. I could hear a female and a male talking. The female had the louder voice, and there was a confidence to it, but I couldn't make out what either of them were saying above the music.

The door across the hallway closed, and I heard more footfalls going back down the stairs, then nothing.

I waited in the darkness for a good five minutes until I was sure everyone was settled in, then opened the bathroom door and stepped back out into the hallway. There was no one out there but I could hear male voices talking quietly somewhere out of sight at the foot of the stairs. These would be Alastair Sheridan's security. For all I knew they could be serving police officers, and I really didn't want to shoot a cop. I was going to have to be very silent and very quick.

I put my ear to the bedroom door. I could hear the faint sound of a woman crying out in pain, and a man's voice calling her a bitch and ordering her to shut up. She cried out again, a scream this time, and I immediately pushed the door.

It was locked.

I was going to have to forget the silent part.

I took a step backwards, ready to launch a kick, but stopped when I heard a commotion at the foot of the stairs and a woman's voice saying to someone angrily 'Let me up there, I need to sort this out', followed immediately by hurried footsteps coming up the stairs.

I darted back inside the bathroom but this time I kept the door ajar a couple of inches, watching as a tall, Amazonian-looking woman with multiple intricate tattoos in a black sleeveless dress appeared. She knocked hard on the door opposite and it was opened by a sobbing woman I couldn't see.

'Get back in there,' the madam told her angrily. 'Do what you're paid to do.'

I opened the door another couple of inches as the madam disappeared inside, leaving the door on the latch. I could hear her simultaneously haranguing the girl and apologizing to Sheridan.

I came out of the bathroom, looking towards the staircase just to check that Sheridan's security weren't standing there (they weren't, and if they had been I'd probably have put bullets in them anyway for tolerating what was going on here), and walked straight into the bedroom, gun outstretched.

The madam had the girl, who was naked, by the hair and was giving her an angry talking-to while a half-naked man stood on the other side of a huge bed that probably slept half a dozen, holding a riding crop limply in his hand, looking surprised that his seduction technique wasn't paying off.

And that was my first big problem.

Because the man wasn't Alastair Sheridan. It was his partner in crime, Cem Kalaman. And in that moment, two things crossed my mind.

One: I'd been set up. Two: Kalaman had been too.

The last time I'd seen him in the flesh was when he'd turned up at my apartment with a group of his thugs fifteen months earlier. Then he'd been a swaggering presence – the all-powerful crime lord. Now he was just a middle-aged sad case with a pot-belly, a flaccid cock, and a face that was a mix of righteous outrage and real fear, but with the fear clearly winning. He dropped the crop and threw his hands in the air, a small, almost feminine gasp escaping his mouth as he realized that his time was up.

I raised the gun, knowing that I would have no problem ending this pervert's life, but as I took a step forward and pulled the trigger, I saw out of the corner of my eye the madam lunging at me as she screamed for help.

I swung round, not wanting to shoot her if I could help it. She grabbed my gun arm and yanked it to one side, still coming at me. I reacted fast, driving an elbow into her face as she got in range, and stopping her in her tracks. But she was still hanging on to my gun arm. I wrenched it free and pulled her into a headlock, just as the bedroom door flew open and one of Kalaman's security people appeared in the doorway, armed with a pistol. He saw me and immediately opened fire, the gun making a loud and very distinct retort. I was already firing back – three shots in all, two of which hit him in the upper body, sending him sprawling. At the same time, the madam cried out and went limp in my arms and I realized she'd been hit.

I eased her to the floor, still keeping my eye on the door. I was certain there were at least two bodyguards with Kalaman, potentially more. And if one was armed, the others would be too. Nobody was helping the other guy though, who'd half fallen through the bathroom door and was now lying on his side trying to move, his shirt bloodied.

I took a quick look over my shoulder. I'd hit Kalaman with that first round and he was curled up in the foetal position, clutching his gut and moaning in pain, and for the moment posing no threat. Neither was the young girl, who was crouching unharmed in the corner, away from the shooting.

She gave me a terrified look, clearly thinking I was going to hurt her. I shook my head, hoping she'd get the message that she was safe from me. I was pretty sure the other bodyguard was waiting on the other side of the door for me to show myself, so I crept diagonally across the room, trying to get as good a view out into the hallway as possible without exposing myself to fire.

I could hear more footfalls and shouting coming from downstairs. My shots had been partially muffled by the suppressor, but the shot from the bodyguard would probably have been audible throughout the building. I needed to hurry.

But rushing something like this is a good way to end up dead.

My view of the hallway widened as I moved towards the wall, but not enough for me to see anyone. I could hear my heart beating. This was a bad position to be in, and I had to force myself to resist the urge to just run out of there.

The footfalls were getting closer, and then from the top of the stairs I heard a male voice call out, 'What the fuck's going on?' He was immediately answered by someone very close to the outside of the bedroom door, who called at him to get back.

That was my cue. While the man outside the door was momentarily distracted, I jumped forward, reached my gun hand round the door frame and pulled the trigger three times, moving the arc of the gun with each shot as I tried to hit an unseen target.

I heard a gasp of pain, and a shot rang out, ricocheting through the hallway.

You never want to think too much on occasions like this. I knew I'd hit the other man so I jumped out into the hallway and saw him stumbling backwards towards the staircase and clutching at his arm, the gun no longer visible. Seeing me, he half leapt, half fell against the wall and landed in a heap at the top of the stairs. Somewhere out of sight, I heard the third guy – the one who'd wanted to know what was going on – racing back down the stairs to avoid being the next victim. Luckily for me, it seemed that Kalaman's bodyguards were a long way off top quality.

I grabbed the discarded gun of the man I'd just shot and shoved it into my waistband. I could have finished him off, but he was no threat so I left him there, walked purposefully back into the bedroom, past the badly injured madam and over to where Cem Kalaman still lay writhing on the floor.

He looked up at me with a fearful expression in his eyes as I pointed the gun down at him, lifting up my balaclava so he, and he alone, could see my face.

'Please,' he said, through gritted teeth. 'I've got money.'

'This is for all your victims,' I told him, leaning forward and firing a single round into his head.

That was when I heard the sirens, far too close and fast for the cops to have just been called. This wasn't good, because it suggested that the set-up didn't only involve me killing the wrong man. It meant I wasn't supposed to get out of this place either.

I moved fast, checking the hallway to see that it was clear. The two bodyguards were still where they'd fallen. The first looked unconscious, while the second one was trying to crawl down the stairs. I was fairly certain no one else was going to want to take me on so I turned and ran back the way I'd come, locking the fire door behind me and running up onto the roof.

I raced along the rooftops, keeping low, conscious of the flashing blue lights of the police cars reflecting off the houses as they raced into the square. It sounded like there were at least three vehicles, but it would take them a few minutes to work out what was going on and start sealing off the streets. I'd originally planned to exit through my flat well before the police arrived, but now going out of the front door there, not much over thirty metres down the street from where the police were arriving, would be way too risky. And for all I knew, whoever had called the police (and my guess was that it was Lane herself) had given them the address I was staying in as well.

The light was on and the French windows still open onto the terrace right near the end of the building, and I ran towards them, clambering over roof terraces, hoping I couldn't be seen from the street, not daring to look. Just like that, it began to rain. Hard. Out of the corner of my eye, I saw the flashing lights of another emergency vehicle entering the square. It couldn't have been much more than three minutes since the first shot had been fired and yet it was as if they'd been waiting round the corner, ready to pounce.

I reached the roof terrace of the house with the open windows and ran straight inside, descending a short flight of stairs into a large open living space. A round-faced man of about sixty in a linen dressing gown, with white hair and a large bald spot, sat on a long L-shaped sofa watching TV and stroking a very fat cat, while another equally fat cat was asleep next to him. The man stared at me, wide-eyed and open-mouthed, and I put a finger to my lips to quieten him.

'I'm not going to hurt you,' I said, approaching him with the gun lowered a little, 'but I need your help. Who else is here?'

He shook his head. 'No one. I'm on my own.'

'Good. Do you own a car?'

He nodded.

'What kind, and where is it?'

'It's a silver Mercedes A-Class saloon. It's parked right outside.'

My luck was in. 'Get me the keys, and fast. The sooner you cooperate, the sooner I'm out of here.'

He got to his feet, much to the annoyance of the cat on his lap, and walked down some stairs into a spacious kitchen. He took a set of car keys off a key holder on the wall and handed them to me.

I told him to lie on his front on the floor. He started to protest and I had to tell him again that I wasn't going to hurt him. 'But I am going to tie your hands behind your back so you don't raise the alarm.'

Gingerly, he got down on his knees, but time was of the essence so I gave him a hard shove, forced him down onto his front, took a pair of the restraints that Lane had supplied from the backpack, and bound his wrists. 'Right, stay there. Do not move for fifteen minutes. Then you can go and get help.'

He said he understood and I left him in there, went out the front door of his flat, and hurried down the communal staircase, putting my balaclava, the pistol I'd picked up from the body-guard, and the suppressor into the backpack, and shoving my own pistol into the back of my jeans, knowing that if it came to it, I'd put a bullet in my own head rather than go back to prison.

But it didn't come to that. I didn't see anyone on the stairs, and as I came out of the front door, a good fifty metres away from where I'd pulled the trigger on Kalaman, I saw that the cluster of police cars, four in all, were parked up at the brothel entrance. A handful of people were on the street looking towards where the action was, but nobody noticed me as I walked over to where the Mercedes was parked and pressed the key fob to unlock it.

I climbed inside, threw the backpack on the passenger seat, drove slowly out of the parking spot and, knowing that any sense of urgency would look suspicious, followed the one-way system round the other side of the square and away from the scene of the crime, even pausing to let an armed response car with lights flashing come through.

Then I turned onto the Bayswater Road heading north and, as soon as there was a gap in the traffic behind me, I threw the burner phone Lane had given me out of the window and into Hyde Park, before accelerating away.

I was free. For now.

14

Alastair Sheridan sipped the glass of Rémy Martin Louis XIII cognac, the type favoured by Winston Churchill, a political hero of his, savouring the taste as he relaxed in his favourite armchair. Mozart was playing in the background – the rousing Piano Concerto No. 17 – while the study's sash window was a few inches open to let in the comforting sound of the rain, and the cool breeze that accompanied it.

Cem Kalaman, his old friend, was now officially dead. Alastair had just received the news in a phone call from an undercover police officer called Chris Lansdowne who'd been working as Cem's driver. Luckily for Alastair, Lansdowne was as corrupt as they came, and a payment of £100,000 into an anonymous bank account in the British Virgin Islands had immediately secured his loyalty. It had been Lansdowne who'd provided Alastair with details of Cem's movements, and by doing so had set up his murder. The assassination itself had required a lot of planning. Money hadn't been a problem. It never was with Alastair, who'd made tens of millions over the years. It had been the logistics. But Alastair had always been a good planner, and setting up Ray Mason to take the rap had been a stroke of genius.

What Alastair hadn't bargained for, however, was Mason escaping the crime scene. And, according to Lansdowne, who was still at the scene himself, this was exactly what had happened. It was nearly an hour and a half since the hit and Mason was nowhere to be found.

Alastair didn't like the idea of Mason being out there, armed and vengeful. He was one of the few people who knew about Alastair's secret life, and who was also crazy enough to come after him. Alastair had good personal security, but he'd feel a lot safer when Mason was back where he belonged behind bars, or better still in the ground.

He took another sip of the brandy, certain that Mason wouldn't come after him tonight. He'd be too busy trying to avoid the attention of the police. Instead, his thoughts turned to Cem. Alastair would miss his company. Theirs had been a close relationship – closer in many ways than any other relationship he'd ever had. But sometimes in business you have to be ruthless and, sadly, Cem had become a liability. As the head of a crime organization with a turnover in the hundreds of millions of pounds, he was too much of a high-profile figure to survive unscathed in the long term, and if he ever talked, he could destroy Alastair.

Alastair was sure that no one in Cem's criminal organization would ever suspect him of having any involvement in their boss's death; few of them even knew there was a connection between the two men. But just to be certain, the important thing now was to make sure that Ray Mason's name was associated with Cem's murder, so that he became the main suspect, and Alastair was just trying to work out how best to do that when the anonymous phone Lansdowne had called him on rang again.

But this time it wasn't Lansdowne calling. It was someone else. Someone with some good news.

Alastair smiled as he listened to the person on the other end of the phone. Things, it seemed, had worked out for him once again.

15

It was 11.15 p.m. and raining steadily as I parked the Mercedes in the shade of a tree at the side of an isolated country lane that, according to Google Maps, was approximately fifty metres behind the house where I'd been staying until two nights ago. The police would find the car eventually – they might even be looking for it now if the guy I'd stolen it from had managed to raise the alarm – but I suspected I'd be long gone before they located it, and just to make things hard for them I'd stopped en route at a piece of waste ground in north London and rubbed dirt on the plates, obscuring them for the cameras.

I'd seen lights on in the house as I'd driven past, so Lane, and possibly her two colleagues, would still be there. I was taking a big risk turning up like this. Some would say that I'd have done a lot better to stay out of sight for a few days, but I needed to know why Lane had set me up.

I cut a rough path through the trees to the back of the property until I came to the familiar leylandii hedge with the wooden gate in the middle. The gate was about eight feet high and I knew from memory that it was bolted from the inside, which meant that the only way in was over it. It didn't sound like there was anyone in the back garden so I jumped up, grabbed the top and hauled myself up, thankful that I'd spent so long in the prison gym practising my pull-ups.

The garden was empty as I slid down the other side of the gate, but all the downstairs curtains were drawn and the lights were on in the rooms. There were people here, I was sure of it.

My suspicion was confirmed a second later when I heard a car door being shut round the front of the house on the driveway. People were either arriving or leaving, and I had a feeling it was going to be leaving. I drew the pistol Lane had provided me with and screwed on the suppressor. I'd reloaded it earlier using bullets from the gun I'd liberated from Cem Kalaman's bodyguard, and I had a full clip. I'd shot three people tonight – it was a strange and unpleasant feeling – and I had no desire to shoot any more. But I also needed answers, and pointing a gun at someone is a very effective way of getting them.

I crept round the side of the house and peered at the driveway. There were two cars there. One was the Range Rover that had transported me to London. The other one was a large black panel van I didn't recognize that looked like it had been reversed in.

The rear doors were open and I could see something wrapped in clear plastic inside.

As I stood there pondering my next move, I heard the front door to the house open and a big red-bearded man came into view dragging something else wrapped in clear plastic. I flinched as I realized it was the body of a woman, and even from this distance, in the glow of the porch light, I knew it was Lane. I might never have seen her face but I recognized the navy trouser suit she had on as the one I'd seen her in two days ago, and I noticed her feet were bare. The man had her by the shoulders, and I watched as he manoeuvred her towards the boot, turning round so he had his back to me as he heaved her inside with a loud grunt of exertion.

That was when I made my move. I covered the ten yards that separated us in the space of a few seconds, moving silently, and I was almost on him when he turned round and saw me.

I pointed the gun at his chest. 'Hands in the air,' I told him.

The man smiled. He had a friendly face beneath the beard, with twinkling blue eyes, and a thick head of curly red hair. 'You scared me, sneaking up like that,' he said. His accent was South African. He lifted his hands above his head and I saw the telltale bulge under his jacket.

'Reach down very slowly with your left hand and take out your gun, then lay it on the ground.' I looked him in the eye as I spoke, my gun hand perfectly steady. 'I want you to know something. I've killed tonight. If you try anything, you'll be next.'

'I know you have,' he said.

He'd stopped smiling but there was still something playful in his expression. He wasn't scared, and that concerned me. But he did as he was told, taking out a pistol and laying it on the ground at his feet.

'Step back three paces away from the gun.'

He stepped back and I glanced in the back of the van, seeing Lane's face for the first time beneath the clear plastic sheeting. She looked about fifty-five, with a strong, almost masculine face that was heavily splattered with blood from a large exit hole on her forehead. Her eyes were closed and her skin was a dead white. She looked grotesque wrapped up like that, with the sleeve of her jacket pulled up to reveal the silver bangle she'd been wearing only two days earlier. Beneath her was the body of a man, doubt-less one of those who'd driven me to London and brought me food every day.

It seemed like we'd all been played. But who had she been working for? Because this didn't feel like anything the security services would have sanctioned.

I stepped away from the van, lowering the gun so it was pointed at the red-bearded man's knee. 'It looks like you've been busy,' I told him. 'Now I'm going to ask you some questions. If you hesitate, or lie, I'm going to put a bullet in your left kneecap, then we'll keep going until you give me the answers I need. First one. Who are you working for?'

'He's working for me,' said a voice behind me – a voice I rec-ognized from the past.

And that was when I knew I was in real trouble.

16

Two years ago, I lost the only man I've ever called a true friend. His name was Chris Leavey and I'd met him when we served together in military intelligence. We'd reunited in the police force and had been working a case together for Counter Terrorism Command which had pitted us against probably the most cunning killer I've ever come across. No one knew her real name. She was simply known by her clients and by the various law enforcement agencies trying to catch her as The Wraith. During the course of that investigation, she'd been responsible for killing a total of six police officers, including three of my team, one of whom was Chris Leavey. She'd been contracted to kill me too and, although she hadn't been successful, I'd always been haunted by the fact that she'd escaped justice from right under my nose.

And now she was right behind me.

Very slowly, I looked back over my shoulder and saw an attractive woman in her early forties with striking dark eyes, dressed in a figure-hugging black spandex top, jeans and running shoes, and holding a pistol very similar to mine with a suppressor attached. There was no effort at disguise but then neither she nor her partner had been expecting to be disturbed.

'Long time no see, Ray Mason,' she said, her voice hard, with a trace of her native South African accent. 'This is a very unexpected surprise. But a pleasant one. What are you doing here?'

It struck me then that The Wraith knew nothing about the execution of Cem Kalaman or my connection to any of the people she'd just killed. 'I had some unfinished business with the people here,' I said, glancing over at Lane's wrapped-up corpse. 'I guess I'm a bit late.'

'It looks that way.'

'I'm happy just to walk away though and leave you to it,' I said, knowing I was far more useful dead than alive to whoever had hired The Wraith and her friend.

She smiled. 'I don't think so. Put the gun on the ground.'

A small part of me thought about shooting it out with her there and then. I'd always wanted revenge on this woman for what she'd done to Chris and my other team members, but in the end, I knew my best option was to do what I could to stay alive just a little bit longer. I put down the gun as the red-bearded guy picked his up.

'So what are we going to do with you, Mr Mason? That's the question. You're the only person who's ever survived me being paid to kill them. It looks like that's about to change. I don't follow events in this country very much but I do know that some very important people want you dead.'

'So why don't we put this gentleman out of his misery?' said Redbeard, giving me a cheery smile, as if he'd just offered to buy me a drink.

'Let's see what the client has to say,' said The Wraith, taking a phone from her pocket and stepping away as she made a call.

I glanced across at Redbeard. He was standing only ten feet away from me. If he was a bad shot and I bolted fast enough he might not be able to put a bullet in me before I made it round the corner and out of sight. But he'd have to be a very bad shot and I'd have to be very, very fast. I was sweating as the adrenalin pumped through me.

'Don't even think about it, Mr Mason,' he said.

'I've got half a million pounds stashed away,' I told him. 'That's a hell of a lot of rands. Let me go, and it's yours. All of it. You could retire.'

'It's a tempting offer, but I'm afraid double-crossing my clients would be no good for my professional reputation.'

'You'll end up dead anyway. She'll double-cross you. She's a snake.'

'I think you're being unduly pessimistic. Even people in our profession have a code of conduct, and my friend here is considered very reliable.'

I looked across at The Wraith as she talked quietly on the phone with her back to me, having a conversation that would effectively decide whether I lived or died in the next few minutes. Now that it was coming to it, I was suddenly terrified.

I swallowed hard. 'Who hired you?' I asked Redbeard.

'I can't tell you that.'

'Why? I'm going to die anyway.' I wanted to keep him talking, hoping he'd let his guard down for just one second, giving me a half chance to do something – anything.

The Wraith ended her call and replaced the phone in her jeans pocket, turning back to face me.

It was the moment of truth. I felt my jaw tighten and my heart beat faster. It made me recall the phrase 'better to die on your feet than live on your knees'. I had a feeling that one was written by someone who wasn't just about to die.

'My client would love to spend some time making you suffer for all the inconvenience you've caused him but there's no time for that. I'm afraid it's goodbye.'

She took a step towards me, a relaxed, almost bored expression on her face, and it occurred to me then, even as she raised the gun, that a woman as strikingly attractive and undoubtedly intelligent as her could have done anything in life, and yet here she was: nothing more than a lowlife, flint-hearted murderer.

My whole body tensed. All my attention was focused on the barrel of the gun. My life didn't even flash before me. I was simply frozen to the spot, knowing that in the next second it would all be over.

And then the shots exploded out of nowhere.

*

I grabbed my gun from the ground as The Wraith spun round and went down, hitting the concrete hard. At the same time, Redbeard, who instinctively seemed to know where the shots were coming from, took cover behind the van doors, already swinging his gun round towards me.

I was already running round the side of the house as I cracked off a shot at Redbeard. It missed, but it did the trick of putting him off as he fired two wild rounds at me, the sound of his bullets cracking across the night sky. Keeping low, I fired twice back, ignoring the shots being returned, and then I was sprinting along the lawn in the direction of the back gate, almost slipping on the wet grass in my haste.

The shooting that had interrupted my execution and saved my life had stopped now. In fact, all the shooting had stopped.

I took a look over my shoulder and saw Redbeard barely ten yards behind me, down on one knee ready to take a shot.

I dived to the ground, swinging round and opening fire at just the moment he started shooting at me. I felt a bullet whistle past my face, but I kept firing and a round struck him in the shoulder, knocking him backwards.

Immediately, I scrambled to my feet and dashed for the gate and freedom.

But before I got there, I heard the back door to the house open and, as I glanced back, I saw The Wraith in the doorway, unhurt and already taking aim at me. I thought she'd been hit, but if she had, she wasn't hurt badly.

I had to give these guys their dues, they were persistent, but neither of them was as desperate as I was. I'd been a split second from death and somehow had been granted a second chance, and I wasn't going to let it go.

The Wraith started firing immediately and I had no doubt she was aiming just in front of me so that I'd literally run straight into her bullets. Instead, I swerved, slipping over on the wet grass in the process, and fired my last two rounds in her general direction. She darted back behind the door frame and I dropped the gun, sprinted like an Olympian towards the back gate and pulled myself up and over it in one go, so that I fell head first over the other side as a round splintered the wood.

I threw out my arms, managing to break the worst of my fall, then rolled over in the dirt, jumped to my feet again, driven by pure adrenalin and the ecstatic joy of survival, and kept running through the woods in the rough direction of where I'd parked the Mercedes. I didn't get in it though, but kept running down the lane and out onto the country road I'd originally turned off.

Headlights temporarily blinded me as a car came into view, moving fast. It screeched to a halt and I jumped in the passenger side as it accelerated away again, heading for the motorway and safety.

For a good minute neither of us spoke. I was still panting from exhaustion. Then, as I finally got my breathing under control, I turned to Tina.

'I didn't want you to have to do that. But thank you. You saved my life.'

She shrugged. 'I know. If I hadn't been there, you'd be dead by now.'

Which was absolutely true. After I fled the scene of Cem Kalaman's killing in the Mercedes, I'd known my options were limited. As I've repeatedly said, I didn't want to involve Tina, but desperate times call for desperate measures and I'd called her on the burner phone, told her about my intention to head back to the house where Lane and her colleagues had held me, and she'd offered to come as back-up. I suppose it could be argued that I'd tried to talk her out of it, but I hadn't really tried too hard. The plan had been simple enough. Although I'd gone in alone, I'd put my phone on speaker and called Tina's number so she could hear what was going on. She'd been positioned on the driveway, just outside the front gates, and had insisted on being armed with the gun I'd picked up from one of Kalaman's bodyguards, even though it had only two rounds in it.

'I couldn't see what was going on from behind the gates,' she said, 'but I could hear it all, so I started shooting. I couldn't even see what I was aiming at.'

'I managed to hit the guy, but I don't think the woman was hurt.'

'It sounded like you knew her.'

'She's the one I've told you about – The Wraith.'

'The one who killed your friend Chris?'

I nodded. 'She didn't actually pull the trigger but she organized his killing, so I hold her responsible. I didn't think I'd ever see her again after she got away last time.'

'So, who's her client now?'

'It's got to be Alastair Sheridan. Cem Kalaman knew all his secrets. He would have always been a threat, especially now that

Sheridan's got his eyes on the PM's job. With him out of the way, there's no one with any evidence of the things he's done. I've got to hand it to him, he's a cunning bastard. Kill Kalaman. Frame me for it. Then sit back and watch while the police hunt me down and kill me.' I shook my head. 'I reckon Lane was part of the plan too, working for Sheridan rather than the security services, and he decided to get rid of her as well.'

Tina slowed the car down, then took the gun I'd given her out from under her jacket and threw it into a hedge.

'You'll need somewhere to stay tonight,' she said, turning back to me.

I took a deep breath, the adrenalin fading now. 'I know. I've got a fake passport on order. It'll be ready tomorrow. I'll pick it up and then try to get out of the country with the cash I've got left.'

The car fell silent as we came onto the M25, heading anti-clockwise in the direction of Tina's house. The wound in my belly that I'd got from the prison knife fight with Troy Ramone was hurting, and when I inspected it, I saw that it was bleeding a little. It was going to need dressing again.

'Come back to mine,' Tina said eventually, 'but after tonight you'll have to leave.'

'I don't want to put you at risk.'

She laughed. 'You've already put me at risk a few times over, but I wanted to help you. And you know what? It felt good tonight, seeing some action again. But now that I've had my dose of it and got away in one piece, I'm happy to go back to my normal life.'

'I'm glad to hear it. I want to think of you living to a ripe old age.' I smiled at her. 'Maybe marry a nice, handsome accountant, even have a couple of kids.'

'I'm not sure that's ever going to happen but I guess you never know. And by the way, you can only stay with me on one condition.'

I looked at her. 'What's that?'

'No trying anything. I know you've been in jail a long time, but you're going to need to keep your hands to yourself. Do you think you can do that?'

'After what's happened tonight, that's the last thing on my mind,' I lied.

17

Jane Kelman hadn't always been a killer. Years ago, she'd been a married mother of two who'd never even been in a fight, let alone murdered anyone. But life has a way of changing things, and the truth was, Jane had enjoyed killing the first time she'd done it. The act itself had been exciting. It had given her a sense of power she'd never experienced before and it didn't take her long to understand why serial killers found murder addictive. The victims too had deserved it. One had been the loan shark she'd been forced to sleep with to help pay off her husband's debts, a low-level gangster and a slimy piece of dirt called Frank Mellon. Another had been his bodyguard. And the third had been her husband himself, set up to make it look like he'd killed Mellon and the bodyguard in a fit of jealous rage.

Three dead men in one night. What had surprised Jane though was her lack of shock or remorse afterwards. And when you've killed once, it becomes easier every time. Some of her victims over the years had deserved their fate, but plenty hadn't, and, as time passed and the bodies started piling up, she stopped giving any of them a second thought.

In fact, aside from a short period when she became interested in the study of psychopaths in an effort to ascertain if she was one or not (she wasn't surprised when she scored very highly on the test), she spent very little time contemplating what she did for a career. She carried out the tasks she was paid to do, and moved on. It was one of the reasons why she was so good at it. Another was that she was a woman and therefore men never seemed to suspect her.

But now she'd failed to kill Ray Mason not once but twice. Admittedly he wasn't supposed to have been there tonight but, even so, it ate at her confidence. She wasn't going to be truly happy until he was dead.

She also had an added complication. Her partner on this job, Voorhess, a fellow South African killer she'd worked with several times before, and who was also her occasional lover, was hurt.

'How bad is it?' she asked as she helped him into the van's passenger seat.

He'd taken a bullet to the shoulder and was pressing a kitchen towel they'd got from inside the house to the wound. 'It hurts,' he said through gritted teeth, 'but it looks like it's gone straight through. I know a doctor in London who can patch it up for the flight home.'

'Let's get over there now then,' she said, taking a last look round. All three bodies were in the back of the van now and the house had been cleaned up so that it would be impossible to tell that anyone had been murdered there.

It was raining hard as Jane shut the van's rear doors and ran round to the driver's side, climbing inside and starting the engine.

'What's your doctor's address?'

'I need to check,' said Voorhess, wincing with pain as he pulled out his phone.

Jane drove slowly forward and the front gates opened automatically. At the same time she brought her pistol up from down by her side and shot Voorhess in the side of the head, the bullet passing out through the open window.

He seemed to rock in his seat and she wondered whether she'd have to shoot him again. But then he toppled sideways against the passenger door, his head lolling out of the window. He was dead.

She yanked him back in and closed the window, contemplating putting him in the back of the van with the others but quickly dismissing the idea. He was too much of a dead weight, and he looked quite peaceful where he was, as if he was asleep, her .22 bullet having not left a lot of blood.

Her next port of call was a farm some forty miles away in rural Suffolk. It was run by a farmer with links to several London crime gangs who offered the occasionally indispensable service of getting rid of inconvenient corpses by feeding them to his pigs. Over the years the pigs had developed a real taste for human flesh and bones, and could be relied upon to leave nothing behind – except teeth, which were gathered up for the incinerator. Jane had got to hear about him through her own underworld contacts (she'd long ago discovered that the black market offered every kind of service imaginable), and had used his services twice before. Because of the risks involved, it wasn't cheap. The farmer charged £10,000 a corpse and, although the client had covered the costs of the three people they'd been sent to kill, Jane was going to have to stump up ten grand of her own money to offload Voorhess. It was another reason to finish the job on Ray Mason.

Ten minutes later, when she was far enough away from the crime scene, she called the client again.

Alastair Sheridan answered on the third ring.

Jane didn't usually know the names of her clients. That wasn't how her business worked. She tended to operate through a middleman who acted as a necessary buffer between her and the person paying the bill, but Sheridan had come to her directly with an offer of a great deal of money. She'd done some work for a close associate of his, Cem Kalaman – he'd commissioned her to get rid of a troublesome witness the previous year – and Sheridan had been impressed enough to want her for this job. It didn't surprise her that a politician would be involved in murder. It happened all the time, including in the supposedly enlightened democracies.

'Is the deed done?' asked Sheridan.

'No,' she said. 'Mason got away.'

'But you just told me you had him.'

'He had armed help. We were ambushed, and he managed to escape. I was lucky not to get hurt myself. But what the hell was he doing there? I was contracted to take out three targets, which I did. You never said anything about Mason. My colleague died because of him.'

'I didn't expect him to be there either,' said Sheridan. 'Look, I'll increase the pay by a hundred thousand dollars to compensate for this. It'll be in your account by Monday morning.'

Jane didn't like complicated jobs, as this one was becoming, but she did like money. 'That's suitable compensation,' she said at last.

'And I want Mason dead.'

'That'll cost you another hundred thousand. It'll be a risky kill.'

'I can go with that,' said Sheridan reluctantly. 'Did you get a look at the people helping him?'

'There was only one of them and no, we never saw him. He was firing from behind a gate. Do you know who it could have been?'

There was a long silence down the other end of the line. 'There's only one person I can think of who would help him on something like this. Her name's Tina Boyd. She's Mason's former lover, and she knows how to handle a gun.'

This was promising. 'Do you want me to do anything about her?'

'Nothing yet. Let me think, but remain on standby.'

He ended the call, and Jane put the phone away. She was suddenly feeling better. Another $200,000 would be a major boost to her retirement fund, and now she had a lead back to Mason.

Whatever happened, she was going to get him this time.

Part Three

18

For the first time in what felt like years I woke up slowly, wondering at first where I was as light shone in through the edges of the curtains, then it came back to me. I was in Tina's bed. Her side was empty but I could hear her moving about downstairs.

It had been long gone midnight when we'd arrived back at her place, one of a row of pretty terraced cottages in a quiet village close to the M25. By then I was utterly exhausted after the events of the evening. I'd told Tina I didn't mind where I slept, but she'd let me stay in her bed. I remembered grabbing a shower, putting fresh dressing on the belly wound, and then climbing into bed beside her, where she was already asleep, or pretending to be. I'd kissed her head, smelling the softness of her hair, and that was pretty much the last thing I remembered until now.

I stretched under the sheets and sat up in bed as Tina came back into the room, already dressed. She was wearing jeans and a plain T-shirt, and her feet were bare, the nails painted red. She looked beautiful and I wanted to pull her into bed with me, but the look on her face suggested this wasn't an option. She had a cup of tea in each hand and she handed me one and sat down at the end of the bed.

'We've got a problem,' she said. 'The police have already named you as a suspect in the Cem Kalaman killing.'

I thought about this. 'They must have had some sort of tip-off. I was wearing a balaclava the whole time.'

'The thing is, you're not just an escaped prisoner any more. You're now the chief suspect in a shooting during which three people died.'

'I didn't shoot the woman. She was hit by one of Kalaman's bodyguards.'

Tina shrugged. 'But you had motive, so whatever happens they're going to pin this on you.'

I sat back in the bed. 'I suppose I should have been expecting this.'

'And guess who they've had on the news talking about how the government has got to get a grip on crime and the prisons, and that your case is just an example of the lawlessness that seems to be sweeping the country?'

I had to laugh. 'Sheridan. Jesus, he knows how to turn a situation to his advantage. You've almost got to admire him.'

'He's obviously been planning this whole thing a long time. And he's got you backed into a corner.'

I was beginning to experience that familiar feeling of being hunted again. It seemed that, whatever happened, there was going to be no rest for me. I'd been set up to do Alastair Sheridan's bidding without even knowing about it and, although I could take at least a sliver of satisfaction from the fact that Cem Kalaman would no longer walk this earth, Sheridan was now more impregnable than ever. In the latest battle between us, he'd won. What was worse, he'd always been winning.

I took a sip from the tea and tried not to look at Tina. She was my weakness, and I guess I was hers too.

And then something occurred to me. A plan. It was vague, but it might work. And best of all, it didn't involve Tina. I just needed to think it through.

'I might have something,' I said.

Which was the moment when there was a loud knock on her front door.

Tina stiffened.

'Make the bed, get rid of those clothes and that tea, and hide in the cupboard,' she hissed at Ray, then got up and headed downstairs with her cup of tea, trying to maintain as casual a pose as possible. Tina didn't get many unexpected visitors. Occasionally her neighbour, Mrs West, knocked on her door to offer her tomatoes from the garden or homemade jam, but she didn't knock as hard as that, and the timing was far too coincidental.

Two men were facing her when she opened the door, both of whom she recognized instantly.

'Morning, Tina,' said Mike Bolt. He was dressed in jeans and a check shirt, while beside him, eight inches shorter, a lot leaner than she remembered, and dressed equally casually, stood his partner, Mo Khan.

Tina had worked with both men for a few years between 2008 and 2010 as a detective in the now defunct Serious and Organized Crime Agency, and had been in a relationship with Mike for part of that time. It had been she who'd ended their relationship but they'd remained good friends afterwards. Mo, however, was different. He'd never liked Tina, and she'd always suspected that it was because he was jealous of her friendship with his partner. Although she'd lost touch with Mike in the last couple of years, she knew he and Mo now worked for the National Crime Agency.

'Morning, gentlemen,' she said. 'Long time no see. I'm assuming this is an official visit.' She nodded towards the jeans. 'Is this the new-look NCA kit?'

Mike smiled. He might have been over fifty now but he was still a good-looking man. Tall, broad-shouldered, with piercing blue eyes and close-cut silver hair, he'd always reminded her of that old Hollywood actor her dad liked, Steve McQueen. Seeing him now, looking happy and healthy, made her wonder why she'd felt the need to finish their relationship.

'It's a Saturday,' he said, looking down at his jeans. 'But yes, this is an official visit. Do you mind if we come in?'

'Please do,' she said, and led them through to the kitchen.

Mike asked her how she was but it was a perfunctory question, offered without much interest. She gave him an equally perfunctory answer and offered them both a coffee, which they declined, and they sat at the kitchen table, her on one side, the two of them on the other. Mo, she noticed, was looking at her suspiciously.

'So what can I do for you both?' she asked, taking a sip from her tea.

'You heard about the shooting of Cem Kalaman last night,' said Mike.

It wasn't a question, and there was no point Tina denying it, since the news was playing on the radio in the background.

'They're saying that Ray Mason's responsible. That's pretty quick, naming him like that. What makes you think it was him?' she asked.

'It was a professional hit,' said Mike. 'The intended victim was Cem Kalaman. The other casualties were one of his bodyguards and a woman caught in the crossfire. According to a reliable witness, the killer said to Kalaman before he shot him a final time: "This is for all your victims." Mason had history with Kalaman, as you know, and he had a motive for wanting him dead.'

'It all seems pretty thin.'

Mike folded his arms on the table and leaned forward, giving Tina an appraising look. 'There are other reasons why we believe it's Mason that we can't discuss with you right now. Now I know your history with him. We believe he had help organizing this hit.'

Tina glared back at him, angry now. 'So what exactly are you asking me? If I'm the one helping him? Be serious.'

'Look, no one's accusing you of anything.'

'Well, it doesn't sound that way. And to answer your question: no, I'm not helping him. From what I saw on the news over a fortnight ago, two people abducted him at gunpoint from a prison van taking him to hospital. Hasn't it occurred to you that he might actually have been taken by people hoping to silence him before his trial came up, and that he could be lying dead in a hole somewhere, rather than going round shooting gangsters, who've got plenty of enemies of their own?'

'Of course that scenario's occurred to us,' said Mike, keeping his voice calm, 'but we've got to look at every possibility, and we've had information that he's still alive. So we're asking if you've seen or heard from him at all.'

'No,' said Tina emphatically, looking at them both in turn. 'I haven't. If I'd heard anything from him I'd have contacted you.'

'Can you tell us where you were last night?' asked Mo.

'Are you not hearing me? I haven't seen him.'

'You were a police officer once,' said Mo. 'You know we have to ask these questions.'

Tina thought fast. She knew that if they wanted to, they'd be able to track her movements using the ANPR, just as she'd been able to track the movements of the Range Rover that had carried Ray to London two days earlier. 'It's none of your business where I was last night,' she told him, 'but what I can tell you is I was nowhere near London, and consequently nowhere near where that shooting took place.'

Mo and Mike exchanged glances.

'Personally, I don't think you're involved in any of this, Tina,' said Mike, 'but we have to do our jobs, so do you mind if we have a quick look round?'

Tina's stomach did a somersault and she had to fight hard to keep a poker face. 'Are you serious?'

'Look, you know how it is, we've got to ask,' said Mike, clearly embarrassed.

'And you can refuse if you want,' added Mo, but Tina knew that if she did they'd almost certainly come back with a warrant. There was too much at stake in the manhunt for Ray. The government, in enough trouble with the riots engulfing the nation's prisons, needed a result fast.

'No, it's OK,' she said, trying to sound as casual as possible as she got up from the table. 'Fill your boots. As you'll see, there aren't that many places here for a grown man to hide.'

Mike gave her a sympathetic smile as he got up from the table, which just annoyed her. He was treating her like a criminal – even though technically that was exactly what she was. Mo's reaction she could understand. He'd never trusted her and she had no doubt that he thought she was hiding something. As he too got up, he was watching her, clearly looking for any signs of nerves in her demeanour.

Tina turned away from him, picking her cigarettes up from the kitchen top and lighting one, determined not to give him the satisfaction of smelling fear on her. She didn't usually smoke in the house, but she knew neither of them liked it, especially in the confined space of her tiny cottage.

Tina followed behind them, watching as they opened cup-boards so small a cat couldn't conceal itself inside, and ludicrously they even looked behind the sofa. But that was the problem. There wasn't really anywhere to hide in this cottage, and Mike would know that. He'd been here enough times before. And Ray wouldn't have been able to hear the conversation they'd been having down here from the bedroom, not with the radio on. Tina had thought about turning it off before she opened the door but had kept it playing because her floorboards creaked so badly and she hadn't wanted them hearing any movement upstairs. Now she recognized it was a mistake.

The search downstairs took Mike and Mo all of two minutes. Mike turned to her at the bottom of the staircase. 'Do you mind if we go up?'

'You know I do, but I don't suppose that's going to make any difference. You remember where everything is, don't you?'

He nodded, looking slightly embarrassed, and they started up the stairs, the floorboards groaning under their combined weight.

Slowly, Tina followed, feeling like a condemned woman. If they caught Ray in here, then that would be it for her. He no longer had a gun so he couldn't hurt either Mike or Mo, but he could still threaten them and make a break for it, leaving Tina behind. She'd be sentenced to the maximum ten years for har-bouring Ray, there was no doubt about it. She had plenty of enemies as it was, and they'd want to make an example of her. She'd serve at least five, and because she was an ex-cop who'd pissed off the wrong people, it would be hard time, like Ray's.

Frankly, the thought terrified her.

When they got to the top of the stairs, Mo turned left into the bathroom while Mike checked in the spare room. Tina had closed her bedroom door when she'd gone downstairs to answer the front door and she tried not to stare at it now. When Mike came out of the spare room, he asked if she had a loft. It was as if he wanted to avoid going in her bedroom and being reminded of something he'd rather forget, which ordinarily might have upset her, but not now.

She pointed out the hatch and gave him the pole to open it with, while she watched Mo open the main bedroom door and walk inside.

The curtains had been drawn and the window was open, the bed was neatly made, and Ray's clothes and cup of tea were gone.

'Don't make a mess,' she said as Mo got on his hands and knees and looked under the bed.

He didn't answer, and she watched as he climbed slowly to his feet and went to the cupboard where she'd told Ray to hide.

Tina stiffened as he opened it, aware of Mike coming slowly back down the loft ladder, knowing that this was the moment of truth. If Ray was in there ...

But the cupboard was empty bar Tina's clothes neatly hanging from the rail.

Mo poked his head inside – just, it seemed, to make doubly sure – then closed it, and turned round.

'I'm assuming you don't want to check if he's hiding in my drawers, do you?' Tina asked, finding it hard to mask her relief.

'We're just doing our job, Tina,' Mo said, stopping at the open window and looking out across her garden before walking past her back into the hallway.

'Well, you're looking in the wrong place,' she told them. 'Now, if you've quite finished, I'd like to get on with my day.'

'Thanks for your help, Tina,' said Mike, motioning for Mo to follow him down the stairs. 'It's good to see you again. You look well.'

She felt like saying that it wasn't so good to see him but she resisted. Even now, she still had a soft spot for him. 'Thanks,' she said, walking down after them. 'You too. How's life treating you?'

'I got married,' he said as they stopped at the front door, showing her the ring she hadn't even noticed. 'A few weeks back now. It was only the two of us in Barbados. We didn't really want any fuss.'

'Well then, congratulations are in order,' she said, forcing a smile, and ignoring Mo's triumphant look. 'I hope you're both happy together.'

She opened the door for them and they stepped out into the morning sunshine.

Mike smiled at her. He did look genuinely happy and she was pleased for him. He was a good man. Which was probably why it hadn't worked for them. 'Thanks, Tina. And if you do hear anything from Ray Mason, please do the right thing and call us. It'll be a lot easier that way.'

She nodded and closed the door, and it was only when she was back in the kitchen that she allowed herself a huge sigh of relief.

She felt a little hurt that Mike had got married without telling her, but that paled into insignificance compared to the fact that she'd just dodged the possibility of a long prison sentence. But where the hell was Ray hiding? He must have got out of the bedroom window but there weren't really any places to hide in Tina's garden, plus they would have heard and seen him from the kitchen.

She stubbed out the cigarette and opened the back door, enjoying the feel of the sun on her face. Her garden backed directly onto a hill that rose up to woodland at the top. It was a lovely view, and was the main reason she'd bought this house. It soothed her to look at it, even though, in truth, it made her home less secure because there was direct access to it from the back. But it was a trade-off she was prepared to tolerate. She kept the gate double-locked, and the fence around it was high and overgrown with thorn bushes she'd planted herself several years earlier, so it was hard to get in. It was also hard to get out, so there was no way Ray would have made it out that way either.

She'd been standing there a good five minutes and was still trying to work out what Houdini-like escape Ray had managed when she heard a whisper from above her.

'Have they gone yet?'

She looked up and there he was, lying flat like a lizard on the cottage roof, his head poking over the guttering.

'They're gone, so get down from there quickly,' she hissed back at him. 'The neighbours might see you.'

He nodded, crawled on his front along the edge of the roof, and manoeuvred his way feet first back inside her bedroom window.

Tina couldn't help but smile as she went back inside the house. Ray was bad news in so many ways but she had to admire his resourcefulness.

When she got back to the bedroom, he was sitting on the bed. He opened his mouth to say something but she shook her head and put a finger to her lips. The reason Tina was alive and free was that she was paranoid. She'd been following Mike and Mo too closely for them to have planted a camera in her house, but they might have managed to slip an audio device somewhere. It would have been totally illegal of course, but that didn't mean it wouldn't happen.

She took a state-of-the-art bug finder she'd bought on the internet a few months earlier from one of the bedroom drawers and proceeded to walk the whole house with it. Only when she was convinced that there was no device anywhere did she finally return to the bedroom.

'Well, Ray,' she said, 'I'll give you this. It's never boring with you around.'

'I'll take that as a compliment,' he said with a grin. 'But you'll be pleased to know I'm going to leave in a couple of hours, as soon as the coast's well clear.'

'They may have this place under surveillance.'

'Would they? They've searched the house so they must be pretty certain I'm not here. I suppose it's possible they might put you under surveillance. But that could work to our advantage. If you drive off somewhere, you'll draw any surveillance team with you. Then I can make my move.'

'But where are you going to go? You're on foot.'
'I think I might have someone who can help.'
Tina frowned. 'Who?'
'Someone who owes me a big favour.'

19

As Mike Bolt walked back to the car with Mo along the village high street, he passed the pub where a long time ago he and Tina had spent some happy evenings. He didn't miss her. It hadn't been a smooth relationship. Mike knew he wasn't easy to be with, and Tina sure as hell wasn't either. But they'd had some good times, and their relationship had ended amicably, and it was for those reasons that he still cared about her. He genuinely wanted her to be innocent of any wrongdoing where Ray Mason was concerned, and he was relieved she hadn't been harbouring him. However, he also knew Tina was a woman who was prepared to risk everything in the pursuit of justice, and this had always made her dangerous and unpredictable.

He looked at his watch. It was a quarter to ten and he'd been at work for three hours already. If the Kalaman killing hadn't occurred last night, he would have been enjoying a day out in Brighton with his new wife, Leanne, something they'd both been looking forward to. He'd be glad when all this was over and he was retired, which if all went well was going to be less than a year away.

'So what do you think, boss?' said Mo. 'Has she been in touch with him?'

Bolt looked at him. 'God knows. To be honest, Tina could be right. Ray Mason may have nothing to do with this. For all we know, he was abducted from that prison van by people who then killed him. He had enough enemies.'

'We've got a witness sighting of a man matching his description leaving the scene,' said Mo.

'An anonymous one. That raises more questions than it does answers.'

'What about Andy Reeves' testimony?'

They'd interviewed the man who'd briefly been taken hostage in his apartment by Kalaman's killer, and whose car the killer had stolen, only an hour earlier. Although the killer's face had been concealed, he fitted the overall description of Mason, and when they'd played Reeves an audio clip of Mason's voice they'd found from a police press conference several years ago, he'd claimed to be 90 per cent sure that the man in the clip was the same one who'd held him hostage. He'd also described his assailant as calm, professional, and even courteous, and that fitted with what Bolt knew of Mason too.

'No, you're right,' said Bolt. 'On balance, I think Mason's still alive, and I think it was him who carried out the killing last night.'

Mo gave him a sidelong smile. 'I know I'm right, boss. Listen, I don't want to speak out of turn, because you know I respect you more than anyone, but don't go soft on Tina because of your past.'

'I won't,' he said, resentful of Mo for pointing out the obvious. 'But the fact remains Mason wasn't at Tina's house just now.'

'That's true, but you know as well as I do that he's been getting help from somewhere, otherwise we'd have found him by now. And he and Tina have got history, you can't deny that. I think it's worth putting surveillance on her, just in case she leads us to him.'

'She'd spot it a mile off.'

'Not if it was done properly.'

'I'll have a word with the boss,' said Bolt, thinking it somehow ironic that he and Mo now worked for Sheryl Trinder, the woman at the NCA who up until a little over a year ago had been Ray Mason's boss.

They were back at the car now and Bolt was just about to get in when his phone rang.

It was DCI Kay Searle of Westminster's Murder Investigation Team, who were assisting the NCA with the Kalaman murder. Bolt had been talking to her down at the crime scene a couple of hours earlier, which meant there had to have been some development.

And there had. 'We've got a CCTV image of a possible suspect leaving Andy Reeves' apartment building last night just after the reported time of the killings. I'm looking at it now, and it's good quality. Something else too – the man in it might be bald and bearded but it looks one hell of a lot like Ray Mason.'

20

Tina needed to know whether or not Mike and his team were keeping her under surveillance, and there was only one way to do that.

An hour after Mike and Mo had gone, she left the house by the front door. It was much cooler than of late and drizzling with rain. Her car was parked in her reserved spot directly outside, and she gave it a thorough examination, both manually and using the bug finder, to make sure it was clear of trackers. Next she checked the street in both directions. The advantage of where she lived was that strangers, either on foot or in vehicles, stood out like sore thumbs. Everyone knew everyone else round here and, although Tina kept herself to herself, the villagers were all aware that she'd been a target of criminals in the past, and were protective of her.

Satisfied that there was no one around, she pulled away, regularly checking the rear-view mirror, and took a winding back route into London, making several circles, before finally relaxing as she pulled onto the Finchley Road, heading south.

She wanted to put Ray out of her mind but it was proving impossible. Their relationship might have lasted only a few months, but those months had been some of her happiest for a long time – happier than when she was with Mike Bolt, who might have cared about her but who'd been unable to set her world on fire as Ray had.

And then, in one bloody night, she and Ray had been torn apart. He'd rescued her from a house where she was being held by two associates of Kalaman and Sheridan, killing both associates in the process. He could have run that night but instead he'd set fire to the house to get rid of any evidence of Tina's presence there, told her to get as far away as possible, and had then remained behind to take responsibility for what had happened so that she wasn't implicated. In the end, he'd gone to prison for her, sacrificing his own freedom so that she didn't have to sacrifice hers.

To have loved again after all those barren years and then to have had it all snatched away in one fell swoop had come close to tearing her apart. It had taken a long time to get over Ray Mason, and then, just as she was coming out the other side, he'd reappeared again, threatening to reignite those feelings. It had taken a lot of self-discipline to hold back the previous night. She'd pretended to be asleep as he'd leaned over and kissed her head, but had been seconds away from turning round, grabbing him and kissing him back. And yet she knew that sleeping with him would just hurt her more in the long term, which was why she was determined to keep as far away as possible from him in these next few hours.

Ray was going to leave after nightfall. He had a plan, which had a solid chance of working. Yet Tina felt conflicted. On the one hand, she wanted him gone before he got her into real trouble. But she also wanted to help him, not only because she still had feelings for him, but also because she too wanted to see the people he was up against suffer.

Which was why she'd volunteered to go in his place to collect the passport and driving licence he'd ordered the previous day. Ray had tried to talk her out of it, stating that it was too risky, and that he would be able to collect them either later tonight or tomorrow, but Tina knew that his plan had a far greater chance of success if he was already in possession of his new ID, and a lot safer for him if she went. So she'd insisted. 'Call it my leaving present,' she'd told him.

Her first port of call was the office where she ran her private detective business, located in a drab residential back street on the Kilburn/Paddington border. She'd considered closing it and working from home several times, but had always demurred. Tina's cottage was her sanctuary, and it felt a lot better not to have to bring work home with her, or have people she didn't know coming there.

She actually had a pile of paperwork to catch up on and she spent the next hour writing a report on an outstanding marital infidelity case she'd been working on, and doing invoicing. It was a good way of getting her mind off her current predicament, and frankly, she needed the money. Private detective work, certainly the mundane kind she dealt with most of the time, didn't pay a huge amount.

At lunchtime, the office phone rang. Tina let it go to answerphone and listened as a distressed-sounding woman left a message saying that, although she knew it sounded foolish, she'd become convinced that her husband of twenty years might be trying to kill her.

Tina was never going to ignore a call like that, so she picked up before the woman had finished leaving her message.

The woman, who immediately introduced herself as Maria Ways, sounded extremely relieved to get Tina on the phone and asked if she could come and see her as soon as possible. 'I don't know if I'm going mad or not, but I think – I really think – he wants me dead.'

'OK, OK,' said Tina, calming her down. 'Of course you can come in.' She looked at her watch. It was 12.45. She had time. And anyway, she was intrigued. This might actually require some proper detective work. They agreed that Maria would come to the office at 1.30.

Tina was careful who she allowed to visit her at the office but Maria's address in Holland Park checked out and when, forty-five minutes later, the outside buzzer sounded and the camera showed a middle-aged, flustered-looking redhead, Tina let her in straight away.

But it wasn't the redhead who came through the door. Two men in suits did. The first was about forty-five, small and wiry with close-cropped dark hair and a scar like a lopsided half smile on his lip; the second was younger, and much, much bigger, with the chiselled yet slightly grotesque look of the long-term body-builder, and a ridiculous deep orange permatan.

Tina had just finished a sandwich and had a takeaway coffee in her hand. She didn't stand up or yell. Instead, she stared them both down. 'I don't know who you are,' she said calmly, 'but if you're here to threaten me then you might want to know you're being recorded on CCTV. Please leave before I call the police.'

The smaller man with the scar looked by far the more dangerous of the two. He sat down opposite her across the desk, while the big one took up a position behind him. 'I'd turn the camera off if I were you,' he said. 'It won't do you any good, and we're not here to hurt you. We just want to know where Ray Mason is.'

'You're not the first person who's asked me that today,' she said. 'I haven't seen him in over a year. But in case he phones me from wherever he's hiding, would you like to leave a message?'

The small one's expression hardened. 'Where is he?'

'I told you, I don't know.' Tina's grip tightened on the coffee cup. It was still two thirds full and hot, and would make a useful weapon. She also had a can of CS gel spray in the desk drawer if it came to it.

The small man read her expression. 'I told you, we're not here to hurt you. But we do want to find Mason, and if we find out you either know or knew where he is, and you haven't told us, then ...' He paused. 'There may be some unfortunate consequences.'

Tina felt her anger grow. 'Are you threatening me?'

The small man wore the expression of a man holding all the cards. He reached inside his jacket, took out a small white envelope and tossed it onto the desk in front of her. 'Your niece Ava's very pretty,' he said. 'I thought you might like to see another photo of her.'

Tina felt a jolt of fear shoot through her. She slammed down the coffee cup so hard the lid came off, and tore open the envelope, terrified of what she might see.

It was a photo of Ava – sweet, blonde and eight years old – walking towards the camera in her school uniform, hand in hand with her mum, Jackie, Tina's sister-in-law. Neither was aware of the camera's presence. Instead they were looking at each other and smiling, total love in both their eyes.

'That was taken a couple of days ago,' continued the small man. 'It's a great shot. The cameraman really knows what he's doing.' He paused, and the scar on his lip curled upwards as he smiled. 'The problem is he's clumsy. You see, he's often transporting acid in his car, and if he's not careful he might spill some of that acid, and some innocent kid or mum, just walking along the street minding their own business, might have their faces burned beyond recognition. Just like that.'

Tina couldn't speak. The thought of anything happening to her family – the one part of her life that was wholesome and undamaged – because of something she'd done filled her with abject terror.

'So I'm going to ask you again,' said the small man, clearly able to see that her shock was genuine. 'Where's Ray Mason?'

Tina knew that these people would carry out their threats. She had no doubt that they'd been sent by the Kalaman organization to find the man who, they thought, had killed their boss. It occurred to her to tell them that Alastair Sheridan had been behind Cem's killing, but in the end she realized that this would be way too risky.

'I don't know,' she said wearily, putting down the photo. 'He hasn't been in touch at all. But if he does I'll tell you. Just don't do anything to my family.' She looked at him. 'Please.'

'As long as you're not lying, they're perfectly safe,' he said.

'I'm not,' she told him firmly.

He nodded and got to his feet. 'Good. That way everyone stays safe and healthy.' He winked at her, and the scar curled upwards once again. 'Have a nice day, Tina.'

For a long time after they'd gone Tina sat there, experiencing first shock, then anger at the way they'd threatened her family. Her eight-year-old niece, for God's sake! There was anger at Ray, too, for coming back into her life and exposing her like this, although she was still confident that there was no way the Kalamans could link her to him.

But the bottom line was she had to protect her family. She couldn't provide protection, but the police would be able to, and if she spoke to Mike Bolt, she felt sure he could put something in place. First, though, she needed to speak to her brother, Tom. She hated the idea of telling him his family might be in danger. As children they'd been close but they'd grown distant over the years, and Tina knew he disapproved of the life she led, and the effect that her dramas had had on their parents. Still, if someone was threatening his children, she had to tell him. Reluctantly, she sat back in the chair, took a deep breath, and called his number.

Tom was one of those people who had his phone on him the whole time, and he answered pretty much as soon as it started ringing.

'Tina! Changed your mind and decided to join us?'

It sounded like he was outside. 'Hey Tom, where are you?'

'Estepona. At the villa we booked. We got here about an hour ago. Don't you remember, I invited you months ago? Mum and Dad are here too. I thought you were ringing to say you were going to get a flight.'

Tina almost laughed out loud with relief. Her family were safe. 'No, sorry, I've got quite a lot on at the moment, but if I get the chance I'll book something short notice and come out for a couple of days. How long are you there for?'

'Two weeks.'

That was enough for Tina. They were too far away for the Kalamans to get to them, and therefore no longer a concern. She made small talk with Tom for a while, said she was going to have a family barbecue for all of them when they got back, then finally rang off, feeling relieved but still very, very angry at the way she'd just been treated.

The anger simmered away in her for another couple of hours as she continued ploughing through the paperwork, until finally it was time to get ready to go and pick up Ray's passport and driving licence so he could be on his way, hopefully to a place where the many people hunting him wouldn't be able to find him. After what had happened earlier, she wasn't taking any chances. Slipping off the loose-fitting sweatshirt she'd travelled here in, she put on a light, custom-fitted Kevlar vest that she'd bought online from a specialist US-based company, before putting the sweatshirt back on over the top, and adding a summer jacket, so that there was no way anyone could tell she was wearing it. She put the can of CS gel in one of the jacket's outside pockets where it was easily in reach, then left the office by the back entrance.

Having adopted her usual anti-surveillance techniques, she drove a round-about route into Hounslow through unusually heavy traffic and found a parking spot on a quiet tree-lined road about half a mile from where Zafir Rasaq lived.

Tina's job often required her to follow people, mainly errant spouses suspected by their partners of having affairs, and in the four years she'd been a PI she'd become very good at getting documentary evidence of their activities, even if sometimes it took her a while. In order to avoid being spotted by the more eagle-eyed of the people she was tracking, she'd also become something of a master of disguise. She had a variety of wigs and props, and with some carefully applied makeup she always amazed herself at the ease with which she became a completely different person, enjoying the anonymity it gave her.

There was no way she wanted either Rasaq or the men she was collecting the documents from to see her real face so she opened a bag on the car's passenger seat, took out what she needed and, using the rear-view mirror, spent the next twenty minutes transforming her appearance into that of a demure, olive-skinned

Die Alone

Muslim woman wearing a black hijab to keep her hair covered, and big black sunglasses.

She checked herself in the mirror, concluded there was no way she'd ever be recognized, and got out of the car, pulling a cheap burner phone she'd never used before from her pocket.

It was time to call Zafir Rasaq.

21

'So what have we got, Mr Bolt?' asked DCS Sheryl Trinder.

Trinder was Mike Bolt's boss, a short, tough, ambitious black woman with more than thirty years on the job, and a definite eye for the NCA director's role. Consequently she was a hard taskmaster, who expected a lot from the people under her, including some very long hours. But she was also fair and honest, and Bolt respected her, even if he didn't much like her. And now, at the end of a Saturday afternoon, with the sun shining outside the window, almost mocking him with its hint of what the seaside could have been like today, he was sitting in her office giving her an update.

'The man on the captured CCTV image looks a lot like Ray Mason,' he told her, passing a photocopy across the desk. 'As you can see, he's done the classic of shaving his head, growing a beard, and throwing on a pair of glasses, which would be enough to confuse people who don't know what they're looking for. But I'm certain it's him. We've released the photo to the media, and it should already have been made public.'

DCS Trinder examined the photo, which had been blown up so that it showed a close-up of the suspect's face. 'That's definitely Mason.' She shook her head. 'The Kalamans are going to be really after him now. The word is, they already had a half-million-pound bounty on his head while he was in prison. God knows what they're going to increase it to now.'

Bolt thought of Tina then, and hoped she'd been telling him the truth, because if she was mixed up in all this and helping Mason, she was potentially in a lot of danger. 'Then it's important we get to him first,' he said. 'We know he had help breaking out. And the chances are someone's helping him now.'

'The person who springs to mind is Tina Boyd,' said Trinder.

'We spoke to Tina this morning,' said Bolt, 'and she gave us permission to search her house. There wasn't any sign that Mason had been there, and she claimed not to have seen or heard from him since his escape.'

'And where was she last night?'

'She refused to say. I think it was because she was pissed off that she was under suspicion. But we checked her car's movements on the ANPR and she made a journey on the M25 yesterday night to somewhere in west Essex. It wasn't possible to get an exact location because it's a pretty rural area, but it's also a long way from where the getaway car was last seen.'

Trinder frowned. 'Do you think we need to put her under surveillance?'

Bolt had been thinking about that a lot. 'I don't think so at the moment. She's hugely surveillance-savvy after everything that's happened to her, so we'd need twelve-strong teams round the clock to make it effective, and there's no evidence that she's been helping Mason. In my opinion, we should keep an eye on her movements on the ANPR and if anything turns up that seems suspect, we can look at her again.'

Trinder was about to say something else when the phone on her desk rang. 'I did ask not to be disturbed, so this has got to be important – excuse me.' She picked up the phone and listened for a moment. 'OK,' she said. 'Put him through.' She mouthed the words 'Home Office minister' at Bolt then made a hand gesture to indicate that the meeting was over.

Bolt got up from his seat as the minister came on the line. It was clear from the conversation that he was after an update on the Kalaman murder and the related search for Ray Mason.

But, as Bolt paused at the door, he picked up something in Trinder's conversation that made him frown momentarily. It was her telling the minister that the NCA had decided for the time being not to put any surveillance on Tina Boyd. It seemed odd to Bolt that the minister would want that level of operational detail. He'd probably have thought about it some more if it hadn't been for the fact that as soon as he walked back into the incident room, it was clear something had changed.

Mo Khan was walking towards him, a big grin on his face. 'We've got a lead. A kid who works in an illegal counterfeiting operation in Hounslow called in. He saw the new-look Ray Mason on the news and said he was there yesterday looking for a passport. Apparently they've done one for him and he's coming in at six to pick it up. The kid wants immunity from prosecution and the fifty thousand reward.'

'Tell him he can have both,' said Bolt with a grin, hoping they could wrap this up quickly. 'Scramble the locals. I'm going to get over there now.'

22

George Bannister sat in the study of his constituency home, knowing he was completely in hock to a murderer. He more than anyone else knew what Alastair Sheridan was capable of, but there was nothing he could do to stop him. The problem was, there never had been.

He and Alastair had known each other since their days at public school. Alastair had always been the handsome and exciting kid, the one with an edge, the one everyone wanted to be friends with. But he didn't give out his friendship easily, and Bannister, who was clever, ambitious, but definitely not one of the cool kids, would ordinarily never have got a look-in. But for some reason Alastair had warmed to him, and even though

Die Alone

Bannister had never been fully accepted into his social circle, they'd got on and Bannister had looked up to him.

They'd both gone to different universities – Alastair to Warwick, Bannister to Oxford, where he'd studied PPE – but they'd remained in periodic contact throughout that time, and when Bannister had graduated with a First, Alastair had been one of the first people to ring and congratulate him.

That was the thing about Alastair. He knew how to make people feel valuable. At the time, Bannister had naively thought it a commendable trait of his. He knew a lot better now.

In those days Bannister had truly been going places, having found his niche at Oxford and built up a cadre of excellent contacts and friendships among the sons of the country's wealthy political elite. He also had a job to go to as a strategist and speech writer for the governing party – his first step on a route that he knew would move him towards a senior role in government. He hadn't needed Alastair any more, yet something always drew him back to his old friend and schoolmate, and when Alastair had suggested that the two of them go travelling in August and September before they started their proper jobs, he'd agreed immediately.

It was 1990, a time when backpacking was taking off among the nation's middle class, and, although he tried not to admit it to himself, Bannister was hugely chuffed that Alastair had chosen him as a travelling companion rather than someone else from his wide circle of friends.

At first it all went well. They travelled to Ko Samui in Thailand, then an unspoiled tropical island with just beach huts for accommodation. From there they went up into the hill country of Chiang Mai, which they made their base for a lazy week which encompassed riding on elephants and smoking a lot of dope. One day they hired a driver to take them right up into the so-called Golden Triangle, close to the Burmese border. It was here that Alastair had persuaded Bannister to try smoking opium. He'd been reluctant at first. He knew as well as anyone how addictive it could be. But Alastair was persuasive, and out there in the jungle with no witnesses, it suddenly didn't seem such a bad idea. So he smoked some, and loved it. He swore to himself he'd never do it again but he remembered feeling very grown up, worldly-wise and adventurous for breaking a societal taboo, and it would always be a secret between him and Alastair.

It was when they got to the Philippines that it all went wrong. Alastair wanted them both to break other taboos. Bannister was realistic enough to know that he wasn't a good-looking young man, nor was he especially successful with women (although he wasn't a complete failure either), but it had never occurred to him to use the services of a prostitute until Alastair had suggested it. Bannister had asked Alastair why he wanted to when it was quite obvious he was already successful with women: by that point he'd slept with seven on their trip, while Bannister had managed a drunken fumble with one. He'd always remembered Alastair's answer: 'Because you can do whatever you fucking well want to them. Especially in a place like this where they're dirt poor.'

Bannister had found this distasteful, but not entirely uncharacteristic. Alastair was an exciting and charismatic character, the life and soul of the party, but he was also superficial and selfish, traits that only became apparent if you were around him long enough, as Bannister had been on that trip. Looking back now, Bannister could see that Alastair had been grooming him, but at the time, although uneasy about it, he'd gone along with the suggestion.

They'd done it in Manila first. Visiting a brothel with its own bar that was stacked with gorgeous Filipina women, they'd picked one each and retired to separate rooms with their escorts. Once again, it had been great fun. Bannister's girl was a tiny doll-like beauty who, in the space of a night, taught him things he'd only ever heard about, or seen on an illegal hardcore videotape. And all, he recalled, for the price of barely three pounds.

After that, he'd been hooked. They'd hired girls – sometimes freelancers they met in bars, other times ones from official establishments – all over the islands of the northern Philippines. One night they shared the same girl. It was another first for Bannister and he remembered it as a huge turn-on. Soon after that they rented a bungalow in a place called White Beach, and shared three girls at the same time.

It seemed to Bannister that Alastair was forever trying to push the boundaries. It should have scared Bannister, because the thing was, Alastair seemed to get a lot of pleasure from being rough with the girls – pulling their hair, slapping them hard, making them cry out in pain. He especially liked sodomizing them. They tolerated it because they were poor and he always paid them well. And Bannister found himself getting swept along by the whole thing, treating it all as a big joke, convincing himself that because the girls were being paid, and the violence against them wouldn't leave physical scarring, it wasn't that bad.

It happened near the end of their time in the Philippines. They were staying in a dump of a town called Angeles City which, it quickly became clear, was the centre of the Filipino sex industry thanks to the huge American military base nearby. Alastair suggested they hire a freelancer, take her back to the cheap hotel room they'd rented, and give her, in his words, 'a real rough seeing to'.

Bannister shuddered when he thought back to how sickeningly he'd behaved. The girl they'd picked up couldn't have been much older than sixteen. It was possible she was even younger. Either way, she'd got a lot more than she bargained for when they got her back to the room. Alastair had gone first. He'd been very rough, and the girl was lying on the bed bruised and crying when he'd finished.

'Now it's your turn,' Alastair had said with a grin, getting up from the bed, naked and sweating.

Bannister had been drinking. That was the excuse he'd always given to himself for doing what he did next. He'd climbed on the bed and, even as the girl had sobbed, he'd forced himself upon her without a thought, revelling in the power he wielded. And then, when he was just about to reach orgasm, holding the girl down by her slender shoulder with one hand, the other hand pushed hard over her mouth to stifle the sobs, he'd caught the flash of a camera. At that point he'd been too far gone to react, and he'd continued in those last few seconds. It was only when he was lying on top of her, still panting, that he realized what had happened.

He'd turned towards Alastair and seen him standing there with that old-fashioned Kodak camera of his in his hand, the one that developed photos instantly. Bannister had often wondered why Alastair carried round such a bulky piece of kit on his travels when he could just as easily use a smaller camera and get the photos done when he got home. Now he knew.

'What the hell are you doing?' he'd asked as Alastair shook the photo to dry the ink.

'Just a little memento,' Alastair had replied, with a grin. 'You can take one of me next time.'

But Bannister had been grimly aware of what he must have looked like in the photo, holding down a very young-looking teenage girl with his hand over her mouth, while having sex with her. 'Give it back,' he'd demanded, getting up from the bed.

But Alastair had been having none of it. 'Hey, relax,' he'd said, slipping the photo into one of his backpack pockets. 'No one's going to see it except us.'

Panicking, Bannister had gone to grab it out of Alastair's backpack, but Alastair had stepped in front of him, blocking his way. He was six inches taller and at least three stone heavier than Bannister, so brute force wasn't going to work. He'd got dressed too, with his shoes on, making Bannister feel suddenly vulnerable against him.

'Give it back to me, Alastair,' Bannister had said, as firmly as he could. 'I'm serious.'

He'd tried to push past him but Alastair shoved him hard in the chest.

'Come on mate, it's only a bit of fun,' he'd said, still smiling, but this time there was an edge to his expression. It was clear he wasn't going to give the photo back. Instead, he'd picked up the backpack, slung it over his shoulder, and pushed past Bannister, almost as if he wasn't there, throwing a couple of one-hundred-peso notes in the direction of the sobbing girl. 'I'm just popping out for a bit. I'll be back in a mo. Keep her here a bit longer if you like. We've paid for all night.'

Bannister had got rid of the girl, paying her an extra two hundred pesos – about the equivalent of three pounds – as a mixture of hush and guilt money. Then he'd gone to bed and waited for Alastair to return, which he did several hours later, sounding inebriated. Bannister had waited until he was fast asleep and snoring lightly before getting up quietly and searching the backpack for the photo.

It wasn't there.

When Bannister had confronted him the next day, Alastair had claimed he'd felt guilty and had ripped the photo up and thrown it in a bin. He'd even offered to let Bannister search his back-pack. 'I'm sorry about taking it, mate,' he'd said with a rueful smile. 'I shouldn't have done.'

Bannister had known he was lying, but there was nothing he could do about it and no more was said. Even so, the atmosphere on the trip had changed, and Bannister was relieved to arrive back in England a few days later. He and Alastair made plans to stay in touch but there was something half-hearted about it, and neither man spoke to the other for several years afterwards.

Eventually, Bannister forgot about what had happened and moved on with his life. He met a girl, got married, and moved steadily up the political ladder, becoming an MP in 2001 and a junior Treasury minister in 2010.

During this time his and Alastair's paths occasionally crossed, and Alastair was always there to congratulate him whenever he moved up a notch, but their relationship had faded to that of mere acquaintances. So when he got a call from Alastair late in 2010 asking for a meeting to discuss a proposed tax change on some new-fangled financial instrument contracts, he was reluctant to say yes. Alastair was now a successful and very wealthy hedge fund manager, and Bannister knew he wanted to use him to lobby the government for tax breaks, so he put him off, saying his diary was very busy.

'I think it would be wise to clear a space in it, George,' Alastair had said coldly. 'You've got an excellent career ahead of you in politics. It would be a real pity if something came up from your past to wreck it.'

Bannister had felt himself go hot all over. 'What do you mean?' he'd asked weakly, even though he'd known exactly what Alastair meant.

'I never got rid of it,' Alastair had told him. 'But you knew that, didn't you? Do you want to see a copy? I had it touched up. You're very clear in it. So's your friend.'

Bannister hadn't known what to say.

'So anyway, mate. How are you fixed over the next two days? I really need to move this along.'

And that had been that. Bannister had had no choice, and he'd belonged to Alastair Sheridan ever since. Alastair was like Don Corleone in *The Godfather*. He called in his favours very sparingly. But when he did, you had to comply. He'd even shown Bannister a copy of the photo he'd taken. It was faded with time, but there was no question that it was a much younger Bannister in the photo. The girl looked even younger than he remembered too. Fifteen at most, possibly as young as thirteen. And the terrified expression on her face as he raped her was something that would consign him to oblivion if it ever got out.

So when Alastair decided he too wanted to go into politics and become an MP, it was Bannister he'd turned to, to sponsor him. By that time Bannister had become Minister of State at the Home Office and already knew about Alastair's shady contacts with Cem Kalaman, but once again he'd done as he was told, and now the man he despised most in the world, who'd been blackmailing him all this time, was possibly going to become Prime Minister within weeks.

Bannister stared out of the window into the street below. It was another glorious sunny late afternoon but his mood was grim because Alastair Sheridan was now dragging him deeper and deeper into the abyss, and it was for this reason that he hesitated before making the call. God knows he wasn't a good man. He'd made mistakes. Huge ones. But he wasn't evil.

Die Alone

Still, in the end, he picked up the phone, dialled the number, and when Alastair Sheridan answered with a cheery greeting, Bannister told him what he wanted to know.

'There's no surveillance on Tina Boyd.'

23

A shortish man in his early thirties who fitted the description Ray
had given her of Zafir Rasaq was standing outside a fried chicken
shop on the corner of Hounslow High Street, looking around
nervously. Tina walked past him twice, checking the area for any
surveillance, before she deemed it safe to approach. Ray trusted
this guy but, even so, he was an informant by trade so in Tina's
eyes someone to be treated with the utmost caution.

'OK, let's get this over with, Zafir,' she said, getting within
feet of him before he noticed her.

He visibly recoiled, then frowned as he looked her up and
down, clearly caught out by her disguise. 'Hey, don't sneak up on
me like that,' he said, making a face. 'Are you—'

'I'm Ray's friend, that's right,' she said, not wanting to give him any more than that.

'Why couldn't Ray come?' he asked.

'It's too dangerous for him.'

'I really don't like this,' said Zafir, shaking his head.

'That makes two of us. Come on, let's go.'

He led the way down the street and she asked him if he trusted the people they were buying from.

He looked at her. 'They're serious criminals. That means you've got to be really careful around them. But they're also reliable. They don't know who Ray is, so all they're interested in is the money. You've got the rest of it, right?'

Tina patted the inside of her jacket. 'I've got it.'

They turned onto a back street dotted with food shops, money exchanges and Poundland-style outlets, and stopped outside a dilapidated curry house that looked like it might have gone out of business.

'This is the place,' said Zafir, taking a phone from his pocket.

Tina eyed him carefully. 'You look worried.'

'They're not going to be pleased when they see it's you and not Ray,' he said.

'Why? My money's as good as his.'

'They don't like not knowing who it is they're dealing with. I'm taking a real risk here.'

'And being paid for it.'

He glared at her. 'Not well enough.' He punched a number into the phone and put it to his ear.

Tina looked up and down the street. It was still fairly busy, with a number of shops open, and plenty of illegally parked vehicles. Two in particular caught her eye. One car was outside an off licence further up on the other side of the road, and had a couple of people sitting in it. The other was a white van with blacked-out rear windows, outside a fruit and veg shop the other way. She didn't like the look of either of them, and was contemplating calling things off when the door to the restaurant opened and Zafir ushered her inside.

The door was immediately locked behind them by a big guy with a beard. He looked at Tina suspiciously then addressed Zafir: 'Who's she?'

'I'm the girlfriend of the man who ordered the passport, and I'm here with the money,' Tina said, eyeing him coolly. At the same time she put her hand in her jacket pocket and gripped the can of CS gel, just in case.

The big guy didn't look happy but walked past them to the back of the restaurant, motioning for them to follow. As they did so, another guy, smaller but more dangerous-looking, appeared out of the shadows and fell into step behind Tina as they mounted the narrow staircase.

She looked round and was about to say something when she saw he had a gun pointed at her back.

'Keep moving,' he said.

Tina tensed but did as she was told, knowing from long and bitter experience that there was no point panicking. No one wants to fire a gun. It's there as a threat.

At the top of the stairs they were led into an office with a desk at the end behind which sat a fat, bald man who Ray had told her was the boss. The big bearded man peeled off so he was standing behind Zafir, who then turned round and saw the gun for the first time.

'Whoa!' he exclaimed, jumping backwards and almost falling over a box on the floor. He turned to the fat man, looking petrified. 'What's going on, Faz?'

The fat man smiled. 'We've got a few questions we need to ask,' he said. 'The first one: where's the man who came here yesterday?'

'He couldn't make it,' said Tina. 'He sent me instead. I've got the money. Where's the passport and the driving licence?'

The fat man reached under a pile of paperwork and produced what looked like the goods, holding them up for her to see. 'They're here. But you know, I've just seen a photo of a wanted fugitive on TV, a Mr Ray Mason, and he looks a lot like the man here.' He poked a stubby finger at the driving licence photo.

Tina swallowed. She hadn't seen the news for a good few hours now. Obviously there'd been some sort of development and they had a new likeness for Ray. This was bad.

'You. Zafir. You brought the man here yesterday. You vouched for him. It's Ray Mason, isn't it?'

Zafir shook his head firmly. 'No. His name's Bobby Fitzsimmons. I served time with him. I told you that yesterday.'

The fat man's face screwed up in anger. 'You're lying. I know the evidence of my own eyes.'

He nodded to the bearded guy, who stepped forward and punched Zafir in the side of the head, knocking him into the wall. Zafir's legs wobbled beneath him and he went down on one knee, clutching his head.

'I'm not putting up with this,' said Tina, who knew that the minute she showed weakness she was finished.

'Shut up and listen to me,' the fat man said. 'I know that the man you represent is Ray Mason. I hear the police are after him, but so are other people. People with deep pockets. So I'm going to ask you once and once only. Where is he?' As he spoke, he nodded to the gunman who came up behind Tina and pushed the end of his gun into the small of her back. He was so close she could smell his deodorant. 'And if you don't answer, my friend will put a bullet in you.'

Survival, in Tina's experience, was all about the ability to make swift decisions. These men were amateurs. Dangerous ones definitely, but amateurs nonetheless, which meant that the gun was very unlikely to be loaded. And the fact was, Tina was angry. She'd already been treated like dirt by the two men who'd threatened her in her office, and she wasn't going to put up with it a second time.

'OK, OK,' she said, raising her hands. 'I know where he is.' She took a step forward away from the gun, half turning as she did so, so that she could see everyone in the room, calculating that no one was going to shoot her while she was cooperating. 'I'll tell you, but get him to lower that gun. I don't want it going off accidentally.'

The fat man made a gesture and the gunman lowered his weapon, giving Tina a cocky look.

'Thank you,' she said with a relieved sigh. Then, in one rapid movement, she swivelled round on her heel and sent a flying snap-kick straight into the gunman's groin, hitting him with such force that he was slammed straight back into the door, his body bent double. The gun flew out of his hand, going off at the same time with a loud bang, which shocked everyone, including Tina.

Taking advantage of the confusion, she kicked the gun out of reach and charged at the bearded guy who'd punched Zafir, yanking the CS gel from her jacket and unloading it in his face before he could react.

She got him right in the eyes and he yelped in pain, covering them with his hands and presenting her with an easy target. She smashed an elbow into his jaw, knocking him sideways, then finished him off with a shin kick delivered to his knee.

He went down like a toppling oak, and she turned her attention to the fat man who was trying to get out from behind the desk, a shocked look on his face. Tina was across the floor in a second, grabbing him by his collar and tie and dragging him back across the desk towards her. 'I'll have those,' she said, grabbing the passport and driving licence out of his hand, and shoving them in the back of her jeans.

She threw him back in his seat and swung round just in time to see the gunman stumble bow-legged across the floor, and grab the gun. He stood back up, still unsteady on his feet, and was in the process of turning the gun in her direction when there was a huge bang as the front door downstairs was kicked in, followed by angry shouts of 'Armed police!'

For a split second the gunman froze. Unfortunately for him, Tina didn't. She stepped over and punched him once in the face then turned round and saw the fat man yank open the side door to the stationery cupboard and run inside. Ray had given Tina the layout of the place so she knew that the cupboard had a false wall at the back, which led into the room where they did the counterfeiting.

Already she could hear the sound of heavy footfalls racing up the stairs. This was obviously an intelligence-led op, which meant they knew where to go. Leaving the two thugs injured on the floor, she grabbed the dazed Zafir and pulled him to his feet, then ran into the stationery cupboard after the fat man, just as the door was being opened from the other side. She slammed both hands into the fat man's back with as much force as she could muster, sending him crashing through the door and straight into a desk, upending a monitor in the process, and knocking over the young man who'd opened the door.

Tina went straight for the window, ignoring the open mouths of the other two men in the room, and climbed out of it onto the fire escape. She raced down the steps and into a narrow alley with rubbish bags piled up against a high wall at the end, astonished that there didn't appear to be any other officers around.

She looked over her shoulder and saw two of the men from the counterfeiting room running down the steps, followed by the fat man and Zafir, both of whom were moving a lot slower.

Tina didn't think that Zafir was going to make it, but that wasn't her problem so, keeping her headscarf pulled up so she couldn't be recognized, and to keep out the stench of the rubbish, she trampled over the bags and did a running jump, getting her hands to the top of the wall and scrambling up and over it, straight into another alley. She took a sharp turn, clambered over another couple of walls, thankful that she'd spent so much time in the gym, and a couple of minutes later she was strolling along a different street, her gait casual, blending into the background in her headscarf and jacket, her breathing finally returning to normal.

That was when she burst out laughing. With shock? Relief? Enjoyment? Who could tell? A week ago she'd been showing photos of a flabby sixty-five-year-old man in flagrante with a rent boy forty years his junior to his frankly devastated wife, just another depressing case among many. And now in the last twenty-four hours she'd aided a fugitive, shot at an assassin, and beaten the crap out of a couple of thugs while only just avoiding the long arm of the law.

It was risky. It was foolish.

But by God it felt good.

24

I awoke with a start just like I'd done so often in prison, as if sleep was a weakness and now I had to be ready for whatever threat was waiting for me.

Except this time none was. I'd fallen asleep on Tina's bed, more out of boredom than anything else. I looked at my watch. 6.15 p.m. Jesus, I must have been out for at least two hours. Hopefully Tina would have picked up the passport by now.

Then I heard it. Outside the window. A shuffling sound, then what might have been a grunt of exertion. I'd only left the window open a couple of inches to let in some fresh air, and hadn't dared shut it in case someone was watching the house.

The noise stopped. Now all I could hear was the sound of birds singing in the trees. I slipped off the bed and crawled over to the window on my hands and knees. I didn't think the police had come back. They'd already searched the house once and I'd been extremely careful to be as unobtrusive as possible all day today, staying upstairs, away from the windows, and only moving when necessary, and I couldn't believe that anyone had spotted me.

I kept my head beneath the window but close to the gap, listening carefully. I thought I heard light footfalls coming from somewhere down below but then there was silence once again and I wasn't sure whether or not I'd imagined it.

I knew from when I'd spent time here before that Tina's cottage was covered front and back by CCTV with a live feed on her phone and laptop. Her laptop was open on the bed. I'd been surfing the net on it earlier looking for any updates on my escape and the Kalaman murder the previous night, and I crawled over now and refreshed the home screen.

Which was when I saw it. A large photo of me at the top of the BBC news page. I'd got used to seeing myself on the news in the weeks after I'd been broken out, but those had been old pictures. This was a brand-new one revealing my supposedly disguised look, and I recognized myself instantly. It must have been taken by a CCTV camera the previous night just after the shooting, when I'd been crossing the road to get to the Mercedes I'd stolen from the householder I'd temporarily taken hostage. They'd named him too for the first time publicly.

My heart sank as I realized I'd just put Tina in real danger. If the counterfeiters had seen this photo they'd know exactly who I was. I cursed, and looked round for the burner phone, found it on the bedside table, and picked it up. There was a missed call from Tina's number that had been made eight minutes earlier.

It was risky to call her back but I needed to know she was OK, and I felt a surge of relief as she picked up on the second ring. I started talking before she had a chance to say anything: 'If you haven't picked up the stuff yet, don't. My new look's plastered all over the news.'

She laughed down the phone, and I could tell she was outside somewhere. 'Yes,' she said. 'So I've found out.'

I felt my jaw tighten. 'Are you OK?'

'I'm fine. And I've got your passport and licence. I've still got your money too. The people you were buying from had worked out who you were. They wanted me to tell them your location, but naturally I was too honourable for that. They got rough, but I got rougher.'

This time it was me who laughed. 'Yeah, I bet you did. Woe betide the man who tangles with you.'

'I'll tell you something else,' she said. 'The place was under police surveillance. They raided it while I was there. I got out. I don't think your friend Zafir was so lucky.'

'Well, that'll do his credibility with the local criminal fraternity some good. He doesn't know who you are so even if he talks to the cops, he won't be able to implicate you. Was your disguise good enough that you won't be recognized?'

'Thankfully, yes. And I didn't drive my own car there, so there's nothing that'll tie me to the scene. It was close though.'

I sighed. 'I'm sorry, Tina. I really am.'

'Look, I care about you. I don't regret it.'

I tensed at her words, knowing that in three hours I'd be on my way, and would almost certainly never see her again. 'Jesus, I'll miss you. I really will.'

'I'll miss you too. But I definitely think it's best for my sanity if you go. Listen, I'll be back in an hour or so, depending on traffic. Is it all sorted your end?'

'Yeah, the pick-up time's 9.30.'

'And he's OK doing it?'

The man picking me up was Steve Brennan, the father of Sheridan and Cem Kalaman's first victim. I'd been loath to call him but had done it because I could see no other way. But I needn't have worried. Steve Brennan had been keen, almost desperate, to help.

'Yeah, he's fine,' I said.

'Good. I'll see you before then to say goodbye.'

It might, I thought, be better if we didn't see each other at all, since it was just a way of prolonging the agony, but in the end I knew I wouldn't be able to face that. I had to hold her one more time. Then no more.

I put the phone back in my pocket and went back into the bedroom. The only sound outside the window was the singing of the birds but I still logged into Tina's account and checked the feeds on her cameras at the front and back of the house, relieved to find that there was no sign of any intruders.

I closed the laptop and smiled. I was just getting jumpy.

25

Mary West had been napping on the sofa, which was something she did more and more these days, and she was making herself a cup of tea in an attempt to wake herself up when she sensed a presence in the cottage. She frowned, wondering if she was just getting senile, sleeping half the day and imagining people in her house. Bill would have told her that this was just part and parcel of getting old, but Bill had been gone ten years now, and she had no one here to tell her not to worry about everything.

But then she'd always been a worrier. Only now, at eighty-five, had she realized how much worry had wasted her time. Sometimes she'd take her grandchildren to one side and tell them that the one thing she'd learned, now that it was far too late, was that you had to embrace life, take risks, not allow it to get the better of you.

Mary thought she could almost hear her bones creaking as she picked up her tea and walked slowly out of the kitchen and into her living room. The light from the gradually setting sun was still strong through the open French windows, bathing everything in a rich golden glow.

Except Mary was sure she'd closed them.

A long shadow fell across her path, and she felt that presence again, knew now that there was someone in her home. Slowly she turned, a shiver of shock running up her spine.

A figure all in black stood there, a mask covering his face, a gun in his hand.

Mary let out a small, terrified gasp and the man put a finger to his lips.

'Don't say a word, and I promise you won't be hurt. You just need to do me a little favour, that's all.'

And that was when Mary realized it wasn't a man at all. It was a woman. And for some reason this scared her even more.

Tina was back in her own car, still parked up in the same back street where she'd left it earlier, removing her makeup and transforming herself back into Tina Boyd, when she got a call on her regular phone.

She thought about leaving it. She was in a hurry, and wanted to find somewhere to dump the disguise, since it was way too risky to be driving around with all this gear in her car after what had just happened. But then she saw who the caller was, and she picked up immediately.

'Mrs West? Are you OK?'

'No, love,' said Mrs West. 'I'm afraid I'm not feeling too well. I'm in bed and I need some things. Are you at home?'

'I'm not, but I can be back in an hour. Are the Morrises not about?'

There was a long pause.

'Mrs West?'

'I tried them, love, and they're not there.'

Mrs West had been her neighbour for almost ten years now, and she'd always been good to Tina, and consequently Tina was very protective of her. 'Don't you worry,' she said, 'I'll sort it out. What do you need?'

'Just some milk and some sugar.'

'OK, I'll buy them on the way home and bring them straight over.'

There was another pause. 'Thank you, love.'

Tina frowned. 'Are you sure you're OK, Mrs West? You don't sound too good.'

But she was already speaking into a dead phone.

26

'You missed all the drama,' said DS Jane Tutill of Hounslow CID.

'I know, I got stuck in traffic,' said Bolt, looking at the caved-in door of the curry house then back at Tutill, who was probably no more than early thirties and thus a couple of decades younger than him. When the police started looking too young to be police then it was definitely time to retire, and in truth, that day couldn't come fast enough for Bolt.

'What happened?' he asked.

'Well, we responded to the NCA's request for help, and had a surveillance team set up on this premises at …' She consulted her notes. '17.24. No one came in or out until at 17.45 the team saw a male IC4 in his thirties, accompanied by a female IC4, age unknown, arrive and stop outside. The male made a call and they were let inside. Then approximately five minutes later, one of the team heard what sounded like a gunshot coming from inside the building. I was in another car and I made the decision to stage an entry in case there was threat to, or loss of, life. We got up there and found two IC4 males with superficial injuries inside a room that was being used as an office. There was also a loaded revolver on the floor which had just been fired, although it doesn't look like anyone was hurt. We arrested three more IC4 males out the back as they were trying to escape, but there was no sign of the IC4 female.'

'Anything else?'

'One of the men we arrested told us that he was the one who gave the initial intelligence tip that Mason was expected this evening to get the passport and driving licence.'

'Where's he now?'

'Down at Hounslow nick with the others, although I did manage to get a quick word with him before he went. He said that Mason came in there yesterday morning with a shaved head and a beard, and had his photo taken. He also told me that he was the one who produced the items for Mason, and he was told that he had to have them ready by six o'clock. Apparently, he finished them this afternoon and gave them to his boss two hours ago. The boss is one of those we arrested, but right now he's not talking. None of them are. The thing is, though, there's no sign of the passport or the driving licence in there, and we've already searched the place twice. And none of the suspects have got them either.'

'Did the informant say why the shot was fired?'

She shook her head. 'He didn't even hear it. He and his colleagues were working in another room, which is soundproofed, and connected by a false wall. The first he knew anything was going on was when his boss, the female and another male came running through. They all went out the fire escape. I guess the female was the fastest, and it's why she got away.' She paused. 'Do you think she was here to pick up Mason's fake ID?'

Bolt thought about this for a minute. 'The timing's very coincidental if she wasn't, and the ID would still be on the premises if she and the other guy had nothing to do with Mason. Have you got her on film?'

Tutill nodded and led him over the road to where an unmarked van was sandwiched between two patrol cars. A small, slightly bored-looking crowd were gathered nearby but since, for the moment, police activity was fairly minimal, it didn't look they'd be hanging around for long.

Tutill pulled open the van doors and they climbed inside. A plainclothes officer sat reviewing pictures on a laptop surrounded by camera equipment, and she asked him if he had some good shots of their female suspect.

'Well, we got shots and video,' he said with a sigh, turning the laptop round so they could see it, 'but I wouldn't say they're good. This is a woman who definitely doesn't want to be seen. This is the best one.' He pressed a couple of keys and an MPEG file came up on the screen with a still image of a man and a woman outside the curry house. The man had his back to the camera while the woman was looking partly towards it. She was dressed in Western clothing – jeans, trainers, a light summer jacket – but with a black hijab scarf covering her head and the bottom half of her face, and sunglasses.

The video started and the cameraman moved into close-up on the woman as she looked up and down the street, constantly moving her head and keeping it down to make it harder to get a decent shot of her. She said a few words to the man as he talked on the phone then she turned and faced the window of the curry house. The camera concentrated on her for a further fifteen seconds or so, during which time she hardly moved, then the curry house door opened and she followed the man inside, pulling the hijab further up her face as she did so.

Bolt asked him to pause it at that point. He stared at the woman's hand as she moved the hijab. The skin didn't seem as dark as the skin on her face, and she was wearing dark nail varnish.

Tina had been wearing exactly the same nail varnish that morning. She'd also been wearing very similar jeans. The woman looked to be about five feet seven and she was of Tina's build.

Bolt made a noise under his breath. He'd known as soon as he'd been told about the mysterious IC4 female who'd managed to escape the scene, leaving behind a couple of injured men and a freshly fired gun, that it was probably Tina. Add to it the coincidental timing and the missing documents, and now the footage of the surveillance-aware woman in the hijab, and he was convinced of it.

His immediate emotion was anger. Tina had lied to him that morning and had clearly been helping Mason all along. Well, if this was how she wanted to play things, then she'd have to accept the consequences.

'Does she look familiar?' Tutill asked him when they were back outside.

'No,' said Bolt wearily, 'I don't think so. She'll have left DNA in there, though. Have you got a SOCO team coming in?'

'We're waiting for one to come available. I don't suppose the NCA have got any spare?'

This was the problem with policing nowadays. Years of government cuts had pared the police service to the bone, to the extent that it was fair to say they could no longer do their jobs properly. He shook his head. 'No, we're as stretched as everyone else. As soon as the team have swept the place and the gun for DNA let me know, and I'll see if I can get a priority on the results.'

Tutill shrugged. 'It's your case, do what you want. It's just a load of extra paperwork for us.'

Bolt smiled. 'I know, and I'm sorry. At least you got a counterfeit operation out of it.'

'There'll be another one opening tomorrow. Maybe the same guys. You know what it's like.'

'I do,' he said. 'We're fighting a losing battle.'

She shook her head. 'No. I think it's already lost.'

Sadly, Bolt shared her sentiment. It was another reason why retirement couldn't come fast enough. He thanked Tutill for her help, told her he'd be in touch, and walked back to where he'd parked his car further down the road, contemplating his next move. If the woman in the hijab was Tina – and he was 95 per cent certain she was – then she'd clearly done everything possible to cover her tracks. That meant she probably hadn't come here in her own car, so unless she'd left DNA it was going to be very hard to prove that she'd been here, and even that alone wasn't going to be enough to arrest her.

But if she had hold of the fake IDs for Mason it meant she was going to have to give them to him at some point. It was time, therefore, to put her under proper surveillance.

He was just about to put in a call to DCS Trinder to get the necessary authorization when his phone rang.

It was Mo. 'Any joy on the op, boss?'

Bolt sighed. 'Mason didn't turn up but I think Tina Boyd did, heavily disguised, and got away with the documents. We need to get people on her ASAP.'

'I think we might have enough to nick her, boss. We've found the car Mason escaped in. It was hidden in woodland near a hamlet in Essex. He'd rubbed mud on the number plates, which was why we weren't able to track it. The local police up there were investigating reports of shots being fired in the vicinity when they found it. And here's the thing. It was only a mile and a half from where Tina Boyd's car was picked up on the ANPR last night.'

Bolt felt a surge of anger. 'There's no way it's a coincidence. She's been playing us, Mo. She must have picked Mason up last night. What do we know about the gunshots?'

'Not a lot. Police got three separate reports of shots being fired at about 11.30 p.m. They sent an ARV but didn't find anyone with gunshot wounds, but they sent another patrol car round there this afternoon, just to take another look, and that's when they found it. The timing looks right for Tina being there too. Her car was picked up twice on the same camera just outside Nazeing, heading towards where the shots were fired at 10.42 p.m. and then heading away in the direction of the M25 at 11.43 p.m. Do you think we missed Mason in the search of the house this morning?'

'I don't see how. But we could have done.'

'What do you want to do, boss?'

Bolt swallowed hard. Tina had lied to him repeatedly. She was involved up to the hilt, just as, deep down, he'd always known she was. 'I want her nicked right away and the house searched from top to bottom. Get onto the locals. Tell them to send ARVs in case Mason's armed. This whole charade's got to end.'

27

The village where Tina lived was picture-postcard, with a single main street containing a corner shop that was still run by a local couple, a twelfth-century church, and a decent pub, which she still popped into occasionally, even though no alcohol had passed her lips for more than a decade now. It was always quiet too, and this evening was no exception. The street was empty, although she could hear laughter coming from the pub beer garden as she drove past with her window open.

She scanned the street carefully as she parked in her spot outside the cottage, just in case the police were keeping an eye on the place. She might have dumped the hijab disguise but she was still carrying Ray's fake IDs, which were taped under the front passenger seat of the Focus, and if she was caught with them she'd have some serious questions to answer.

She left them where they were and got out of the car with a bag carrying the milk and sugar for Mrs West. It felt strange knowing that Ray was inside the cottage, only feet away from her, and yet here she was doing everything possible to avoid him. Him leaving was for the best, she kept telling herself. And the sooner he went the easier it would be for them both.

She knocked on Mrs West's door, and when there was no answer, she looked in the front window. The living room and kitchen were empty and the French windows to the garden were open. She was probably out back somewhere, although there was a distinct chill in the air now, and if she wasn't feeling too good, the garden wouldn't be the best place for her.

Mrs West had only once been ill in the nine years they'd lived next door to each other, and even then she'd tried to make as little fuss as possible and Tina had had to insist on doing things for her, so the timing of this latest call, with everything else that was going on, had rung a small alarm bell.

Tina tried the handle. The door was open. Feeling just a little bit wary she stepped slowly inside, shutting the door gently behind her but leaving it on the latch.

'Hello, Mrs West,' she called out. 'I've got your stuff.'

There was a pause, then a weak voice called out: 'I'm up here, love.'

Tina relaxed a little, putting the milk in the fridge and the sugar on the side.

'Do you need anything?' she called out as she climbed the stairs. 'A cup of tea or anything like that?'

She opened Mrs West's bedroom door, and the moment she walked in she realized she'd made a big mistake.

Mrs West was sitting up on her bed, fully clothed, while standing off to one side near the window was the woman Tina had shot at the previous night. She was wearing a black balaclava but Tina knew who it was by the long black hair poking out of the bottom. She was holding the same gun as well, a pistol with a suppressor attached, which was now pointed at Tina. This, then, was The Wraith, the professional assassin who'd come so close to killing Ray on two occasions.

'Come on in, so I can see you,' The Wraith said, her accent a curious mixture of South African and American.

Tina knew she was already too far inside the door to escape without risking getting shot, so she stepped further inside, trying hard to keep calm.

'I'm sorry, Tina,' said Mrs West. 'I didn't mean to—'

'It's OK, Mrs West,' said Tina, giving her a reassuring smile. 'It'll all be fine, I promise.'

'Get round the other side of the bed, away from the door,' The Wraith demanded.

Tina did as she was told. It was a small room, very similar to her own, and she had to pass close to the woman as she walked round the front of the bed to get to the other side. She didn't try anything though. The woman's gun hand was steady and it was clear from all Tina had heard that she'd had a lot of practice at killing.

'What do you want?' Tina asked, retreating until she was standing against the wall, only a few feet from Mrs West.

'Ray Mason,' said The Wraith emphatically, still keeping her position by the window where she could see across Mrs West's and Tina's back gardens. 'I don't want to have to kill either of you, which is why I'm wearing this mask.'

'I don't know where he is.'

'Of course you do. It was you last night, wasn't it? The one who shot at me. And don't bother to deny it.'

Tina thought fast. If she lied too much, she risked either her or Mrs West getting hurt. She had no idea how this woman had got to her but she was clearly not to be trifled with.

'You're hesitating. I don't like that.'

'Yes, it was me,' she said. 'I was trying to save his life.'

'I don't take it personally. It was business. Just like this is.' She paused. 'Where's Mason now? And please don't lie.'

'I don't know,' said Tina instinctively.

Two shots rang out, their sounds muffled to a loud pop by the suppressor, and Mrs West let out a strangled gasp and fell backwards on the bed, her head hitting the wall. As Tina watched, horrified, Mrs West's eyes closed and her body went limp. There were two smoking holes in the middle of her chest.

For a long moment the room was silent. Then Tina spoke, anger overtaking her fear. 'You bitch. She was an old lady.'

'She didn't have long to live,' said The Wraith evenly. 'I could smell it on her. I just helped her on her way. But the point is, you've got to stop lying, or you're next. So I ask again, where's Ray Mason?'

Tina had stared down gun barrels before, but she didn't think she'd ever faced an adversary as cold-blooded as this. It was the casualness with which she'd murdered Mrs West, as if she was doing nothing more than swatting a fly. She knew now that a wrong answer could be fatal.

'When I left him earlier he was in my house. I think he's still there now.'

The Wraith nodded. 'Good answer, because I think he is too. I heard the toilet flush on the other side of the wall a few minutes ago. That's the problem with these quaint little English cottages. You can hear everything. Now, take out your phone very slowly, put the phone on speaker, and call him. Say that you've just seen the police in the village, and tell him to go out the back way into the garden. And make it sound like you mean it or I'll put a bullet in your belly.'

Tina hesitated.

'Do it now,' The Wraith snapped. 'Don't test my patience. It won't end well.'

And that was the problem. Tina knew it wasn't going to end well, whether she made the call or not. But she knew she had to do whatever it took to prolong her life so she took out her burner phone and called Ray, thinking fast.

'Hey Tina, where are you?' he asked. 'I thought I heard your car pull up.'

Tina stared at The Wraith and the gun in her hand. She knew that if Ray went out the back entrance, he'd be a sitting duck. The distance from Mrs West's bedroom window to her back patio was no more than twenty-five feet. The Wraith wouldn't miss from there. But she also wouldn't want to be looking out of the window with Tina at her back, which meant as soon as Tina finished the phone call, she was dead.

She watched the woman's finger tighten on the trigger.

'That's right, I've just arrived now,' said Tina, feeling awful that she was about to sentence him to death. 'But there are police all over the village. Plainclothes. I've seen them. You need to get out the back way now. Go.'

'Thanks, hun,' he said, using his old pet name for her. 'I'm gone. I'll call you when I can.'

He ended the call, and Tina slowly put the phone back in her pocket, her whole body tensing, suddenly feeling terribly vulnerable because she knew there was no way the woman opposite her was going to let her walk free from here.

And she was right.

'Thanks, Tina, that wasn't so hard, was it?' said The Wraith, and shot her twice in the chest.

I was in Tina's bedroom when I got the call. I was on my feet in an instant, throwing on the backpack that contained my meagre possessions and crawling over to the bedroom window. If the police were going to raid the place they'd come from the back and the front, but when I lifted my eyes just above the bottom of the frame, I could see that the hill rising up beyond Tina's back garden to the woodland at the top was empty.

Moving fast, I crawled out onto the landing to the front bedroom, which looked out over the high street, and peered out of the window as surreptitiously as possible. The street too was empty.

Completely. And Tina's car was parked directly outside, with no sign of Tina herself.

Something was wrong here, but staying put wasn't an option. Crawling back away from the window, I pulled out the burner phone and called Steve Brennan's mobile number.

Brennan answered on the third ring.

'There's been a change of plan,' I whispered, getting to my feet and running down the stairs. 'How soon can you get to the rendezvous point?'

'I drove up early. I can be there in about ...' He paused. 'The satnav says fourteen minutes.'

'Do me a favour, Steve, and put your foot down. I'll meet you in ten.'

28

This whole thing was turning into a messy job for Jane Kelman. Two more people dead, and she still hadn't taken out Mason.

Now she stood in the shadows behind the old lady's open bedroom window, waiting for her target to come out of the back of Tina's house and into view. The light was beginning to fade, which suited her fine. She could still get a good shot at Mason, and with no witnesses either as the temperature was dropping fast and none of the neighbours were outside. She'd make the kill and escape the way she'd come in, up the hill and into the woods beyond, where she'd parked her car earlier.

She didn't like waiting around like this. Her usual MO was to take someone out then put as much distance between them and her as possible. The only reason she was putting this much effort into taking out Mason was because of the amount of money on offer for his death. Three hundred thousand dollars, including the bonus the client had just paid her to keep going with the job. With everything else she'd made and invested over the years, she was only a couple more jobs away from a comfortable retirement at her condo in Panama.

Unfortunately, for a man with the police on his tail, Mason didn't seem to be in any particular hurry to emerge. She looked at her watch. Five minutes since Tina Boyd had ended the call and there was still no sign of him.

'Come on, come on,' she whispered.

And then she saw the back door to Tina's house fly open and Mason come running out, keeping low, turning round and looking up just as she aimed the pistol at him and pulled the trigger.

He was already diving for cover and the bullet struck his backpack in a puff of smoke. But now he was down on his hands and knees on the patio and she took aim again, this time at his head, her finger tightening on the trigger, only vaguely aware of movement behind her.

Tina had still been wearing the Kevlar vest under her sweatshirt and jacket when The Wraith had shot her and, although she fell down hard, banging her head in the process, she was still very much alive, if badly winded. She'd lain utterly still, holding her breath with her eyes closed, knowing that at any moment the woman could walk over and put a third and final bullet in her head. It had been an utterly terrifying few minutes, made worse because she'd been so helpless.

But then, as it had become clear that this wasn't going to happen, Tina had opened one eye and watched the woman as she stood at the window, all her concentration now on her new target.

Tina had known that the chances of her creeping up on the woman without being heard were almost zero. Her best bet was to stay where she was. But that way she was sentencing Ray to death.

Her mind had been in utter torment, until she'd seen the woman stiffen and raise her gun.

Pushing down on the palms of her hands, Tina had slowly lifted herself up and was in a crouching position as the woman fired her first shot.

She was still pointing the gun out of the window as Tina took a silent step forward, then another. Then, holding her breath in an effort to stay completely silent, Tina sprinted across the room.

The Wraith heard her at the last second, and was already turning round as Tina slammed into her, yanking her gun arm up and away from her body and launching an elbow strike to her face. But The Wraith was quick. She blocked the elbow strike with her forearm even as the momentum of Tina's attack sent the whole of her top half out of the window. Tina kept going, trying to push her out completely. Out of the corner of her eye she could see Ray. He was getting to his feet, looking slightly disorientated, but as he saw what was happening, he ran towards, then vaulted, Mrs West's fence.

Tina just had time to feel a pang of relief that he was OK before The Wraith launched herself upwards, keeping hold of Tina and trying to drive a knee into her groin. The two of them stumbled back into the room and Tina fell backwards onto the bed, landing on Mrs West's legs, with The Wraith on top ofher.

Now the momentum was with The Wraith as, with a snarl, she yanked her gun arm free, her dark eyes burning behind the mask.

But Tina had rage on her side, and that gave her strength. She sat up suddenly and punched The Wraith in the side of the head before she had a chance to turn her gun on her. The woman stumbled, the gun went off, and Tina broke free, punching her in the head a second time, sending her sprawling over the bed and down the other side.

Leaping up, Tina sprinted through the bedroom door, hitting the wall on the other side of the landing, then took a hard left turn towards the stairs as a single round flew past her head and struck the wall.

Ray was already coming up the stairs, obviously in the middle of some sort of rescue attempt, but now he was just in the way.

'Run! Run!' she screamed, and he immediately turned round and together they scrambled down the narrow staircase, almost falling over themselves in their haste.

As they made the turning at the bottom, Tina shoved Ray bodily into the living room, taking a half glance over her shoulder to see The Wraith already at the top of the stairs, taking aim with the gun.

Tina dived out of her field of vision, landing in a heap on top of Ray as The Wraith fired a second round. She rolled off him in an instant and then she was on her feet, motioning for him to follow her out the front door, knowing that if they went out the back they'd be easy targets.

Her car keys were already in her hand as she opened the front door. 'Get in the back,' she hissed at Ray as they made a dash for the car, knowing that if The Wraith had moved fast enough she would already have got to the front of the house and could get a shot at them from the upstairs window.

But there was no time for hesitation and she pulled open the driver's door and jumped inside, keeping her head down. She heard rather than saw Ray come flying into the back and, shoving the key into the ignition and starting the engine, she pulled away in a screech of tyres.

No shots came, and Tina was halfway through a sigh of relief when she glanced in her rear-view mirror and saw two marked police cars driving fast down the high street in the direction of her house.

'Oh shit.'

'What is it?' asked Ray from the back.

'Stay down. It's the police.'

Tina put the Focus into third gear, rounding the bend so they were out of sight, then put her foot to the floor.

'What the hell are they doing here?'

'I have no idea,' said Tina, accelerating fast then slowing rapidly and taking a right-hand turn onto one of the back roads at the end of the village, spotting the lead police car just as she pulled across the road. She'd guessed that they were coming to her house but had hoped they hadn't spotted her driving away. Now she knew they had.

'Jesus, what happened back there?'

'I'm sorry, Ray. The woman with the gun – The Wraith – she used Mrs West to lure me round there. Then she killed her and told me I'd be next if I didn't call you.'

Ray shook his head. 'I'm sorry too. Jesus, what a mess.'

'It is,' she said as calmly as she could as she accelerated along the narrow, winding, tree-lined road, hoping she didn't meet anything coming in the other direction. 'And now we're going to have to say goodbye. Your passport and licence are taped under the passenger seat so grab them, then when I slow the car, you jump out and get your arse into the woods fast, because if you get caught, it's going to look very bad for me. And ditch the burner phone somewhere safe. I'm getting rid of mine.'

She heard him rip the documents free and then he appeared in her rear-view mirror – balding, bearded, but still undeniably handsome – and smiled at her. 'Thank you for this. I owe you big time.'

A couple of middle-aged bike riders in full leather gear came hurtling down the hill, and Tina dodged to avoid them, mounting the bank at the side of the road before righting herself. They were close to the edge of the woods here. In a few moments the woods would give way to farmland, followed by the next village along.

She slammed on the brakes, slowing to only a few miles an hour. 'OK, go, go, go!'

Die Alone

They looked at each other one last time in the mirror and Ray said the words he'd used only a handful of times before with Tina: 'I love you.'

Then he was out the door, across the road, and racing into the trees, as she sped away, wondering how much more of this day she could take.

29

Almost as soon as I hit the tree line I heard the police cars coming up the hill. I dived down in some ferns and crawled behind a beech tree, watching as they drove past, barely thirty seconds behind Tina. There were two of them and I waited for them to pass, counted to ten and, confident that they were the only ones coming, jumped to my feet and continued running through the woods. The light was disappearing but the trees, a mixture of beech and oak, were too far apart to provide much cover. If the police flooded the area it wouldn't take them long to find me.

I knew from experience, however, that it would take them time to get organized and, if I moved fast enough, I could still get away. In the short time Tina and I had been together we'd spent a lot of time walking round these woods and I knew exactly where I was. To the right of me was the grassy hill that led directly down to the back of Tina's cottage, whereas to the left, the wood was bordered by a single-track road that ran along its top, and it was here where I was supposed to be meeting Steve Brennan.

My heart was still pounding from how close I'd come to getting killed. Some sixth sense had told me to look round just as I'd come out of Tina's back door, and there she was. The Wraith, a balaclava covering her head, standing in the upstairs window pointing a gun straight at me. I'd felt the bullet strike the back-pack like a punch as I dived to the ground, not sure if I'd been injured or not, but knowing that either way I was totally exposed.

But the second bullet never came, and when I looked round I'd seen The Wraith and Tina struggling.

I looked at my watch. 8.12 p.m. Exactly ten minutes since I'd made the call to Brennan, so the other man should be close by. Somewhere way off in the distance I could hear the sound of a police siren. There'd be a full pursuit of Tina now, and once again I felt a pang of guilt. And for involving Steve Brennan, a man who'd already suffered far too much in life to have to face the indignity of prison. But I quickly pushed the guilt aside. When you're on the run and desperate, and when of course you believe you're acting in the greater good, guilt's a luxury you can't afford.

The road was about a hundred yards to my left if I remembered correctly, and I turned towards it now, pulling the burner phone free from my pocket.

'I'm up here,' I whispered into the phone. 'Where are you?'

'I should be at the spot where we're meant to meet in about two minutes,' Brennan replied. 'A police car just came whizzing past me on the main road, with all its lights flashing. Is everything OK?'

I could have spared Brennan the risk of getting caught by telling him just to turn round and go home, but self-preservation was standing right in the way. 'We'll be fine,' I said, 'but the sooner you're here the better. Keep driving until you see me.'

I ended the call and picked up the pace, running fast now, seeing the outline of the road up ahead. The siren I'd heard earlier had stopped and all was once again quiet, except for the birds in the trees, and the faint rumble of an engine coming from ahead of me. This would be Brennan.

When I was a few yards from the road, I stopped behind a tree and crouched down.

Which was when I saw it. A car parked in the shadow of a large holly bush a few yards in from the road. It could have been a dog walker but, with darkness about to fall and the temperature dropping, it was a bit late, and I hadn't seen anyone else in the woods.

Realization hit me. The Wraith would have had to come out either at the front or the back of Tina's neighbour's house after the shooting, and to avoid detection she'd almost certainly have chosen the back, which meant she'd have come up the hill and into these woods.

Where she'd probably hidden her car.

I turned round, and saw her immediately, no more than thirty yards away, creeping up on me like a hunter, using the trees as cover. She was still wearing the balaclava and her hair was tied back in a ponytail. She saw me looking at her and stopped.

For a few seconds we simply observed each other. There was no anger, no real emotion at all. Just an interest, born possibly of mutual respect. Three times we'd been brought together now. Three times she'd tried to kill me. Three times she'd failed, but still she came back. I admired her determination. I suspected she admired mine.

And then, just like that, the spell was broken as she whipped up the pistol from her side and started firing in rapid succession.

But thirty yards is a long distance from which to hit someone with a pistol shot, especially in poor light, even if you're a good shot. And The Wraith was definitely a good shot, as was clear by the closeness of the bullets as I crouched low, darted behind a tree, and then sprinted for the road, zigzagging as much as possible.

But she didn't hit me.

And then the shots stopped.

As I reached the road, I saw a silver Audi estate round the corner a hundred yards away, driving towards me. It was Steve Brennan.

I broke into a mad dash towards him, stealing a look over my shoulder. I couldn't see her. I kept running. The Audi was slowing down, now only thirty yards away. Once again I glanced over my shoulder, only this time I saw her, still within the tree line, running parallel to me but slightly behind, reloading her gun as she went. And she was moving fast too. Faster than I was.

After shoving in a fresh magazine, she again took aim and fired off three more rounds.

They flew wide and I kept running, gesticulating wildly for Brennan to stop the car and get into the passenger seat.

At first the other man looked confused. Then, as I came alongside the driver's door, he seemed to get the message and clambered out of the way. I jumped inside, shoving him the rest of the way across. Thankfully the car was an automatic and Brennan had put it in park. Without missing a beat, I shoved it into reverse and slammed my foot down on the accelerator, just as The Wraith ran out into the road, barely ten yards ahead of us. 'Keep your head down!' I yelled as the car shot backwards down the road, turning the ten yards into twenty, then thirty.

The Wraith lowered her gun and took aim at the tyres, but before she could crack off a shot I spotted a gap in the trees and reversed the car into it, then slammed the gearstick into drive and drove back out, wheel-spinning as we went. In the rear-view mirror I could see her standing in the road, the gun down by her side, her posture one of defeat. Then she was off again into the trees.

A minute later I brought the car to a halt at the side of the road, still panting with adrenalin. 'Nice to see you, Steve,' I said with a smile, looking across to where Brennan was crouched in his seat with his hands over his head. 'I think you'd better take the wheel now.'

30

'I love you.'

It was less than three days since Ray Mason had re-entered Tina's life, and now he was gone again, leaving chaos and trauma in his wake. It had taken her months to get over him, and she'd come so close. She was proud of the way she hadn't slept with him the previous night. It would have been very easy. She'd slept with a couple of men this past year, but they'd been as much to forget him as anything else. But she knew if she'd done anything with Ray then it would have brought back all the memories of the intimacy and the desire – the closeness – that they'd experienced together, and that would have been too much to bear. It was why she'd fled the cottage today. Anything to avoid temptation.

And now, just with those three single-syllable words, he'd drawn her right back in, because the truth was she loved him right back, which was why she'd risked her life and her freedom for him – not once, but twice. And all to no avail, because he was gone. Very likely for ever. Leaving behind the body of her poor, innocent neighbour, Mrs West, a woman who'd always been so kind to Tina. She knew it wasn't Ray's fault. The responsibility lay with the woman who'd murdered her, and the people who'd paid for her services. But even so, if Ray hadn't come back, none of this would have happened. The euphoria and excitement of earlier that day were long gone now, replaced with anger, grief, shock.

And fear too. Because Tina was scared, not only about the consequences of her actions in the last twenty-four hours, but also because she had no idea who might be coming for her next. Her family was safe for the time being, but they'd be back in two weeks, and the people ranged against her had long memories.

Yet even now she was protecting Ray by drawing the police away from him. She'd shaken off the patrol cars chasing her in the warren of back roads around her village and now, forty-five minutes later, at close to nine p.m., she was on a B road in Essex, just north of the town of Shenfield, some thirty miles away from her house. She had no doubt that by now the police would be tracking her car using the ANPR, and were doubtless closing in on her, which meant she didn't have much time.

She was in open farmland with no one following her, or coming the other way. Slowing the car down, she opened the passenger window and flung the burner phone she'd been using to communicate with Ray into a hedge, before accelerating away. Then, pulling out her regular phone, she put it on hands-free and dialled 999.

As soon as the operator answered, Tina identified herself with her full name and address, and claimed she'd witnessed the murder of her next-door neighbour but had fled the scene, fearing for her own life. 'I'm going to attend the nearest police station in the next hour. I'll give my statement then.'

The operator tried to get more details but Tina ended the call. She was going to do things her way. She checked the satnav on the phone. She was only eighteen minutes from her lawyer's house, and was expected. They'd go to the nearest police station together and face the music, and most likely Mike Bolt. Tina knew Mike would be furious. He'd helped get her out of some serious scrapes before, but it would be her lies that hurt him the most. And if she was going to avoid charges and prison, she was going to need to keep lying.

She'd just lit a cigarette when she saw car headlights approaching fast in her rear-view mirror. She kept her speed at a steady fifty, and when the car got to about twenty yards behind her, its flashing blue lights started. And then, as she rounded the corner, she saw two more police cars with flashing lights blocking the road.

Tensing, she slammed on the brakes and brought the car to a halt, just as black-clad armed officers appeared on both sides of her, screaming at her to turn off the engine.

It struck her then, in one of those rare moments of epiphany, how hollow, lonely and disjointed her life had become. Here she was, a decorated former police officer, alone in the middle of nowhere on a Saturday night, being nicked at gunpoint like the worst kind of thug.

She switched off the engine as the driver's side door was yanked open by one of the armed officers and she was dragged from the car and forced to kneel in the road with her hands clasped behind her head. 'It's all right, I know the drill,' she snapped as one of the cops continued to bark orders, the barrel of his gun only inches from her face. Behind her she could hear other officers searching her car. It didn't take them long to discover it was empty.

The officer who looked to be in charge walked over to her, standing a few feet away with his MP5 pointed straight at her.

'Where the hell's Ray Mason?' he demanded.

Tina managed a shrug. 'I don't know what you're talking about,' she said.

31

'We're here,' said Steve Brennan, opening the boot of the car.

I emerged from where I'd spent the journey, under a thick blanket behind a box of painting equipment.

'Thanks, Steve,' I said, climbing out with my backpack and stretching. 'I'm sorry about earlier. Are you OK?'

Brennan didn't look OK. He looked badly shaken, and every inch of his sixty-five years plus at least five extra. He'd hardly spoken on the journey down here.

'I'm fine,' he said. 'But I wasn't expecting that.'

'Neither was I. If I'd known I was at risk like that, I'd never have involved you.'

I gave his shoulder a gentle squeeze, trying to calm him. He was obviously shocked by what had just happened. Like most people, he'd probably never encountered violence like that first hand.

'It's probably best not to mention what happened to Karen,' he said, leading me up the driveway to the pretty cottage where he and his wife had lived since long before their daughter Dana had been abducted. Dana had grown up here, and I wondered how different all their lives would have been had she not been snatched that sunny summer's day all those years ago.

'My lips are sealed,' I told him, following him inside, through a narrow hallway with low-hanging beams and into a cosy living room where Karen Brennan sat with a book. The TV was on in the background with the volume turned low, playing a nature documentary.

As I came into the room she got to her feet and shook my hand but her demeanour was less than welcoming. 'Hello, Mr Mason,' she said, not looking me in the eye.

'Call me Ray, please,' I said.

She nodded tightly and looked past me towards her husband. 'Are you OK, love? You shouldn't be out doing all of this.'

'I'm fine, don't worry about me,' said Brennan, giving her a tender kiss.

She held him for a long moment, and I found myself feeling jealous for what they had, even though their closeness had been cemented by tragedy. They clearly adored each other, and their love simply served to amplify my solitude.

'Please sit down, Ray,' said Brennan. 'Can I get you a drink of something?'

I sank into one of the armchairs, still stiff from the hour-long journey down here in the boot of the Audi. I felt like I was intruding on them but the desire to relax with some company trumped the feeling, as did the idea of a drink. I hadn't had alcohol in over a year, but I wasn't going to turn it down now. 'Yes please. Have you got a brandy?'

Brennan said he had and went to get it while I faced Karen Brennan across the room.

'They're saying on the news you killed three people last night,' she said, finally meeting my eye. 'Did you?'

I'd never given either of them the full details of the Bone Field case or told them who the suspects were. In the run-up to my arrest I'd done my utmost to keep them abreast of developments, but that had been more to show them that I was working on their behalf. All they knew was that their daughter's killers had yet to be brought to justice.

Brennan returned with two glasses of brandy while I was still working out how much to tell her. 'Don't question him too much, Karen, please,' he said, handing me one of the glasses.

I took a big sip, reeling at the burning sensation as it ran down my throat. I'd never really been a spirit drinker, preferring good red wine, but the brandy had a soothing effect and I took another sip before speaking. 'It's OK,' I said. 'I've asked you for help so I owe you a full explanation.' I looked at them both in turn. 'I believe – in fact, I know – that there were three men involved in Dana's abduction and murder, and they're the same people I was investigating for the Bone Field murders.' Neither said anything but both were listening closely. 'I killed one of them last year. He was a long-term associate and confidant of Cem Kalaman. Yes, I did kill Kalaman last night, along with one of his bodyguards who was trying to shoot me at the time. Kalaman was also one of Dana's killers, and I don't make any apology for ending his life. He was responsible for a lot of murders and the world's a better place without him in it.'

The room fell silent as they took this in, and I took another sip of the brandy.

Karen spoke, and there was a mixture of disapproval and anxiety in her expression: 'I wanted justice for Dana, but I didn't want you to kill people.'

I remembered the first time I'd visited them the day after Dana's remains had been discovered, the best part of thirty years after she'd gone missing. Karen Brennan had been utterly distraught, desperate for me to find her daughter's killers, showing me her final school report, pressing a photo of her into my hands and asking me to keep it to remind myself of how kind and beautiful she'd been. And I remembered feeling so sorry for her that I'd committed the cardinal sin of detective work and become emotionally involved in a case, making that fateful promise to bring Dana's killers to justice, whatever it took.

Whatever it took.

'I know,' I said. 'I understand that.'

'You said there were three killers,' said Steve Brennan. 'Who's the other one?'

'I can't tell you that,' I answered, deciding that knowing Alastair Sheridan's identity would do them no good. 'But he's someone with power. Someone who'll be very hard to get to.'

'But if you know who he is, why can't the police do something about him?' asked Karen.

'There's no evidence against him. He's clever, he's well protected, and he's ruthless.'

She looked frustrated. 'So he's going to get away with it?'

'I don't know,' I said truthfully. 'Look, I'm so sorry to involve you both like this. It was the only way.'

'We're old, Mr Mason ... Ray. We've suffered enough. We don't need this.'

Karen Brennan's words hurt because I knew she was absolutely right.

'Come on, love,' said her husband. 'Ray's a good man. He's tried to do the right thing for Dana. It's more than anyone else has ever done.'

She looked up at him. 'But at what cost? You're risking our last few months together for this.'

I frowned. 'Your last few months? What does that mean?'

Steve Brennan sat down next to his wife and took her hand. 'I've got cancer,' he said after a pause. 'Oesophageal. I was diagnosed a month ago. It's already spread to the lungs. They've given me a year at most with treatment. No more than six without.' He looked down at his lap, then back at me. 'I've opted for without.'

I didn't know what to say. Finally I took a deep breath, musing on the utter injustices of this world. 'I'm sorry. I really am. Listen, I can take it on my own from here. I'll be out of your home tomorrow at first light, I promise.'

Brennan shook his head firmly. 'You know, for twenty-seven years we had to sit here waiting for news that they'd found our daughter. Twenty-seven years! Just not knowing. Wanting to die but knowing we couldn't because we had another daughter ... But the pain ... it was hell. It *is* hell. You know, sometimes, very occasionally, I'd have this little sliver of hope that she was somewhere alive, like that Austrian girl, that she'd be found. And then one day the last bit of hope just disappeared when they dug up her bones miles away. And to find out that she'd been brutally murdered ... God, it was like being hit with it all over again.' He paused. 'And then you came, and you offered to help us. You were the only one who did. And for the first time I actually felt some hope. Then you got put away, and you didn't write back when I wrote to you.'

'I thought I'd failed you,' I said quietly, 'and my correspondence was checked so I couldn't tell you what I'd done or hadn't done.'

'I understand. But we were ignored all over again. The inquiry into Dana's killing ground to a halt. But you never stopped, Ray. You promised us you'd do everything to bring to justice the people who killed our daughter. And you've done that, and spent time in prison for it. I know Karen doesn't share my sentiments but, I'll be honest, I feel a lot better knowing these men are dead. It gives me some peace.' He turned to his wife and squeezed her hand. 'You've got to understand that, love. I want to do this for Ray. I've booked the ferry to St Malo for tomorrow morning. I'm taking him over. It'll be safer that way.'

Karen nodded slowly and her face tightened as a tear rolled steadily down one cheek.

I bowed my head, not wanting to intrude upon her grief – a grief that had gripped her since the summer of 1989. Someone, an old girlfriend, had once said to me while we were watching a real-life crime documentary that if murderers could see the grief they left behind, they'd never want to commit a crime again. In truth, she'd had a point. Most killers weren't psychopaths, and plenty had the capacity for regret, but there were some for whom the suffering they left behind was part of the enjoyment of the act itself. Alastair Sheridan was one of those people, and I had no doubt he wouldn't care less about the deep, all-consuming pain in this room tonight.

I finished my drink and got to my feet. A framed headshot of Dana, caught for ever in childhood, grinned across at me from the mantelpiece and I looked at it for a long moment, thinking that if I had my time again, I'd still hunt down her killers just as ruthlessly.

'I'll leave you two in peace,' I said.

'I'll show you to your room,' said Steve. 'We've got an early start tomorrow.'

As I walked past Karen she looked up at me, the tears still running down her face. 'Good luck,' she said at last, but she didn't get up.

I thanked her, thinking that, whatever happened, I was going to go after Alastair Sheridan. I didn't know how I'd do it. Or where or when. But it would happen. And when it was over, one of us would be dead.

32

When Jane Kelman got back to her hotel room in the Hilton at Heathrow Airport, she was angry and frustrated. Somehow Mason had thwarted her once again. In the last twenty-four hours she'd almost had him not once, not twice, but three damn times. And still he'd got away.

Jane was a businesswoman first and foremost and one of her selling points was that she never got emotionally connected with her jobs. She'd killed for money many times now (she didn't know the exact number because she thought it vulgar and disrespectful to keep count), and until she'd come across Ray Mason she'd had an enviable hundred per cent success record. He now stood out as a symbol of her failure. What was more, she was taking unnecessary risks to get to him, and that was going to have to stop right now.

She poured herself a glass of Chenin blanc from the mini bar and sat down in the tub chair next to the bed to review the events of the night. She didn't think anyone had seen her either arriving at or leaving the old lady's house, but she couldn't be sure of that. She hadn't passed any police cars leaving the scene and had been wearing a balaclava when she'd fired on Mason in the woods, so the driver of the car he'd escaped in wouldn't have seen her face.

En route back to the airport, she'd pulled off the M25, driven down a rural back lane and buried the gun and the silencer about twenty yards apart in woodland, where they were unlikely to be found. The gloves she'd dropped in an industrial waste bin close to the short stay car park where she'd left the rental car, which had been hired using a fake name and credit card that couldn't be traced back to her.

She took a large gulp of the wine, which tasted cheap and dull, and, concluding that she'd done everything she needed to, put in a phone call to the number Sheridan had given her, and gave him the bad news. Not only that she'd failed to kill Mason, and Boyd, but that she was quitting while she was ahead and leaving the country the next morning.

Sheridan wasn't pleased. 'I thought you were meant to be the best,' he told her. 'You can't just leave a job half finished.'

'I have no idea where Mason is. He escaped in a car. And there's no point trying to go after Tina Boyd now either. Or him for that matter. He won't risk coming after you now.'

'That's easy for you to say. It's not you he's after.'

'Look,' she told him coldly. 'You deceived me. I thought I was cleaning up a minor problem for you. I had no idea that Ray Mason was involved, or that you'd organized for him to kill the head of the Kalaman crime organization. If I'd known that, I'd never have taken the job. You made the mess. You clear it up. And if you're scared Mason might come after you, then get some security.'

'I'll pay you half a million to deal with it,' he said, a note of pleading in his voice.

And that, she knew, was Alastair Sheridan's problem. He was like a spoiled child, too used to getting what he wanted, and when things went wrong, he got desperate. It made him an unreliable client, and she didn't need that.

'I'm sorry, I can't help you,' she said. 'Make sure you have the hundred thousand dollars' compensation for the loss of my colleague in my account by Monday at opening of business.'

She ended the call, switching off the phone. She'd get rid of it in the terminal tomorrow before she boarded her plane to Miami, and home. Sheridan had already paid her for the first part of the job and she'd subcontracted Voorhess, who clearly now no longer needed paying since what was left of him was sitting in a pig's belly, so she was up on the deal, and the fact that she was still alive was also a bonus.

Jane's degree had been in finance and consequently she looked after her money very carefully. She had $1.7 million in liquid investments, a rental property in Panama on the Pacific coast, and no mortgage on her condominium in Fort Lauderdale. She'd already paid for her sons to get through university, so there were no outstanding debts. But her cash target was $2.5 million. When she had that amount, she could leave the life for ever. She'd fallen into killing by accident and, although she was good at it, it was no career for a lady. At forty-six, it was definitely time for a change. Maybe even meet a nice man and settle down somewhere.

That was her dream, and it was why, when she'd finished the wine and poured herself a second glass, she checked the private hotmail account she used for business to see if there were any other jobs in the pipeline. She wanted something nice and easy. An unsuspecting wife or husband she could take out with minimal fuss for a nice flat payment. Instead there was a message from an address she recognized immediately: DWolf119@hotmail.com.

The message was to the point: 'Are you free for an urgent job. Need to be in London next 24 hours. Payment 750 pounds.'

'750 pounds' meant three quarters of a million, which equated to nearly a million US. An almost unheard-of sum for a hit. Except DWolf was a representative of the Kalamans. It was he who'd hired her the previous year to kill the man in witness protection.

If they wanted to pay her three quarters of a million now it could only mean one target. Ray Mason.

Jane couldn't resist a small chuckle. The Kalamans clearly didn't have a clue that it was Alastair Sheridan who had ordered their boss's murder, and that he'd already hired Jane to sort out the mess. But then, why should they? What it meant for her, though, was a double payday. If she played this right, she could kill Mason and collect payment both from Sheridan and the

Kalamans. She was looking at well over a million dollars. She'd have to kill at least a dozen individual spouses for that kind of money, and would probably have to wait years for that number of jobs to come along. This way, she could be completely retired within the next few weeks.

It was too tempting a possibility to turn down, and even though she didn't have a clue where Mason was, she knew that with the combined resources of the Kalamans and Alastair Sheridan hunting him down, he wasn't going to be that hard to find.

'I'll be in London tomorrow morning,' she wrote, not wanting to let DWolf know she was already in the country, in case it aroused suspicions. 'Consider me in. I'll need clean tools and a down payment.'

She had to wait less than five minutes before she received a reply: 'Good. Both are available. Call this number as soon as you arrive.'

She wrote down the number using the hotel stationery, shut down the laptop, and finished off the wine.

She was back in the game.

33

Tina and her lawyer, Arley Dale, were sitting next to each other in an interview room at NCA HQ, facing a very pissed-off-looking Mike Bolt across the desk, while Mo Khan sat next to him, his own face making little attempt to hide the contempt he felt for Tina. It was 11.45 p.m. but she was feeling wide awake.

Arley had once been a high-ranking commander in the Met and been groomed for the top job of commissioner. Then one day, seven years earlier, when she'd been forty-five years old, her life had been torn apart. Her husband had been murdered and her two teenage children abducted and used as pawns to blackmail her by a terrorist group. It had been Tina who'd managed to get the children back safely, killing their captor in the process, but unfortunately, before that happened, the terrorists had forced Arley to reveal secrets that had resulted in a number of police officers being killed, and because of this she'd spent the next four years of her life in prison where she'd spent the time studying for a law degree, and on her release had started a small but successful legal practice.

She and Tina weren't close, but they'd remained in touch, and when Tina had called on her for help earlier, Arley hadn't hesitated to offer her assistance.

The air in the interview room was warm and close as Bolt exhaled loudly and ran a hand through his closely cropped hair. He was dressed in the same clothes he'd been in when he'd come to see Tina fourteen hours earlier so he had clearly had a long day. Weirdly, it made her feel sorry for him.

'Where's Ray Mason?' he asked her now.

She met his gaze with confidence. 'I told you both this morning, I don't know. I haven't seen him since before his arrest last year.'

He and Mo exchanged noncommittal glances.

'Where were you last night between nine p.m. and midnight?'

'What's this got to do with anything, DI Bolt?' asked Arley. Her tone was firm but not confrontational. 'Tina's come in tonight to give you her witness statement regarding the murder of her neighbour, Mrs Mary West.'

'Tina's come here tonight because she was arrested on suspicion of assisting an offender,' said Mo.

'Which is a claim she completely denies, and which you have, as far as we can see, absolutely no evidence to back up.'

'Listen,' said Bolt, 'you're both former career police officers, so why don't you just cooperate and answer the questions as they're put to you?'

Tina sighed. 'Last night, I went for a drive. I needed to think. I've been having a tough time of it recently.'

Bolt looked exasperated. 'Come on, Tina. Your car was picked up on CCTV less than a mile from where the car used in the Kalaman hit was abandoned.'

'One point six miles to be precise,' said Arley, 'and you're not trying to accuse her of that, are you?'

'No,' said Mo. 'But we believe Ray Mason was responsible for it, and we believe you picked him up after he abandoned his car. There were also reports of shots being fired.'

'But I don't know anything about it,' said Tina. 'You've tested my hands for gunshot residue, it'll show there was none.' She was well aware, just as Bolt and Mo were, and indeed Arley, that gunshot residue only stays on the skin for a maximum of six hours.

'We're not saying you fired the shots,' said Mo. 'But we believe you were there.'

'Well, I wasn't.'

'Tina,' said Bolt, doing little to hide his exasperation, 'if you're lying, you're going to be in a lot more trouble than if you tell us the truth now, and help us find Mason. As you know, we're searching your car and your house for DNA samples, so if he has been with you, we'll know.'

'I can't help you because I don't know where he is,' said Tina, but she knew she was on much shakier ground here. She'd got the car valeted on the way home from London earlier that evening, and she'd got Ray to wash the bed sheets, but if they searched hard enough, it surely wouldn't take them long to find DNA evidence of his presence, and it would be hard for her to argue that it was from the time before Ray had been arrested. DNA traces of a person tended to disappear after a few weeks. Luckily for Tina, the survival of DNA at a crime scene was still a very inexact science, and it was possible she could argue that Ray's had simply lasted an unusually long time. With no other evidence against her, she was confident her chances of acquittal on any charges would be a lot better than fifty/fifty.

'OK,' said Bolt, changing tack. 'Take us through the events of tonight, starting with how you came to be running out of Mrs West's front door.'

Tina told them everything, from the call to her mobile from Mrs West, which she knew they'd be able to confirm from her phone records, to the moment she'd driven away, giving as good a description as possible of the woman Ray had said was The Wraith. The only thing she missed out was any mention of Ray himself.

'So even this killer believed that you knew where Mason was,' said Mo, raising an eyebrow.

Tina shrugged. 'It seems like everyone does.'

'Why did you wear a bulletproof vest round to your neighbour's?'

It was another thing she was going to have to blag. 'Because it wasn't like Mrs West to phone for help, and with everything else that's been going on, I've just been getting suspicious.'

Mo sat back in his chair and laughed. 'You don't expect us to believe that, do you? I get nervous on the job sometimes but I don't wear a bulletproof vest.'

'As far as I know, no one's ever tried to kill you,' Tina countered. 'I've had attempts on my life going back fifteen years. It makes you paranoid.'

Tina knew she'd got Mo with that one, but that was the thing with police interviews: if you wanted to look innocent on the tape, you had to play the game. Answer everything. Don't hesitate. Parry and thrust. Never take the 'no comment' route, which just makes you look guilty. At the moment she was parrying well, knowing that events backed up her story.

But now Mike spoke again. 'We have a witness who saw you pick up a man in your car who came running out of your house.'

Tina felt her insides tighten. She'd known there was a risk she'd been spotted but thought she'd got away with it. 'Whoever it was must be mistaken,' she said, adopting a puzzled expression for the camera. 'I didn't pick up anyone.'

'You just ran out of Mrs West's house and drove away?'

'That's right.'

'Why?'

Tina rolled her eyes. 'Because I was scared. Someone was trying to kill me.'

'But you must have seen the police in the rear-view mirror. They saw you easily enough.'

'I didn't see them. I was trying to put as much distance as possible between me and Mrs West's killer.'

'If you didn't see the police, why didn't you dial 999?'

'I did, once I'd calmed down from the shock of what had happened.'

Tina knew they knew she was lying. But she wasn't playing to Mike and Mo right now. She was playing to a potential jury, and she'd long ago learned that if you wanted to be believed, it wasn't necessarily what you said, it was the confidence with which you said it that counted.

For the next twenty minutes they tried to break down her story. They even pulled out a photo of her in a hijab and tried to pin the passport incident on her. But Tina was too much of an old hand to waver, and it was clear they both knew that.

'I think you need to get out and look for the killer,' said Arley eventually, 'rather than go round in circles here. My client has answered every one of your questions in detail, as well giving you a description of the killer. You've examined her. You can see she's received injuries and come very close to death. So I'm requesting that you de-arrest her so that we can go and get her some treatment.'

De-arresting someone exonerates them of all wrongdoing, and Tina knew that Mike and Mo wouldn't go for that, and they didn't. However, after a few more minutes of wrangling, they agreed to let her go for now.

'You can't go back home though,' said Mike. 'Your house is a crime scene.'

'My client can stay with me for the time being,' said Arley.

Tina smiled at her, feeling grateful. Her chest hurt where the two bullets had struck her, and two large bruises had already formed when the police doctor examined her, but thankfully he didn't think she had broken anything.

As they were leaving HQ, Mike turned to Tina and asked for a quick word in private.

Both Arley and Mo looked surprised but stayed back as Mike led Tina outside onto the street.

'What the hell do you think you're doing?' he demanded, grabbing her by the arm when they were out of earshot of everyone. 'Protecting Mason like this? Whatever the rights and wrongs of the case against him, he's a dangerous fugitive.'

Tina yanked her arm free and glared at him. 'There are much bigger criminals than him out there, Mike. Right under your noses in fact. Try digging a bit deeper on Alastair Sheridan and see what you find.'

Mike tried to hide his surprise at the mention of Sheridan's name but Tina saw it in his eyes.

'Didn't anyone tell you that Sheridan is one of the Bone Field killers?'

'That's bullshit, Tina.'

'It's not though, is it? Last year, Ray tracked down that lawyer, Hugh Manning. Remember him? The one who got murdered on, what was it, his fourth day in witness protection?'

'The one who was going to testify against Cem Kalaman?'

'It was Sheridan he was going to testify against. The man who's possibly going to be the next Prime Minister.'

Mike shook his head. 'Look, you can't come up with conspiracy theories and expect them to exonerate you from your own actions. If by some chance Sheridan is involved we'll get him for it.'

'Forgive me for saying so, but you're taking your time.'

Mike's eyes flashed with anger. 'That's your problem, Tina. It always has been. You ride roughshod over the rulebook, totally convinced of the rightness of your cause. Just like Mason. The man who just over twenty-four hours ago executed an unarmed man in his underwear and shot several others. You can't operate like that. It makes you part of the problem, not the solution. And I'll tell you this: if we find any evidence that you've been harbouring him, don't expect any favours from me.'

'I won't,' she said. 'Have you finished?'

He stared at her for several seconds. 'For now,' he said finally, then turned and walked away.

'You had a fling with Mike Bolt, didn't you?' said Arley when she and Tina were in her car and driving back to her house in Essex.

Tina settled back in the seat. Arley's car was a Mercedes so obviously the lawyering was paying her well. 'I did. A long time ago. We're still friends, or at least we were until tonight.'

'He's a good-looking man.'

'He's a good detective too.'

Arley nodded slowly. 'I've heard that. I'm not going to ask you whether or not you did harbour Ray Mason, because I don't want to know. What I do want to know is whether the police are going to find his DNA traces in your car and house.'

'Almost certainly. But we were in a relationship so he's been in both places before often enough. What do you think my chances of being charged are?'

Arley sighed. 'I think if they turn up DNA evidence showing that Mason's been in your house and car, and the witness they've got who saw a man running out of your house and into your car can ID him as Mason, then they'll definitely charge you. If the witness is wavering, I don't think they will, not without some other hard evidence, because it'll be too hard to get a conviction. You'll be good in court, they know that. Because you're a decorated former police officer, a jury will probably want to believe you. And because Mason's been in your car and house before, albeit a year ago, we'll be able to find an expert witness who'll argue that it's not entirely impossible for the DNA traces to have lasted that long, and the NCA and CPS know that too. But that's all assuming they don't find anything else that ties you to him.'

'They won't,' said Tina, with more confidence than she was feeling.

34

'And in conclusion, ladies and gentlemen, what we need is not just strong leadership, not just a clear, ambitious vision of a streamlined, forward-looking Great Britain which rewards hard work and where rich and poor alike have a real stake, but the unwavering strength and self-belief needed to make it happen.'

Alastair Sheridan paused for effect, looking confidently round the huge U-shaped table at which thirty-six MPs, including five junior ministers, sat hanging onto his every word, all having consumed a huge dinner and copious quantities of alcohol.

'And if the Prime Minister does not possess those three traits – and although it truly saddens me to say it, it seems quite clear by her performance these past two years that she doesn't – then it's high time she was replaced by someone who does. Thank you.'

There were shouts of hear-hear, and some of the more raucous of the group banged their empty wine glasses on the table in appreciation. Alastair was also pleased to see the MP for Ely South, the statuesque blonde Hannah Walker, grinning and nodding her head enthusiastically. He'd always wanted to have a go on her, and had never understood why she'd lasted as long as she had married to Geoffrey bloody Barker, a sweaty, slap-headed creep fifteen years her senior. One day he'd have her, he thought. One day. Then he'd wipe the smile off her face, by God.

At that moment, Alastair was in his absolute element. He found this whole process of infiltrating the party and plotting against the leadership, while simultaneously giving the appearance of being a loyal servant forced into disloyalty out of a desire for the greater good, hugely entertaining. And these fools, the supposed elite of the country, were lapping it up. Politics, Alastair had found, was like finance. In other words, it was largely about using your common sense and sounding confident. You didn't really have to learn anything in any detail. You didn't even have to be that bright. And like everything else in life, it was simply a race to the finish line, by which time you'd either tripped up your opponents along the way, or persuaded others to do the tripping for you, until you were the only one left in the race.

What you did after that was anyone's guess. Alastair had no real vision at all for what he'd do for the country if, as was looking increasingly likely, he became Prime Minister. In truth, he was only interested in the status and power that such a role gave, and the respect people would be forced to give him.

The dinner, which was being held in the private upstairs room of a country house hotel just outside the M25 in Berkshire, finally finished. All those present had offered their support to Alastair should he choose to run against the Prime Minister for the leadership of the party, and Alastair had suggested that each of them spend the parliamentary summer recess canvassing the opinions of their constituents on whether or not they supported a leadership election. Alastair, of course, had no intention of canvassing the opinion of his constituents on anything, but it sounded like the sensible thing to say. Instead, he was looking forward to going on holiday the day after tomorrow, flying on a private jet with his family to Dubrovnik, for a well-earned break.

When it was only Alastair and George Bannister left at the venue, they settled down for a final brandy in one of the adjoining private rooms.

'I've just seen the headline on my phone. What happened earlier this evening?' said Bannister quietly. He looked both angry and concerned, something he'd done a good job of hiding during the dinner. 'Tina Boyd's neighbour, the old lady who was shot. Did that have anything to do with you?'

Alastair knew there was no point in denying it. In truth, he'd been annoyed himself. He'd expected The Wraith, as she liked to style herself, to kill Ray Mason, and possibly Tina Boyd too (which would have been a nice bonus). Instead she hadn't managed to do in either of them. Killing old ladies might have been permissible in South Africa, or wherever it was she came from, but over here it was like killing kids or dogs. It meant a whole lot of trouble.

'It was a mistake,' he told Bannister equally quietly. 'It wasn't meant to happen.'

'You can't just do this kind of thing, Alastair. It's too danger-ous. It could get us into huge amounts of trouble.'

'It won't if we keep our nerve.'

'It's getting out of hand. Things can't continue like this.'

Alastair knew there were only two ways to deal with Ban-nister. With threats or reassurance. He decided to go for the latter and put a hand on Bannister's shoulder. 'They won't con-tinue like this, I promise. Have you been kept abreast of the latest developments on the hunt for Mason, and the old lady's murder?'

'Obviously,' Bannister answered testily. 'I spoke to the NCA commander this morning and this evening.'

'And still Mason stays on the run. This is becoming some-thing of a humiliation for the NCA. For the government as a whole. It brings our entire policy on cutting police numbers to the forefront,' Alastair continued, warming to his theme. 'I'm going to authorize a big increase in police numbers if I become PM, and pay for it with an equal cut in the foreign aid budget, so no one can accuse me of not trying to balance the books. Have they any idea where Mason is?'

Bannister shook his head. He looked uncomfortable, and Alastair could tell it wasn't just about the fact that the authorities hadn't been able to locate Mason. 'No, but he's not your average prisoner on the run. He's ex-military intelligence, and he's clearly resourceful.'

'Do you think he's out of the country?' asked Alastair, who was keenly aware that his security might not be enough to stop a concerted attempt by Mason to kill him.

'I really don't know where he is, Alastair,' said Bannister. 'But we have a lot of people looking for him and his capture is top priority.'

'What about Boyd?'

'What about her?'

'She could still be in touch with him.'

'If she is, we'll find out. But I don't want any attempts on her life. Call off your dogs, Alastair, and let things settle. Boyd's no threat. And right now, Mason will be too preoccupied trying to remain free to bother with you.'

Alastair wasn't so sure. Mason was one of those fanatical types who seemed prepared to risk everything in the pursuit of revenge. But he was more concerned with Bannister, whose attitude seemed testy. He'd been fine over dinner – then again, like most politicians, he was a good actor – but the news about the old lady had clearly got to him.

'Fine,' he said. 'I'll let things lie.' He stopped, and looked Bannister right in the eye. 'Don't lose faith in me, George. I'll take us both to the top.'

Bannister sighed and turned away from his gaze. 'I know you will, Alastair,' he said, but his tone was weary, as if he'd had enough.

Alastair leaned down close to his ear, deciding that it might be time to replace the carrot with the stick. 'Don't ever fucking forget that photo of you throttling an underage prostitute, George,' he whispered, feeling the other man tense. 'Because I won't. And if anything happens to me, I'll make sure the whole world sees it.'

35

Driving home that night through the largely quiet streets of Clerk-
enwell, a place he'd always considered an oasis in the centre of
London, Mike Bolt thought about what Tina had told him about
Alastair Sheridan.

It seemed ludicrous to believe that the man who could potentially be the next Prime Minister was a killer. Bolt himself hadn't
had any involvement in the Bone Field investigation, but he knew
that it was ongoing, and that it was being overseen by the NCA.
It had been, and to a large degree still was, a very high-profile
case, which had started off with the discovery of the remains of
seven women buried in the grounds of a private farm in mid-
Wales some fifteen months back now. Only one of the women

had been identified and it was believed that the other six had been illegal immigrants from eastern Europe, and their deaths had happened over a number of years.

At the time, there'd been the usual clamour for results from the press and the public, and the ownership of the farm had eventually been traced via a series of shell companies to a lawyer called Hugh Manning. But Manning had been murdered while in police custody, which had got plenty of conspiracy theories going as it seemed he was going to name names of people involved.

Since Manning's death, the case had still periodically made the headlines, mainly because of the lack of progress in bringing anyone else to justice, but Bolt had always believed there'd been a lot more to it than met the eye. He also knew that it had been Ray Mason and Tina who'd discovered both the location of the Bone Field farm and what had gone on there, so they both knew more about the case than most people.

Bolt had always trusted Tina's judgement. She'd worked for him for several years on some important cases, and she was undoubtedly a good detective. From what Bolt knew of Ray Mason, he'd been a very good detective too. And so he had to concede that it was therefore unlikely they were wrong about Sheridan's involvement, which put him in something of a dilemma. What did he do about it?

Twenty years ago, maybe even ten, he would have known the answer instantly. He'd have started digging deeper, regardless of the consequences. Bolt considered himself an honest, conscientious cop, one who genuinely wanted to keep the streets safe for law-abiding citizens. But he was no blind rule taker either. Like Ray Mason, he'd once executed a man in cold blood. The man's name was Lench and he'd been by some distance the most brutal murderer Bolt had ever come across. Even so, he'd been unarmed and offering no resistance when Bolt, overcome with anger and emotion, had shot him dead. In those days he'd been prepared to take major risks in pursuit of what he perceived to be natural justice.

But those days were long gone. He was only eleven months away from retirement. He and Leanne had a plan worked out. Leanne was going to take early retirement from her teaching job. She'd sold her house just before the Brexit vote and the collapse of the London property market and had moved into Bolt's penthouse loft conversion in Clerkenwell, which he rented from a man he'd once done a huge favour for, so they were ready and able to start a new life elsewhere at the drop of a hat. They'd both fallen in love with the south of France and were looking for a house with gites attached to do up and start a holiday rental business. It was the classic pipe dream of middle-class Brits everywhere, and with their combined pensions and the capital they'd built up over the years it was eminently doable. Leanne's mother was French, and she spoke the language fluently. The knowledge that they were going to do it together was what kept him going in the day-to-day humdrum and difficult hours of the NCA. He couldn't afford to do anything that compromised that dream, and digging deeper into a case that didn't concern him was a real risk. He could already see quite plainly what it had done to Ray Mason.

As he parked the car in the building's underground car park and climbed the stairs to the loft, he'd already decided that he wasn't going to do anything foolish.

It had just turned two a.m. when Bolt climbed into bed beside Leanne, trying to be as quiet as possible, though he was secretly pleased when she stirred and put a hand in his.

'Go back to sleep,' he whispered, kissing her neck.

'Love you,' she managed to whisper back, then did exactly that, her breathing soft and steady.

Bolt lay beside her, one arm encircling her waist, and closed his eyes. But he couldn't help thinking about Alastair Shcridan and the possibility that he might get away with his crimes, and for a long time sleep didn't come.

Part Four

Part Four

36

It was ten o'clock on a sunny, if noticeably cool, Sunday morning when Jane Kelman took a seat on a bench facing the Serpentine in Hyde Park. Because of the time, the park was relatively quiet, peopled mainly with joggers and cyclists, and there were no boats out on the water.

She was dressed casually in a coat and jeans, with walking boots. Her hair was blonde now and shorter, and tied into a bun, and she was wearing outsize sunglasses. Just like Tina Boyd, she was an expert in changing her appearance. She knew she was physically attractive, with her best feature her eyes, which were almond-shaped and a deep brown in colour, so she tended to wear sunglasses wherever possible to deflect attention from them.

Today she looked positively ordinary and, unlike most women in their mid-forties, this pleased her. The worst thing for a hired killer is to be memorable, especially one who was killing with the frequency she was. Jane knew she was taking a significant risk by remaining in the UK and taking on a new job so soon after the others, but like most people, she found it very hard to turn down a life-changing sum of money.

She didn't have to wait long until a short, wiry man with a large scar on his lip sat down on the bench next to her. He was dressed in a thick coat and carrying a small backpack, which he placed on the seat between them.

It was extremely rare for her to meet a client. Anonymity was far safer for both parties. But she'd killed for the Kalamans before, and this gave the relationship a rare measure of mutual trust.

She glanced across at the man and used the agreed code: 'Do you have the time? I left my watch at home.'

'I did too, but I believe we said ten,' he replied, uttering the return code phrase, the scar curling his lip into a sneer.

It was an unfortunate disfigurement, she thought. It made him look hard, but that didn't necessarily mean he was. She was reminded of a couple of lines from her father's favourite movie, *The Magnificent Seven*. 'Don't hire the man with the scar. Hire the man who gave him it.'

'Ten it is then,' she said.

He nodded, seemingly satisfied, and looked out across the water. 'Thanks for coming at such short notice. We need you to move fast. Did you get the dossier you were sent on the target?'

She nodded. It had been comprehensive, not that she'd needed to read it. 'I've come across him before on another job. He's slippery.'

'He is. And the police are having a hard time finding him.'

'So what makes you so confident that you can?'

'We know someone who knows where he is. She just needs to be made to talk. We'll deliver her to you. You get the information. Then you take him. Your tools are in the backpack. Check your email account at least once every half hour. That's how you'll hear from us from now on.'

'I'll need a down payment.'

'A hundred thousand's already been deposited in the account we sent your last payment to. You'll receive the remainder as soon as we have confirmation that the job's done. It would also be very useful if you could get the chance to speak to him before you pull the trigger. We'd ideally like a filmed confession. We want to know who else was involved. He wasn't acting alone.'

Fat chance of that, thought Jane. There was no way she wanted Mason talking. The deader he was the better.

'I'll see what I can do,' she said, getting to her feet with the backpack.

37

Tina enjoyed staying at Arley's place. Her kids, both now in their early twenties, still had vivid memories of the day seven years earlier when their father and nanny had been murdered and they'd been abducted at gunpoint. According to Arley, they'd undergone extensive therapy afterwards to help them come to terms with what had happened. Considering they'd spent the next four years apart from their mum while she'd been in prison, twins Oliver and India seemed remarkably confident and well adjusted.

They hadn't seen Tina since the night she'd rescued them from their abductor, killing him in the process, and when they first saw her on Sunday morning they'd both hugged her tight and thanked her profusely for what she'd done for them. Tina had to fight hard to keep her emotions in check but, as always, she tried to deflect attention away from her role, remembering that night all too well herself, and wanting to keep it in the past where it belonged. Even so, it did make her feel good to know that, because of what she'd done, these two were here now. Oliver was about to go travelling in the Far East, just as Tina had done at his age, and India had a job in London working for a charity.

'The pay's crap but at least it's doing something worthwhile,' she said when she was telling Tina about it.

The four of them had a barbecue in Arley's back garden. The sun was shining but the weather had cooled down substantially and they sat around the patio heater. Tina felt comfortable in the company of this happy family that had come so close to being torn apart and wiped out in one bloody day. The kids bombarded her with questions about the famous cases in her career, and were endearingly blunt.

'So Mum says you're in trouble again,' said Oliver, who'd grown into a good-looking young man, and was the more confident of the twins.

'I didn't say that,' said Arley, 'and you need to leave Tina alone. You know we can't talk about an ongoing case.'

'Mum'll sort you out,' said India. 'She's a shit-hot lawyer.'

Tina laughed. 'I'm innocent, so justice will prevail. But you're right. She is shit hot.'

After they'd cleared away, Tina and Arley sat together in the lounge.

'You know you can stay here for as long as you want, Tina,' said Arley. 'I like your company, and I'll never stop owing you for what you did for me.'

'There was never any debt to pay,' Tina told her. 'I did it because it was the right thing to do. And seeing your kids now, healthy and happy – you know, it makes me feel good. But I don't like imposing on you. I may still be in danger and people around me seem to have a very unfortunate habit of dying. I don't want that to happen to you.'

'It won't, Tina. It was Ray they wanted, not you. It'll be too dangerous for them to try again. And in case you hadn't noticed there's a police car parked at the end of the road. They'll be keeping an eye on you now.'

'In that case, I'll take you up on your offer. I don't know when the police are going to let me back into my house, or give me my car back.'

'I'll chase them tomorrow, but it's unlikely they'll let you go home before the end of the week.'

Tina sighed, suddenly feeling very down. 'I'm not sure I want to go back. Not after what's happened to Mrs West. It won't feel right.'

Arley leaned over and put a hand on her arm. 'Then don't. Do something else. Stop sticking your neck out waiting for someone to chop it off, because one day someone will. When we were sat outside with the twins talking about your past, it made me realize how many needless risks you've taken over the years.' She sat back and gave Tina an appraising look. 'Look at you. You're young, you're gorgeous.'

'You should be my PR woman, not my lawyer.'

'Why don't you go out and date, rather than hold a candle up for men who are never going to be there for you?'

'Says the single woman.'

Arley chuckled. 'I'll admit it's not easy finding a decent guy out there, especially online, but remember, I'm ten years older than you and I've been in prison. I'm not a catch. You are. You can find someone.'

'I've been dating,' said Tina, remembering all the meaningless, unsatisfying encounters of the past year, and the date with Matt that had had some promise but still hadn't made it off the ground. 'In fact I met someone last week. Do you mind if I borrow your PC? I need to check my profile and send him a message, and the police have got my smartphone.'

Arley gave her the kind of look she'd employed a lot when she was a senior detective. Authoritative and slightly condescending. 'You're not planning on doing anything dodgy, are you?'

'Arley, please,' said Tina. 'I never do anything until the third date at least.'

'I meant anything illegal, like try to get in touch with Ray Mason.'

'Don't worry, I've had my fill of illegal. I just want to get on with my life now. And I promise you, Arley, hand on heart, that I have no idea where he is.'

'Good. My laptop's on the table. And show me a photo of this man you met. I want to see if he passes muster.'

Tina sat back down with the laptop and quickly logged on to her account. She hadn't logged on in close to a week and she had eighty-nine new messages. That was the thing about online dating. It was a numbers game, and you had to kiss a hell of a lot of frogs before you had a chance of finding a prince. Tina skimmed through the messages, more out of curiosity than anything else, but there was no one whose words or photos even came close to attracting her. She then brought up Matt's profile. He was forty-two, six feet tall, an engineer with a daughter aged ten from a previous relationship, and he was a really nice guy. But it was this that was putting Tina off. She just couldn't bring herself to involve someone like him, and by extension his daughter (whom he seemed to dote on), in the violence and chaos of her life. It would just make her feel scared for him.

Still, she showed Arley his photos, including one he'd posted of him in a pair of swim shorts.

'Yes, I like him,' said Arley. 'Definitely. I hope you're going to see him again?'

'I think so,' Tina lied.

'Well, make sure you do, but maybe not for a few days yet. It might be hard to explain what you've been up to this weekend. Keep him on ice.'

'Will do,' said Tina.

She returned to her seat with the laptop and, as Arley started checking her phone, Tina checked the emails on her two official addresses, cancelled a couple of deliveries to her house, and then logged on to an email address that only she and Ray had access to. She was certain that the police wouldn't be monitoring Arley's laptop – they'd need a warrant for that – and she didn't think either Sheridan or the Kalamans would have been able to break into it already. In fact, it was unlikely they knew where she even was.

Even so, she felt more than a little guilty as she typed in the password and saw that there was a single message saved in the drafts section, which could only be from one person. She opened it up and started reading.

Hey you. All good. Now safely out of UK. Planning next move. I'm sorry we had to leave under the circumstances we did. I'm sorry I said I love you too. It was a heat of the moment thing. But I want you to know that I will miss you deeply like I've always missed you since the day I was arrested. But I also want you to get on with your life. I saw on the news that they'd arrested you but that now you've been released. Take care for God's sake. And stick to your story. I got rid of the phone and I don't think there's anything tying me to you. You won't see me again now and I won't give you my location because I don't want you to be compromised. But just know that I'm truly thankful not just for your help but for everything else as well. Take care Tina.

Tina read the message through a second time, deleted it and, remembering her promise to Arley, didn't write anything back. When Ray logged back on and saw that his draft was deleted, he'd change the password to one they'd agreed yesterday. That way it would be impossible for anyone to monitor any communications between them. Not that she thought they'd be speaking again.

She briefly considered dropping a message to Matt and giving him a second chance, but decided to leave it for a few days. Instead, she put down the laptop and settled back with Arley, who'd now been joined by Oliver and India, to watch an episode of *Midsomer Murders*.

Ray was safe. It was time to move on.

38

Mike Bolt sat at his desk in the far corner of the loft's open-plan living area. He hated working Sunday evenings, especially when he'd been working all weekend.

Behind him, Leanne was lounging on the sofa watching a re-run of *The Vicar of Dibley* on TV. Ordinarily, Bolt would have joined her. He was exhausted. There was still no sign of Mason, and the witness from Tina's village who'd apparently seen her leaving with a man in her car the previous night after the Mary West murder was now unsure if he'd seen a man after all. And so far they hadn't found any useful traces of Mason's DNA in Tina's cottage. So, although they had plenty of circumstantial evidence linking the two of them, they didn't have a shred of proof.

The pressure from above to find Mason was relentless, made worse by the number of killings connected to his escape, and the complete absence of any leads. Sheryl Trinder had torn a strip off him and Mo in her office that day for their perceived failures, and had effectively told them they'd be fired for misconduct if it turned out that Mason had been hiding at Tina's place when they'd searched it.

However, this wasn't why Bolt was still working. He was working because he couldn't seem to let go of what Tina had told him last night.

Like most people, he'd been surprised by the lack of arrests in the Bone Field case. The remains of seven women had been found at the house in Wales, which made their killer or killers some of the worst in British criminal history. Bolt was realistic enough to know that, because only one of the women had been positively identified, and she was a working-class woman in her early twenties, the case hadn't captured the public's imagination in the way it might otherwise have done, and so, as time had passed, the clamour for results had died down. But there were still plenty of unanswered questions. The ownership of the farm-house had been traced back through numerous shell companies to Hugh Manning, the lawyer who'd done a lot of work for Alastair Sheridan's hedge fund, and he'd handed himself in with Tina Boyd a year earlier, on the same night Ray Mason had been arrested for murder. But Manning had then been assassinated less than a week later while in a secret location under police protec-tion, presumably to stop him naming other people who'd been involved in the Bone Field murders. Only a handful of people would have known his whereabouts, yet somehow the killers had got to him, suggesting they were people on the inside with powerful connections.

Under ordinary circumstances, Bolt might have thought Tina mistaken in thinking that Alastair Sheridan was a serial killer. She was a good detective, but prone to letting emotion get the better of her. Yet the fact that the NCA investigation into the Bone Field murders now had only a handful of people on it, none of whom had turned up anything new in months, was now bothering him.

The problem was that the two people who did have an idea of what was going on weren't helping him. It was too risky to talk to Tina off the record. And Mason had disappeared into thin air. Except, as Bolt knew from years as a detective, no one disappears into thin air. Tina had been helping Mason, he was convinced of that, but there had to be other people involved for him to evade detection.

So Bolt was going back in time, looking for likely helpers. According to the prison records, Mason had only had one visitor in his whole time behind bars, and that was his lawyer, Edward Kleinman, who at sixty-three, with an unblemished record, was unlikely to be caught up in anything illegal.

Mason's phone records for the six months up to and including the day of his arrest were spread out on the desk in front of him. He started from the most recent statement, crossing out the calls he wasn't interested in with a red pen. There were at least two a day to Tina, sometimes more, and Bolt felt a twinge of jealousy that irritated him as he crossed those out too. In the weeks leading up to his arrest, Mason had been one of the main investigators on the Bone Field case and there were plenty of calls between him and his fellow investigator, DS Dan Watts, who'd died in mysterious circumstances on the night of Mason's arrest. There were also ones to and from Sheryl Trinder, who'd been Mason's boss at the time, but Bolt wasn't interested in any of these. He was interested in people they didn't know about and, after he'd gone through all the statements with the red pen, there weren't that many numbers left.

One number did catch his eye. It turned up eight times in the three months running up to Mason's arrest, including four times in the space of a week. It was a landline belonging to a Steve and Karen Brennan.

Bolt rubbed his eyes and took a sip from the glass of Pinot Noir he had on the desk next to him. The names sounded familiar.

Then he remembered. They were the parents of Dana Brennan, the thirteen-year-old girl who'd gone missing in Hampshire decades before, and whose remains had been found in school grounds in Buckinghamshire the previous year, alongside those of a young woman in her twenties called Katherine Sinn, who herself had gone missing the year after Dana. Bolt recalled now that Mason had been investigating those cases too, not for the NCA, but for one of the Met's Murder Investigation Teams. The murders of Dana Brennan and Katherine Sinn had never been officially linked to the Bone Field murders, although Bolt remembered that Sinn had been Alastair Sheridan's cousin.

The series of four calls had been made between Mason and the Brennans in the week after the discovery of Dana's body, which stood to reason as he'd been investigating their daughter's murder. Bolt's team had produced a detailed dossier on Mason, which Bolt had read and re-read a dozen times since his escape. It was how he knew immediately that Mason had been suspended from the investigating team before he'd made the fourth call to the Brennans. It was possible, of course, that Mason had just been telling them that he'd been removed from the case. But he'd still been under suspension when he'd made the fifth call two weeks later. According to the records, they'd talked for eleven minutes. And there were two more – one by Mason, one by the Brennans – over the next six weeks, each one lasting close to fifteen minutes, before Mason made a final one, a few minutes before his arrest, lasting eight minutes.

The thing was, there was no reason for Mason to be talking to the Brennans in any of those last four calls. He wasn't on the case, and the couple would already have been assigned a special-ist liaison officer to keep them informed of any progress on the reopened inquiry into the murder of their daughter. But Mason had still been talking to them. Why? There was only one reason Bolt could think of: he'd become emotionally involved in the case. It would also explain his actions since being broken out of prison. Rather than make a run for it like any ordinary escaped prisoner, he'd gunned down Cem Kalaman, a man Tina Boyd had claimed was one of the Bone Field killers.

But who'd broken him out of prison in the first place? Steve Brennan was in his mid-sixties. It wouldn't have been him. But at the very least he was worth looking at further. It wouldn't take Bolt long to get hold of the Brennans' phone records. He thought about doing it now, but it was already close to ten p.m.

He yawned, finished off the Rioja, and looked over at Leanne. It could wait until tomorrow.

39

Alastair Sheridan missed the hunt.

The hunt had been their thing, the three of them – he, Cem, and their mentor, the man they'd called Mr Bone. After their first two murders they'd worked out a system. Victims were selected from those unlikely to be missed. These included prostitutes, runaways and, more recently, illegal immigrants, usually brought into the country by Cem's own criminal organization. Only very trusted operatives were involved in procuring the victims and transporting them down to the farm in Wales they'd bought for the specific purpose of the hunt, and even those operatives had no idea what was going to become of the girls.

Over the years, nineteen young women, aged from mid-teens to late twenties, had died at the farm. The police had only found the remains of seven because Cem and Mr Bone had used acid, and more recently pigs, to get rid of the corpses. It had worked well. Sometimes the victims were hunted through the surrounding forest for sport, but more often they were imprisoned in a specially built basement, tortured and raped, usually over the course of a weekend (although one particular beauty had been kept alive for weeks), before finally being put to death. Their ends were always filmed and, although Alastair had learned never to hang onto mementoes of what he'd done, he did enjoy watching the films afterwards when the three of them were together. Reliving those moments gave him a sense of power that he found hard to put into words.

It was highly unlikely they'd ever have been caught if it hadn't been for Ray Mason. Surprisingly enough, though, Alastair didn't hold any ill feelings towards him. He wasn't the kind to brood. Nor was his sadism all-consuming. He was a planner, a man who always had to be in control of a situation. Only when he felt perfectly safe did he let the savagery that resided deep within him out of its box and give it free rein. Then it would be put back in again until the next time. And that was why Alastair had survived and prospered. Because, unlike Mr Bone or even Cem, he was able to live very easily among people who were not like him. He was charming; he could pretend to be kind without anyone noticing his innate fakery. He made people *want* to like him. That was his genius.

And that, of course, was why he'd be Prime Minister.

It was late when his driver pulled inside the gates of the family home and came to a halt on the large turning circle in front of the main house. Both the driver and the man next to him were armed police officers. Alastair had requested them: he might have been the man who'd organized Ray Mason's escape from prison but he'd also been prudent enough to know that it might be better to have another layer of protection in place in case, as had happened, Mason disappeared. Obviously, with no known connection between him and Mason, Alastair could hardly have cited him as a reason for needing the bodyguards, so instead he'd sent some threatening letters to himself, and bingo, the bodyguards had materialized. It always amazed him how easy it was to fool people.

The two officers – young, professional, and not easily fazed – got out of the car along with Alastair and walked on either side of him to the front door. They kept their hands close to their guns and a vigilant eye out for any danger. But with each passing hour the threat from Mason receded, and Alastair was feeling safe enough to admire the beauty of the beautifully restored ten-bedroom Georgian mansion he called home, lit up tonight in ethereal green by a dozen strategically placed spotlights. Alastair had bought it outright seven years ago for a little over £6 million, and he'd just had it valued at £8.2 million. His father would have been proud of him.

The Asian officer, Asif (it was always first names with Alastair), placed a phone call to a third officer inside the house, whose job it was to look after Katherine and his son, and she answered the door to them.

'They've both gone to bed, sir,' she said as Alastair stepped inside followed by the other two, giving him a smile.

She was young, late twenties, handsome rather than pretty, and big-boned, but attractive nonetheless. He gave her a dazzling smile in return, imagining her naked and chained to a bed while he whipped and beat her mercilessly. 'Thanks, Susie. I think I'll join them. I'll see you guys in the morning. Thanks so much for doing this. I really appreciate it.'

He mounted the stairs to the master bedroom, satisfied with how the day had gone. It would have been nicer to know that Mason was riddled with bullets somewhere but he was far less of a threat now that Alastair had police protection. It was time to move into holiday mode, but sleep was far from his mind, and the thought of a naked and bleeding Susie had aroused him.

As he slipped inside the bedroom, quietly closing the door behind him, he saw that Katherine was indeed asleep. He stopped by the bed and looked down at her. She was still a good-looking woman, and she kept herself in excellent shape thanks to her personal trainer and yoga sessions, but she'd never really done that much for him, mainly because – like a fragile, priceless artefact – he'd never been able to treat her roughly. She was there to project his family-man image, and deflect any suspicion of sexual wrongdoing, and as such he'd never even raised a hand to her – a feat that had taken huge amounts of self-discipline. Whenever they had sex, Alastair had to fantasize that she was a prospective victim and that he was pretending to be tender to lull her into a false sense of security.

He leaned over and touched her hair, wanting to pull it hard, and she stirred.

'Is that you, Alastair?' she whispered without moving or opening her eyes.

He ran a hand over her naked shoulder, stroking it. 'It is. Sorry I'm late.'

'Come to bed, we've got to be up early,' she grunted testily.

God, he wanted to hurt her then. To leap on top of her and beat her into submission so she was choking on her own blood and begging for mercy.

One day, he thought. One day I'll do you too.

He turned away to avoid temptation and masturbated quickly in the en suite bathroom to rid himself of the mood, knowing that it would just get worse if left unchecked. Then he cleaned his teeth, got undressed, and slipped into bed, where he fell quickly into the warm, dreamless sleep of those who have no conscience.

40

Going on the run can be done. I'd proved that. I'd been free for over two weeks now, with the police, the NCA and most of the British underworld after me. But in a digital age, where your every transaction, your every footstep even, is recorded somewhere, and if there are enough resources against you, the whole thing becomes an increasingly precarious balancing act. One wrong move and it's all over.

So far, though, I was still ahead of the game. Steve Brennan and I had caught the Portsmouth ferry to St Malo with me hidden in the boot of the Audi estate under a blanket with empty suitcases piled on top, and screened from the outside world by a couple of boxes filled with the kind of bits and pieces you take with you when you're travelling to your house in France. Security is a lot looser going out of the UK on ferries than coming in, because the illegal immigrant stowaways customs officers are looking for are usually coming the other way. It had been an uncomfortable journey down in the hold where the movements of the sea are far more pronounced, but a small price to pay to escape the UK.

At the other end Brennan's car had been stopped at passport control, but after a brief conversation with the passport officer he'd been let through and, a few minutes later, when we were safely clear of the terminal, I'd joined him in the front. It had been that easy.

However, the next step was always going to be the hard part. I was going to need transport so, after some discussion, we'd stopped at a car rental place in the town of Fougères and, while I waited in the Audi, Brennan had rented a Renault Megane for two weeks in his own name. As soon as he was done, I'd followed him in the Megane to the holiday home they'd bought some years before, after their surviving daughter had left home.

And now, on Sunday night, here we were, Steve Brennan and me, sitting in armchairs in the cottage's olde worlde living room, having consumed a huge chicken and vegetable stew, washed down with a bottle each of Fleurie. We'd talked all evening and the thing was, it hadn't been maudlin. Brennan had spoken happily about the first half of his life: a childhood growing up by the sea in Dorset, meeting Karen, having two wonderful daughters, the family holidays. The fun, the laughter. Memories someone like Alastair Sheridan could never erase. And I'd told

Brennan about my life, about my experiences in the police and military, as well as the failures. The pain of losing friends, the pain of prison, but the good things too. The camaraderie I'd had in the army; the one happy relationship before Tina which I still remembered with fondness years later. And the fact that I'd brought people to justice whose crimes would otherwise have gone undetected.

'And you said there's one more man responsible for Dana's murder,' said Brennan, his words slightly slurred from the wine. 'Someone who's going to get away with it.' He looked incredulous. 'And the police still aren't interested in charging him?'

I sighed, wondering whether it had been such a good idea emphasizing the fact that there was still someone out there. But I opted for the truth. 'The problem is, Dana died nearly thirty years ago, and the evidence against this third man is sketchy and circumstantial, which means no police officer would even think about charging him, and the CPS would throw it out way before it ever came to court. But I know for an absolute fact it's him.'

'And you can't tell me who it is?'

'I don't want to. It won't help. But let me tell you this. If an opportunity shows itself, I will get him. I promise.'

Brennan looked at me sadly. 'I don't want you to do any more on our account, Ray. Let it go. You've got a chance to build a new life now. Do it.'

I took a generous sip of the Fleurie, savouring the taste. It was the first time I'd relaxed in more than a year. I could see the light at the end of the tunnel. The possibility of change. Of reinventing myself. Of finally finding a measure of peace after a lifetime of violent upheavals.

But I could also see Alastair Sheridan's smug, laughing face. A man who revelled in killing. Who knew he'd got away with it time and time again. A man who could be Prime Minister.

And I knew that if I let him live, Alastair Sheridan would haunt my dreams for ever.

Part Five

41

To gain full access to someone's telephone and financial records, the NCA simply have to have that individual declared a person of interest by a senior officer. So at eight a.m. the next morning, Mike Bolt told DCS Sheryl Trinder about what he'd found the previous night in Ray Mason's old phone records. She wasn't hugely enthusiastic that it would lead anywhere but, given the lack of progress in every other area of the inquiry, she was willing to give it a shot, and gave him the authorization he needed.

Things can move fast in a police inquiry if the will is there to drive them forward, and the will to apprehend Mason either dead or alive was most definitely there, so it took less than an hour for copies of the Brennans' bank, credit card and phone statements to be on Bolt's desk. Rather than waste the time of any of his team, he closed his office door and scanned them himself with his second large Americano of the day.

A few small things stood out, most particularly a phone call from an unidentified mobile number to the Brennans' home landline a couple of days earlier that had lasted nine minutes. It stood out not only because it was one of only seven calls made to the number in the previous two weeks (the others all appeared to be sales calls), but because of the timing. The call had been made two days ago at 11.39 a.m. – the morning after the Kalaman killings, the same day that Tina almost certainly collected fake documents for Mason, and was then subsequently arrested after the murder of her neighbour and the police chase. A search of Brennan's mobile phone records also showed that he'd received a call from the same number at 20.02 that same Saturday night, and another eleven minutes later.

There was also a payment on Steve Brennan's Visa debit card to P&O Ferries, made three hours after the phone call to his landline, followed by a second payment, made yesterday, to a branch of Hertz in Fougères, France. The payment was for more than €800, suggesting that he'd rented a car for a reasonably substantial length of time. Bolt had no idea where Fougères was but when he checked on Google Maps, he saw that it was some fifty miles east of the ferry port of St Malo.

Now all of these things could have simply been coincidence, but if the Brennans had travelled to France by ferry, it did seem strange that they'd hire a car that far from the port. Either way, as far as Bolt was concerned, it merited further investigation.

He called Mo in and suggested he use a couple of the analysts on the team to help him get a better picture of Steve Brennan's movements over the past forty-eight hours.

While that was going on, Bolt got an update from the SIO on the Mary West murder. There was no real progress, although one witness reported seeing a woman walking briskly up the hill behind Mrs West's house around the time of the shooting. Unfortunately the witness could give no further details of what the woman looked like as she'd been too far away. Next he called the SIO on the Kalaman killings. Her team hadn't turned up any further clues either during the extensive search of the crime scene and were still trying to work out how Mason had got onto the rooftop.

'He either broke into an apartment or rented one,' Bolt told her.

'I know that,' she answered testily, 'but it's hard to get inside any of the apartment buildings. That whole block's like a ghost town. No one lives there. Most of the owners aren't even on the same continent.'

And that was the problem. Mason had planned his assassination well, and he'd had help. The two men who'd broken him free from the prison van still hadn't been accounted for. Who the hell were they? And where had they been hiding Mason?

It was just short of midday and Bolt was contemplating an early lunch when Mo knocked on the office door and walked in, carrying some papers in his hand. It was immediately obvious from the look in his eyes that there'd been a development.

'Steve Brennan's helping Mason,' he said, sitting down opposite Bolt and putting the papers on the desk. 'So's Tina.'

Bolt sighed. 'So what have we got?'

'That call from the unidentified number to the Brennans' landline on Saturday morning belongs to an unregistered burner phone. But we triangulated its location, and the call was made from Tina Boyd's house. As you know, there was a second call made from the burner phone to Brennan's mobile number at 20.13, which was around the time Mrs West was shot dead and Tina fled the scene. That call was made from woods about half a mile east of Tina's house.'

'You can get to those woods from Tina's back garden,' said Bolt. He'd often walked there with Tina himself.

'We also triangulated Brennan's phone's location when he took the call. It was two miles away from Tina's place, and it's definitely him because his car was picked up on ANPR cameras on the M25 four minutes earlier, and then again thirteen minutes later driving the other way. The phone and the car then travelled back to the Brennans' home in Hampshire where they stopped overnight. And then yesterday morning, the phone and car were at the ferry port at Portsmouth. P&O Ferries have confirmed that Steve Brennan and his Audi travelled to St Malo on the ferry. We can't track the car any further without help from the French police but, according to Brennan's mobile provider, his phone was in a rural area about two hours inland, stayed there overnight, and is at this moment crossing the Channel from St Malo back to Portsmouth.'

'So Steve Brennan goes to a rendezvous near Tina's place, picks up Ray Mason, takes him back home, then smuggles him out of the country. And if he was driving in his own car, the only reason he'd stop to rent one from Hertz is if he's doing it for Mason. Any idea where they stopped last night? I didn't see any hotel payments on his credit cards.'

'The Brennans own a property there. They've got a mortgage with HSBC for it. I've just pulled it up on Google Maps.' Mo handed Bolt a sheet of paper with a satellite image of a group of three detached houses set amid fields, with a copse of trees running along their back. 'As you can see, it's a nice rural location.'

Bolt examined the photo and thought how hard it was for anyone to evade the long arm of the law these days once they'd been identified as a suspect. The day was coming when it would be all but impossible to commit a crime undetected – and not a moment too soon as far as he was concerned.

'This is good work, Mo.'

'Mason could still be at the Brennans' house in France.'

'You're right. If they stayed there last night it means it's not currently being rented out. If I was Mason, I'd probably want to stay put for a couple of days and work out my next move. He's had a couple of narrow escapes. But even if he keeps moving, we now know he's in a rental car. We need to get onto our French counterparts and Interpol. Find out what car it is, and see if they're prepared to put the Brennans' place under surveillance for us. I'll clear that with the boss.'

'Is it worth leaning on Tina some more?'

'Not yet. This is all conjecture. What we need is proof. Did P&O say whether Karen Brennan travelled with her husband to France?'

'They said it was just him,' said Mo.

Bolt sighed. 'Well, I think our best bet right now would be to pay Karen Brennan a visit.'

42

'I'm not looking forward to this,' said Bolt as they turned into the Brennans' driveway. 'I remember when Dana Brennan disappeared. I can still picture her mum and dad on TV press conferences begging for whoever abducted her to bring her back. It was heartbreaking.'

'I remember it too,' said Mo. 'I was only about fifteen but it was all over the news. I can't imagine what it'd be like to lose one of my kids.' He shook his head. 'It would kill me.'

Mo was one of the most doting dads Bolt knew, and he had three lovely children who were now all well into their teenage years. Bolt might not have had children himself, but he'd still been deeply affected by the sheer pain the Brennans were clearly going through. At the time he was twenty-three and a uniformed officer. It was one of the cases that made him think he'd made the right choice joining the police.

Bolt pulled up directly behind a red Skoda that he knew belonged to Karen Brennan and they got out of the car.

'I can't believe the Brennans would help Mason,' said Mo as they walked up to the front door. 'I know he was trying to find their daughter's killer, but this is going way beyond that.'

Bolt hadn't told Mo about Tina's claims that Alastair Sheridan was involved in the Bone Field killings. 'Well, let's hope Mrs Brennan wants to talk to us.' He rang the doorbell. As was always the case with policework, they hadn't announced they were coming.

Karen Brennan was a small woman in her sixties who looked worn by her experiences, and as soon as she answered the door and they introduced themselves, Bolt knew their suspicions about the Brennans' involvement were correct. Her face went pale and she grabbed the door frame to steady herself.

'Are you all right, Mrs Brennan?' asked Mo.

'Yes, yes, I'm fine,' she said. But she didn't look fine at all. She looked like she might burst into tears.

'We'd like to talk to you about Ray Mason,' said Bolt gently.

'I don't know what you're talking about,' she said, but her jaw was quivering.

'I think you do,' continued Bolt, still talking gently, keen not to intimidate her. 'I think it would be best if we talk inside.'

'Oh God,' she whispered, her tight features pinched into an expression that veered between resignation and outright panic.

Then she nodded and turned away, leaving the door open for them.

Bolt exchanged a glance with Mo and they followed her into a small living room, Bolt having to duck to avoid the overhead beams.

They sat down opposite her, and Bolt leaned forward. 'Mrs Brennan, we know that your husband's been helping Ray Mason.' She started to protest but stopped as Bolt raised a hand. 'We've checked the movements of his car and his phone and we know that he picked up Mason on Saturday evening and brought him back here, then smuggled him by ferry to France yesterday. If we were to search your house and your husband's car, I have no doubt we'd find DNA evidence of Mr Mason's presence. So you need to tell us the truth. Where are they now?'

Mrs Brennan sat bolt upright, kneading her hands in her lap. 'I don't want to say anything to get my husband in trouble.'

'I'm afraid he's already in trouble, Mrs Brennan,' said Mo. 'Mr Mason is a fugitive from justice. Aiding and abetting him is a serious offence.'

'But given your circumstances, there may be room for some leniency if you both cooperate with us,' put in Bolt.

She had a tissue up the sleeve of the cardigan she was wearing and she took it out now and dabbed her eyes. 'I told Steve not to do it but he said he owed Ray for all he'd done for us.'

'What exactly did Mr Mason do for you?' asked Mo.

'He promised he'd bring Dana's killers to justice. He said the man he killed on the night he was arrested last year was one of them, and that the gangster, Kalaman, was another.'

'Did he say he had killed Kalaman?' asked Bolt.

She nodded.

This was a big breakthrough. It also condemned her husband and threatened to drag Tina Boyd deeper into the conspiracy.

'And when Mason called your husband on Saturday, do you know where he was phoning from?'

She looked at them both. 'I don't know. I didn't know much about it. I didn't want to get involved. But I also feel bad because when Ray – Mr Mason – first came here, I gave him a picture of Dana, and I ... I suppose I put pressure on him to find her killers.'

'Giving him a picture is not putting pressure on him,' Bolt told her.

She nodded, dabbing her eyes again. There were tears running down her face and Bolt could see that she was having a hard time holding herself together.

'I don't want Steve to go to prison. He and Katie are all I've got. And he's only got a few months left. He's got cancer. It's terminal.'

The room was silent for a few seconds. Mo looked uncomfortable, and Bolt felt terrible.

'I'm very sorry to hear that, Mrs Brennan,' Bolt said. 'We'll see what we can do to help you and your husband. We know there are extenuating circumstances.'

She stared at Bolt. 'Please don't send us to prison.'

Bolt swallowed. 'We'll do what we can for your husband. You definitely won't have to go to prison.'

'But you said if you searched this house you'd find his DNA and then—'

'We're not going to search this house,' said Bolt. 'OK, Mo?'

Mo nodded. 'I've got no objection.'

'Do you know where Mr Mason is now?'

'Steve left him at our holiday home in France. I don't know if he was intending to stay there or not. Steve's on his way back now. He should be home by five.'

'When he gets back, tell him to call me,' said Bolt, handing her a card. 'In the meantime, don't call him. I don't want your husband calling Mr Mason to warn him. If he does that, he really will go to prison.'

She nodded nervously. 'I won't. I promise.'

'Good. Your husband needs to get himself a lawyer and we'll arrange for him to come in and be interviewed under caution. I can't guarantee what'll happen but we'll do what we can to go easy on him.'

'Thank you,' she said quietly, the tears coming freely now.

They left her there, and Bolt was pleased to get back outside in the fresh air.

'It looks like we've got a result,' said Mo.

Bolt sighed. 'It doesn't feel like it though, does it? And I'm not sure how the boss is going to feel about us not arresting Mrs Brennan.'

'She won't care if it means we get hold of Mason.'

'That's what I'm hoping.'

Bolt took out his phone and dialled Sheryl Trinder's number. She answered on the second ring and he gave her the good news: 'Ma'am, we have a possible location for Ray Mason.'

43

The day was warm and sunny and I was sitting in the Brennans'
back garden, which effectively consisted of a small round swim-
ming pool that you'd need to do a hell of a lot of lengths in to get
fit, and a wooden deck that wasn't a lot bigger. The garden was
surrounded by a bland wooden fence that needed some plants to
screen it, but which at least gave some privacy from the next-
door cottage.

I knew I couldn't stay here long. I was too conspicuous,
even in a place as quiet as this. The Brennans' was the end
house in a row of three, and I knew from the cars outside and
the voices I'd heard that the other two were occupied by English
holidaymakers who were probably getting their news from the

British media, and right now I still looked a lot like my latest mugshot photo.

But I had to admit, I liked it here. I'd found a bakery earlier on and bought a crusty baguette from a young man who hadn't given me a second glance, then came back here, stuffed it with jambon and Roquefort cheese, and demolished the lot with a pot of good coffee, thinking I might not have made it yet, but I was getting close.

The first part of my plan was complete. I'd got to France with fake ID and I had a car. The second part was to open a bank account into which I could transfer some of my bitcoin once I'd cashed it in. The problem was, with all the money-laundering legislation in force across the Western world, it wasn't so easy to open a bank account any more, even in some of the traditional tax havens. At the very least I was going to need fake address documentation. I was also going to need a credit card with some money behind it in order to secure longer-term accommodation.

Not surprisingly, I had no idea where to find anyone who could supply me with any of these. But one of the things I'd learned during my time in the police was that the criminal underworld, though vast and sprawling, was also full of connecting parts. And there were people out there – call them criminal networkers or facilitators if you like – who knew everyone who was anyone, and who specialized in bringing these different parts together.

The cheerily named Archie Barker was one of those people. Back in the day, they'd called him the gentleman dope dealer. Public school educated, with a degree in politics and Spanish, he'd worked as a lecturer at various universities in Colombia, Mexico and Spain, and during that time had somehow managed to make some excellent contacts in the drug-trafficking world. The word was he'd even spent a weekend at Hacienda Nápoles, Pablo Escobar's estate outside Medellín, back at the end of the eighties.

Whether that particular story was true or not, one thing wasn't in dispute: he definitely knew the right people. Using his lecturing as a front, he'd reached out to several London-based organized crime groups (including, allegedly, the Kalamans), made some introductions between the buyers in the UK and the sellers in South and Central America, and had helped to set up some very effective coke and heroin smuggling routes into Europe – and all this simply through some old-fashioned charm.

It said something about Archie's skill as a criminal operator that it had only been six years earlier, when he was already in his mid-fifties, that he finally came to our attention. I was working organized crime at the time and we'd got wind that he was the person brokering a huge coke deal between the Gulf Cartel in Mexico and a Chechen outfit who'd recently arrived in London and were looking to become significant players.

And that, in essence, was Archie's Achilles heel. Because he acted as a free agent, with no particular affiliation, he ran the risk of upsetting people, and unfortunately didn't have the muscle backing him up for that not to matter. And it turned out that someone didn't like the idea of him helping the Chechens because one night, while a surveillance team I was leading were watching his house, there was an attempt on his life.

It all happened very quickly. Archie came out of the front door of his beautiful townhouse deep in the wealthy heart of Belgravia en route to one of the flashy London restaurants he liked to eat in and was on his way down the steps when the back doors of a van parked further down the road opened and two men in balaclavas jumped out and ran down the street towards him, holding pistols. Archie spotted them almost immediately, but by that point they were barely twenty yards away, and he knew there was nothing he could do. He'd never have made it to the front door, or his car for that matter, which was further down the street.

Luckily for Archie, the cavalry were on the scene, and before the gunmen could open fire my team of twelve armed surveillance officers were out of their vehicles and drawing their weapons. Stunned, the gunmen had dropped their own weapons immediately and thrown their hands in the air and, while my team searched and cuffed them, I'd marched up to a simultaneously relieved and stricken-looking Archie and arrested him for conspiracy to supply a controlled substance. I remember him smiling then as he realized for the first time what had just happened, and thanking me profusely for saving his life. He'd even said those classic words: 'I'm forever in your debt.'

It wasn't the usual reaction from an arrested suspect and, of course, once we got to the station he denied any wrongdoing whatsoever. However, he was courteous and jovial, a real character, and I have to admit, I liked the guy. We didn't have enough to charge him but he was temporarily placed under police protection while an investigation started into who'd targeted him. During those weeks I got to spend a bit of time with him, my objective being to get him to cooperate with us in return for a new identity and permanent witness protection. Archie was old school, though. He never gave us a thing we could use. We never did find out who'd targeted him either, but the experience had made him realize it was best to retire while the going was good and he'd headed off to Ibiza and bought a boutique hotel in one of the more picturesque parts of the island. I'd occasionally get an email from him saying that if I ever fancied coming out to Ibiza, I could stay at his hotel for free for as long as I liked.

I'd never taken him up on his offer, although once, when I'd needed some help on a case, he'd given me some off-the-record information that had proved useful. But I'd never properly called in his debt to me, and now was my opportunity.

I still had his mobile number. Like a lot of numbers I thought I might one day need again, I'd learned it off by heart. I doubted if he'd have changed it.

But I was taking a risk calling him. Courteous, jovial and in my debt he might have been, but he was still a criminal, and there was still a big reward on my head, from the police and from the Kalamans, with whom I'm sure he still had contacts.

I was drinking a cup of coffee and mulling over whether to call him when the landline phone started ringing inside the house. I wondered if it was Steve Brennan telling me he'd made it back home safely, although I'd told him before he left that it was safer for everyone concerned if we had no further contact.

I let it ring until I heard the answerphone kick in, but the caller hung up without leaving a message.

I put down my coffee and stood up. The call had made me nervous. Perhaps Brennan was trying to warn me about something. Either way, I decided it might be best if I made myself scarce.

I went back inside the house and I was halfway up the stairs when the phone started ringing again. Again, I let it go, going into the bedroom and chucking all my stuff into my backpack.

When it hit answerphone, the caller hung up again.

Ten seconds passed. And then it started ringing a third time.

There was a handset next to the bed in the master bedroom and I went inside and picked it up.

'Ray Mason. Get out of the house now,' said a male voice that sounded vaguely familiar. 'The police are on the way. The car you are driving's not safe. Change it when you can.'

The line went dead.

I put down the receiver, grabbed the backpack from my room and went over to the window from where I had a view of the narrow country road that led down to the cottage.

I saw them straight away. Three cars travelling in convoy, two unmarked, the first only twenty seconds from the entrance to the driveway.

I bolted down the stairs and out the back through the open French windows, shutting them quickly behind me to at least make it look like the place was empty. I could already hear the cars pulling onto the gravel at the front of the house.

One thing I've learned in life is there's no such thing as being over-prepared. And when you're on the run and you stop somewhere, you always need an escape route. And thankfully I had one.

Rather than park the rental car in the driveway where it might have attracted attention from the neighbours, I'd left it next to the narrow lane that ran down the side of the house, making sure it was screened from view by some trees. I'd seen from Google Maps that the lane wound down past a farm for about a mile and a half before joining another road that led back to the main highway.

I ran across the deck to the fence then, as quietly as I could, climbed over it and slipped down the other side, taking a very quick look round. The lane was empty and I jogged down it, keeping to the grassy bank, trying to minimize the noise I made as much as possible, before turning into the trees where the car was parked.

Fishing out my car keys, I unlocked it and got in, throwing down the backpack. I started the engine and pulled away in silence. That was the joy of hybrid cars. They're powered by electricity until they get to a certain speed and that means you can't hear them. Driving slowly down the lane to prevent the wheels making too much noise on the stones, I kept my eyes fixed firmly on the rear-view mirror until I'd put a good hundred metres between me and the house. Only then did I begin to pick up speed.

And only then did I start to think about what had just happened. I had no idea how I'd been found. I was 98 per cent certain I'd covered my tracks well enough that I wouldn't have been followed here, but that wasn't what was preying on my mind now. Someone had called to warn me to leave. Someone with Brennan's number and knowledge of the police operation to arrest me.

Die Alone

Who?

And in one of those moments of epiphany, I remembered where I'd heard that voice before.

And now, suddenly, nothing made sense.

44

It was Monday afternoon and Tina had got her phone and car back earlier than expected. She'd just left her cottage where the forensic team had let her in to get some more clothes. She'd seen one of her neighbours, Diane, as she was leaving. Tina didn't know Diane especially well but they always exchanged pleasantries when they saw each other. But not this time. Diane had turned away rather than speak to her, and it had saddened Tina. This village had always been her sanctuary through thick and thin. Now she was unwelcome here.

At least, she thought, she was welcome at Arley's. Tonight, Arley's son Oliver was cooking dinner. Some kind of vegetarian Sri Lankan curry apparently. If Tina hadn't killed his kidnapper all those years ago, he'd have been dead now, along with his sister, no question about it. Amid everything else, the thought gave her some comfort. 'Put that one in your pipe and smoke it, Diane,' she whispered aloud.

Tina had been told by the senior SOCO officer searching her cottage that it could be as long as two days before they were finished. While she was in no hurry to go back in, she didn't think the police needed to be poking round in there for that long, so she decided to put a call in to Mike and see if he was feeling charitable enough to speed things up for her. She knew he probably wouldn't but wanted to speak to him anyway. She respected Mike and didn't like the fact that he was angry with her.

She put the phone on hands-free and called him, wondering if he'd answer, given how things had been left between them.

But he did.

'So are you finally going to come clean, Tina?' he said brusquely.

'If you're talking about Ray Mason, then I've already told you everything I know.'

'Bullshit. Tina, we're building a case against you. The sooner you cooperate the better it'll be for you. I'm serious.'

His tone sounded almost sympathetic, and this worried her. 'I'm sorry, Mike, I can't help. But I wanted to know if you could speed SOCO up in my cottage. They're telling me they won't be finished until Wednesday.'

As Tina spoke, she slowed to round a sharp bend. Her satnav was taking her on a quiet back road away from the M25 so she was surprised to see a car in front of her going slowly while behind her another one, a black SUV, came up behind her fast.

That was when she knew it was a trap. 'Shit,' she said quickly. 'I think I'm about to be attacked.'

'What's going on?' demanded Bolt, sounding concerned.

The car in front did an emergency stop, partially blocking the road, and immediately two men with scarves pulled up over their faces jumped out and ran over, pointing pistols straight at her. There was no way past them, and no way of reversing either as the SUV behind was blocking her way. Two other men jumped out of it, again with scarves pulled up over their faces. One of them looked like he had a taser.

One of the gunmen appeared at the driver's side window, pulling at the handle. 'Open the fucking door!' he shouted, banging the pistol's barrel against the window.

'Mike, I'm being kidnapped! The reg is EF14 3DW!'

'Open up now or I'll put one in your leg!' screamed the gunman.

'All right, all right, I'm coming!' she shouted, as much for Mike's benefit as anyone else, then opened the door.

The gunman yanked her out by the arm and pushed her towards the one with the taser, who immediately discharged it.

The electric shock was all-consuming. Tina's knees went from under her and she crumpled to the ground, landing on her side. She felt herself being picked up by several hands and dragged rapidly over to the open boot of the lead car. She just had time to see another gunman jump into her car, and then she was being lifted up and shoved inside like an unwieldy parcel, unable to do anything to resist.

Then the boot slammed shut and the world went dark.

'Jesus Christ,' said Bolt. 'Tina's been abducted.'

He and Mo were on the M3 eastbound, heading back to HQ. Mo was driving and Bolt was writing down the registration number Tina had given him in his notebook.

'I thought we had people watching her,' said Mo.

'We've got a car watching her lawyer's house 24/7, but she's not under surveillance. We haven't got the manpower for that, and anyway we've got her passport so she isn't a flight risk. I didn't think she'd be in danger.' But even as he spoke the words, he knew he'd made a serious mistake.

'Who do you think's got her?'

'I don't know, but there's a half-million bounty on Mason's head and there are people out there who think she knows where he is. She managed to give me the reg of the car the kidnappers were driving. We've got to find it before she comes to any harm.'

45

Tina was trapped in the boot for what felt like an interminably long time. Her abduction had been highly professional. These guys knew exactly what they were doing. The most obvious suspects were the Kalamans – the same people who'd visited her in the office two days earlier. She wasn't sure if that was a good thing or not. What they wanted was also pretty obvious. The question Tina was asking herself was, would she give up Ray?

And right at that moment, feeling scared, dizzy and claustrophobic, she wasn't at all sure of the answer.

The car eventually stopped and she heard footsteps coming round the back followed by bright light flooding in as the boot lid was opened. Two sets of hands roughly pulled her out and she was forced to her knees and a hood placed over her head before she could properly take in her surroundings.

A voice spoke close to her ear in a rough London accent. She wasn't sure but she thought it might be the man with the scar on his lip from her office. 'You've got a reputation as a fighter so a word of advice,' he said. 'Put a lid on it this time. My friend's got a gun pointed at you, he's ex-army, and he's got orders to put a bullet in your kneecap if you start playing up. But if you do what you're told, you won't get hurt. Nod to show you understand.'

Tina nodded.

She was lifted to her feet and marched inside a building with hard floors that smelled of grease and engine oil, the door shutting with a loud clang behind her. No one spoke as she was led through another door, and then a few seconds later she was pushed into a metal chair that felt cold against her bare forearms. Two thick straps were forced round her torso and arms, pulling them tight. Two more tied her to the chair's arms and a final two were used to tie her to the legs. She was now completely helpless and it gave her a sick, cold feeling in her stomach.

'What do you want?' she asked, already knowing the answer.

But there was no reply, and she heard footsteps moving away from her, then the door shutting and a lock being turned. She tried to move around in the chair but it was held fast to the floor and her bonds were tight. The room was cool, and Tina suddenly felt very thirsty. Her only hope was rescue. Mike had the registration of the car they'd brought her here in and she hadn't heard it being driven away. But any rescue would take time. They'd have to find the car, and it wasn't like tracking a mobile phone. If there were no cameras in the vicinity then it would make their task almost impossible.

Was this the place where she would die? The Kalamans were ruthless enough to kill her, and once they'd extracted the information they needed, there really wouldn't be much incentive for them to let her go. The thought scared her, but not as much as it would have done many years ago, before the job and her own innate self-destruct button had turned her life upside down. She'd been held at gunpoint before, too many times, and had always survived, but if this was the end, then so be it. It was a waste of life – that was the worst thing – but it wasn't as if her life was worth that much any more, and at least it would mean that her family would be safe.

She just hoped it would be quick.

But right now, her abductors were taking their time. The minutes passed. She could hear the faint sound of muffled voices coming from outside the room, and an even fainter sound of traffic coming from somewhere further away. She wondered why they weren't questioning her already. Maybe they wanted to let her stew for a while to make her more compliant. If so, it was working. Her thirst grew more pronounced as the time continued to drag, and now she needed to pee.

She thought about calling out but knew it would do no good. She shut her eyes and tried to think of something else, knowing that the longer they left her here, the better her chances of being rescued.

And then, after she'd been in the room for what must have been at least an hour, maybe even longer, she heard the outside door shut and the sound of muffled voices again.

There was a pause. Tina took a deep breath, steadying herself as the fear came seeping back. Then the door to the room she was in opened and someone came inside. She could just about make out footsteps coming closer, so light she thought she might even be imagining it.

Except she could feel a presence. Closer now. Right beside her.

'Hello Tina,' whispered a voice in her ear, and her blood ran cold.

Because the presence of the woman Ray called The Wraith meant only one thing. She wasn't getting out of here alive.

46

It was 4.29 p.m. Exactly ninety-nine minutes since Mike Bolt had received Tina's frantic call, and he and Mo were now in the middle of Tottenham, driving on a quiet residential road just north of Lordship Lane, with Bolt behind the wheel.

The ANPR cameras had tracked the car the kidnappers had used to abduct Tina along the M25 heading clockwise, then down the A10 into north London, before it turned left onto the A406. It had last been picked up sixty-four minutes ago by a camera going south on the Tottenham High Road, so it was likely to be parked up somewhere close by.

Even in an area as busy as Tottenham, which was very well covered by ANPR cameras, this meant it could still be anywhere in a heavily populated warren of streets covering as much as a square mile, which might not have been quite the proverbial needle in a haystack, but was still going to be a serious challenge. Because of the seriousness of the offence, and the fact that the perpetrators were likely to be armed, Bolt had managed to acquire the assistance of four armed response vehicles, an armed surveillance unit, and half a dozen other marked and unmarked patrol cars to aid in the search.

By rights, Bolt and Mo shouldn't have been there. They both had more than enough to do back at HQ. The French police had arrived at the Brennans' house in France and found no sign of Mason, which was a setback, and now a lawyer representing Steve Brennan had called Bolt and arranged for them both to arrive at NCA HQ at 6.30 p.m. for a formal interview. But there was no way Bolt was going to stop searching for Tina. Whatever her failings – and, Jesus, she had plenty of them – she was still a former cop, a former lover, and a former friend of his, and that meant he felt duty-bound to help her. DCS Trinder hadn't been keen but, given that Tina was a person of interest to the NCA in the Ray Mason case, it was in Trinder's and the NCA's interests to get Tina back unharmed.

The radio crackled into life. It was HQ. 'Alpha One to all vehicles. We've got movement on suspect car. Just been picked up on camera going west on Creighton Road at the junction with White Hart Lane. Hard stop has been authorized. Repeat. Hard stop has been authorized.'

There was a clatter of reaction on the radio from the other cars, several of which were in the immediate vicinity, as they now converged on the suspect car.

Bolt felt the adrenalin surge through him as he took a quick look at the satnav, got their bearings, and made a rapid three-point turn before accelerating north towards Creighton Road.

The chatter over the radio was coming thick and fast. Within the space of a minute, Tango 3, one of the ARVs, had got a visual on the suspect car, and was following at a distance of about fifty metres. Seconds after that, a second ARV announced that it had just turned onto Creighton Road, ahead of the suspect car, and now had it in sight in its rear-view mirror.

'This is Tango 4. Two male suspects in front of vehicle,' the driver intoned, his tone calm but tense. 'We are unmarked so they haven't picked us up, but they are now directly behind us. We are ready to move. Over.'

'Tango 3 to Tango 4. We have car between us and are ready to move when you are.'

'Tango 4. We're ready. Go, go, go!'

Bolt heard the sound of car doors slamming and yells of 'Armed police!' over the radio, and his hands gripped the wheel tightly as he pulled onto Creighton Road, cutting up a car that immediately let rip on the horn. Bolt ignored it, annoyed by the fact that the pool car he was driving didn't have a flashing light, which would automatically have given him right of way. Up ahead, he could see the marked ARV parked up in the road with its own lights flashing, the traffic already backing up behind it.

Knowing he wouldn't get any closer, he pulled the car up on the pavement, threw on the hazards, and jumped out, followed more cautiously by Mo.

A total of six officers – three in plainclothes and wearing black police baseball caps, and three in full uniform – had the two suspects, both white males and already cuffed, lined up against the car at gunpoint, while a handful of passers-by stopped and stared. The boot was already open and one of the cops was looking inside.

Bolt felt the tension shooting through him, fearful that Tina was in the boot, already feeling his anger growing from somewhere deep within. As he ran, he touched the handle of the Glock 26 pistol in his shoulder holster, wanting to pull it out but resisting the urge. The suspects were compliant and under control so there was no point. Instead, he pulled out his warrant card as one of the cops turned to face him.

He lifted it up for them to see. 'NCA, DI Mike Bolt,' he said, using his police rank. 'Any sign of the victim?' He could already see that the boot was empty.

'No, she's not in there,' said one of the uniforms who was pointing an MP5 at the nearest suspect's back. 'And these two are both unarmed.'

'Where the hell is she?' demanded Bolt, grabbing the nearest suspect by the collar of his shirt and dragging him round.

The suspect – short, wiry, mid-forties, with a scar curling up from his lip – stared back at him blankly. 'I don't know what you're talking about. And get your hand off my collar or my brief'll have you for assault.'

Bolt felt rage building in him. He wanted to draw the Glock and shove the barrel against this arrogant bastard's forehead, knowing that that way he'd get an answer in seconds, but he also knew that this one simple, three-second act of madness would cost him his job, his pension, and possibly even his freedom. He was powerless, and the cocky expression on the other man's face told him he knew it too.

'I know you abducted Tina Boyd,' snarled Bolt, still holding onto his collar and pulling him closer. 'And I know you did it in this car. And do you know how I know? Because I was on the phone with her at the time and she gave me your registration number. So what's the betting we'll find her DNA in your car?'

The suspect turned to the other cops. 'This man's assaulting me. Are you going to stop him? I don't know why he's accusing me of all this.'

'Sir, I think you'd better let him go,' said one of the cops.

Mo appeared at his shoulder. 'Come on, boss, leave it alone.'

'Yeah, do what your mate says, eh, boss? Leave it alone.'

The suspect smirked as Bolt's grip on his shirt tightened. He thought of Tina, maybe dead already. Then he thought of Leanne. Their life together. Their retirement plans.

He let go, and shoved the suspect back against the car.

'If we find Tina Boyd's body, then I swear to God you'll go down for murder. Twenty-five years minimum.' He looked over at the second suspect, a younger guy in his thirties who was standing facing the car with his head down. 'And that goes for you too. Twenty-five years.'

The second suspect didn't react.

Mo tugged at Bolt's arm. 'Come on boss, we've got to keep looking for her.'

Bolt turned to the armed cops. 'All right, take these two to the nearest station and keep them there. We'll take this up later.'

With that he turned and walked back to the car, knowing that for Tina time was running out fast.

If it hadn't run out already.

47

'I once had a client who despised her husband so much that she didn't just want him dead, she wanted him to suffer very, very badly beforehand. I didn't ask why. That wasn't my concern. My concern was, as it always is, to do my job and get paid, and this particular job was comparatively lucrative. It took some planning and some help from a colleague who's no longer with us, but eventually I managed to get our target, shaken but unhurt, to a nice quiet place, just like this one. My client wanted to have her husband's death live-streamed to her at home, so we set up a link. I changed into some splash-proof clothing, and got to work. I used a cordless drill on him. It was a long, unpleasant job because the client was very specific about what she wanted done, and it took him well over an hour to die. I got no pleasure from it. None at all. Contrary to what you might think, I'm not a sadist. But I was paid to do a job and I did it efficiently and well. I've been paid to do a job here too, Tina, and it's entirely up to you how painful we make it.'

The hood was ripped off Tina's head, and she stared up at the woman she knew as The Wraith.

She cut a terrifying figure. She was wearing a 'Scream' mask and a white plastic painter's smock that ran all the way from her neck to her knees, and in a gloved hand she was holding a cord-less power drill, with a thin bit already attached.

'I'm going to ask you some questions,' she said, 'and if you give me the right answers you'll be left here alone and alive, and once I'm safely on my way out of the country, an anonymous call will be made to the police and you'll be freed.'

'I don't believe you,' said Tina. 'You said that last time. Then you shot me.'

The Wraith smiled. 'And somehow you survived. I've read up on you, Tina. You're a survivor. I admire that. I'd rather let you live if I can. We can never have enough strong women in the world.'

Tina watched as she placed the drill on a nearby worktop, then looked round the room. They were in what looked like a cavernous mechanic's workshop with large ramps on either side of them, and tools littering the floor, but no cars. The chair she was tied to was made of wrought iron and had been chained to each of the ramps, which was why it was impossible for her to move it.

She took a deep breath. Behind the door opposite her she could hear the muffled voices of the men who were guarding her. There was no escape. She knew that.

'So what do you want?' she said at last.

The Wraith turned back to face her. 'What I want is not to have to use the drill on you, Tina. I also heard you were stubborn. Sometimes that's a good trait. Today, it definitely isn't. So, my first question to you is this: who was the individual who collected Mason by car from the woodland near your house on Saturday evening?'

Tina hesitated. It was one thing betraying Ray when he was out of the country, but to give up the names of Steve and Karen Brennan, a retired couple grieving for the loss of their daughter, to the Kalamans was a much harder proposition, especially as the Kalamans were ruthless enough to go after them. Or worse still, send this psycho bitch to get them.

'I won't tolerate hesitation, Tina. Answer me.'

'I don't know,' said Tina. 'Ray organized it all. He told me the less I knew about the details the better.'

There was a pause. Then The Wraith picked up the drill again. She switched it on, the sound a thin, metallic shriek, reminding Tina of long-ago, stomach-churning visits to the dentist.

She stood in front of Tina, the bit whirring manically. 'Perhaps we should start with an easier question,' she said above the noise of the drill. 'Are you right-handed or left-handed?'

Tina swallowed, knowing what was coming. Suddenly absolutely terrified, she knew that she was going to have to give the Brennans up.

Still she hesitated.

Without warning, The Wraith drove the bit into Tina's left hand between two of the knuckles, pushing down hard.

Tina writhed in agony, eyes shut, teeth tightly clenched, a low, desperate howl rising up from inside her, but she was being held firmly in place by the straps, and The Wraith's free hand which was on her forearm.

The pain seemed to last for ever. Tina tried to lurch forward to headbutt her tormentor but she could hardly move. Helpless as the bit split through her palm before being slowly, ever so slowly, withdrawn.

The Wraith turned off the drill and quickly and expertly placed a strip of dressing over the hole in Tina's hand. Blood ran out from under it, dripping first onto the chair arm, then onto her leg.

The pain began to fade as shock and adrenalin took over, but Tina's fear remained exactly the same.

'You did well keeping quiet while I did that – I'd thought we might need a gag,' said The Wraith amiably, stepping back and looking down at her, her dark eyes sparkling behind the mask. 'Now that was just a little taster. The next insertion is going to be through your anklebone, and I can tell you, having administered it before, that the pain dwarfs what you've just experienced. So once again, who was the person who picked up Mason?'

Tina took a series of deep breaths as she tried to stop herself from panicking. Knowing that if she gave the answers, she was signing her own death warrant. Knowing that if she didn't, the torture would simply continue until the woman got the answers she wanted. It was an impossible choice. She was damned both ways.

Once again she hesitated.

It was a bad move. The Wraith's eyes narrowed in anger beneath the mask and she picked up the drill again, switched it on, and grabbed Tina's face, coming in close. 'You're trying my patience, bitch,' she snarled, and pushed the drill into Tina's hand a second time, forcing it all the way through to the palm before ripping it back out.

This time Tina screamed, or tried to, but The Wraith's gloved hand was covering her mouth.

Suddenly all she could see was the drill bit, dripping blood and torn flesh, taking up her field of vision, coming closer and closer.

'Are you going to talk, bitch? Or do we miss out the ankle altogether and just go for your eye?'

Tina nodded frantically.

The Wraith removed her hand and took a step backwards, looking down on her with eyes like flint.

Tina swallowed, trying to ignore the pain and the blood pumping out of her hand, trying to fight down the rising panic that threatened to overwhelm her.

'OK,' she said tightly. 'I'll talk.'

48

Mike Bolt was driving in the direction of Tottenham High Road while Mo sat beside him with a laptop open on his lap, trying to narrow down a location for Tina into something manageable, when the radio burst into life.

'Tango 4 to all cars, we have an issue here. Over.'

Tango 4 was one of the ARVs carrying the suspects who'd been arrested a few minutes earlier. Bolt knew that each suspect had been put in a separate car so they could no longer communicate.

'Tango 4, this is Beta 1,' said Bolt urgently. 'What's the situation?'

'I'm the situation, Beta 1,' said another voice. 'I'm one of the men you've just nicked. I'm a UCO in deep cover with the Kalamans. I can't even give you my real name.'

'But you know where Tina Boyd is?'

'Yes I do. My problem is, if her location comes from me, it could blow my cover and jeopardize the whole Kalaman op, and I can't have that.'

'Is she all right?'

'She is at the moment.'

'What the hell's that meant to mean?' demanded Bolt, who was losing patience fast.

'They're bringing someone in to question her. They're sure she knows where Ray Mason is.'

'This is life and death,' Bolt told him. 'Where is she?'

The UCO sighed loudly. 'Jesus, this isn't good. OK, they've got her at a place called Premier Motors. It's down at the bottom of Hartland Road, close to the railway line. You reach it down an alleyway. There's a signpost at the end.'

Mo was already typing the details into his laptop. 'I've got it,' he said. 'Take the next left. According to this, it's a four-minute drive.'

Bolt slowed the car down to take the turning. 'Beta 1 to all units, did you get that?' he shouted into the radio. 'Go to Premier Motors Hartland Road now. Tango 4, how many suspects are holding her? And are they armed?'

'This is UCO, Tango 4. When I left, there were two suspects, both IC1 males, both armed, guarding Tina Boyd. And as I said, I think there may be a third either en route or there now. But you have to do this without blowing my cover.'

'We'll be able to come up with something,' Bolt promised, taking the turn and accelerating as other units announced that they too were on their way.

'See, that wasn't so hard, was it?' said The Wraith with a smile.

Tina felt sick. Dressing had been applied on the second wound but she was still bleeding from the palm, and a grape-fruit-sized bloodstain had formed on her jeans. But her sickness didn't come from pain, it came from her guilt. She'd betrayed the Brennans, told this monster who they were, and how Steve Brennan had picked up Ray and transferred him to France.

The Wraith finished typing something into her phone, then picked up the drill. 'Next question. What's Ray Mason's phone number?'

'I don't know. We both threw away our burner phones.'

'But you're communicating with him. I know that. And if you say you're not, then this is going in your ankle right now.' She had already removed Tina's left shoe and sock ready for, as she put it, 'a quick insertion'. Tina knew the injury would make her lame for life, but also that if she gave out this last bit of information then her life could almost certainly be measured in minutes, if not seconds.

But what choice did she have?

'Yes, we are.'

'How?'

Tina took a deep breath, gutted about what she was on the brink of doing, the thought of that drill through her ankle making her do it. 'Email. We communicate in the drafts section so no messages actually get sent.'

'Ah, a very useful method,' said The Wraith. 'I use it myself sometimes. And what is the email address?'

Tina told her, giving away her final nugget of information.

'Down to the end and turn right, boss,' said Mo, holding onto the dashboard as Bolt raced down the road, wondering what kind of undercover operation allowed a UCO to take part in an armed abduction of a civilian without telling his superiors about it. But he had little time to think about that now. If the Kalamans were sending someone to get Ray Mason's whereabouts out of Tina they would almost certainly have her killed afterwards. Which meant they might already be too late.

He braked hard as he came to the junction then turned right in a screech of tyres.

'OK boss, we're on Hartland Road now. Straight down, and it's just before the railway arch on the right.'

Bolt could see the arch already, a quarter of a mile ahead, and he pushed his foot down hard on the floor, barely slowing as he came to a speed bump, hitting it so hard the car actually lifted off the ground, hoping no one was foolish enough to step out in front of him.

'This is Beta 1, our ETA is thirty seconds,' he shouted into the radio. 'I repeat: thirty seconds. We're going straight in.'

'Beta 1, this is Tango 1, we're right behind you, heading west on Hartland Road.'

Bolt glanced in his rear-view mirror and saw one of the unmarked armed surveillance cars following. He looked at

Mo, who'd now put away the laptop and had a hand hovering above his gun holster. He looked utterly terrified, and Bolt felt for him. Mo had never fired a gun before. He wasn't an action man cop. He was a detective. Bolt was different. It had been a long, long time since he'd fired a gun, but even now, this close to retirement, he felt that familiar buzz at the prospect of action.

'It's going to be OK, Mo,' he said. 'We'll resolve this peacefully. No one's going to do anything stupid.'

The arch loomed up in front of them, and Bolt saw a yellow signpost saying Premier Motors on the wall just in front of it. He slowed the car and swung it into a huge turn, driving straight at the set of locked gates at the end of the alley, just as a train rumbled by overhead.

'Thank you for that, Tina,' said The Wraith, putting the phone away in the front pocket of her jeans, and taking off the splash-proof smock, letting it fall to the floor. 'I'm glad it didn't have to get too messy.' She turned round and pulled a short-barrelled pistol from her waistband, chambering a round as she turned back towards Tina.

Tina's insides did a somersault as she stared down the gun barrel. 'You lied,' she said.

The Wraith smiled beneath her mask. 'You knew I would.'

'I haven't given you all the information,' Tina blurted out, thinking fast. Doing anything to extend these last few seconds. 'Ray and I have a code we always use. Kill me and you'll never know it.'

'Don't waste my time,' said The Wraith, still pointing the gun at Tina's head. 'You've got three seconds to tell me, or I pull the trigger anyway. One ...'

A sudden burst of shouting came from the room next door, and seconds later the door to the workshop was flung open from the outside, and a man in jeans and a shirt appeared in the doorway, already in a firing stance.

The Wraith was already ducking behind Tina, using her as a shield, and the man was still in the process of shouting 'Armed police!' when she opened fire on him, the noise of the gunshots intensely loud in the room. It was that quick.

He fell backwards, landing on his back, as The Wraith ran behind one of the raised ramps, keeping her gun trained on the doorway.

A second later an arm holding a gun emerged round the frame and Tina saw Mike Bolt's head appear.

'Get back!' yelled Tina as The Wraith fired another shot, the bullet bouncing off the frame in an angry wisp of smoke, narrowly missing Mike.

Tina's first thought was that The Wraith was trapped, but then she ran towards the other end of the room, using the ramp and the shell of an old car as cover, and Tina saw that there was a roller door there through which vehicles could be driven in.

The Wraith hit a button and the roller door started to rise. At the same time, Mike poked his head back round the frame, saw what was happening, and ran inside the room, pointing his gun towards her.

'Armed police, drop your weapon!'

The roller door had only opened about a foot but that was enough for The Wraith and she dived down and rolled through the gap, out of sight.

Bolt didn't get a good shot at the shooter in the Scream mask, and even if he had it would have been unlawful to take it if his life wasn't in danger, and at that point it wasn't. That was the thing about being a police firearms officer in the UK. You had to make split-second decisions, knowing that the onus was always on you not to pull the trigger. Because in the worst-case scenario – and he'd seen it happen several times before – you ended up facing a murder charge just for doing your job.

As the shooter rolled under the door and out of sight, Bolt stole a quick glance over at Tina who was sitting tied to a chair in the middle of the cavernous workshop, looking pale and shocked but still very much alive – and felt an immediate burst of relief.

'We've got you, Tina!' he shouted as he raced towards the roller door, gun outstretched, taking a quick look over his shoulder to see Mo come running into the room, a gun in his hand and a phone to his ear as he called an ambulance for the plainclothes cop who'd just been shot.

Everything had happened incredibly fast, but that was the way with extreme violence. It exploded out of nowhere, and you had to know how to react to it. Bolt had been in this kind of situation before, albeit a long time ago, and he knew what he had to do. They had one man down, two more with the prisoners, and the other ARVs were still en route.

Bolt was on his own. And he knew he couldn't let this shooter get away because by the way she moved, she was a woman, which meant she was almost certainly the person who'd killed Mary West.

As he took off after her, he felt a burst of exhilaration. There was no fear. There wasn't time for that. He didn't think about Leanne or the fact his life was good and a sunny, warm retirement for them both beckoned. He was in the moment. Concentrating with every ounce of his being; he raced towards the roller door, now already risen a good five feet, and, bending down, ran under it, and out into a yard facing the railway line.

He spotted her almost immediately. Unlike virtually all other suspects in a similar situation, she wasn't running. Instead, she was in a two-handed shooting stance, less than fifteen yards away.

He reacted instantaneously, bringing his own gun round to fire, already having made the decision to pull the trigger.

But he was too late. He felt her first bullet hit him with the force of a cricket bat, somewhere in his upper body, then the second straight afterwards, just as powerful.

And then he was falling, the gun gone, the world seeming to melt and fade around him, no longer even conscious of the impact as he landed on the ground.

49

Even with the ringing in her ears, Tina clearly heard the two shots outside, and from where she was sitting she could just make out Mike falling to the ground beyond the now fully open roller doors.

At that precise moment, Mo was removing her wrist straps with shaky hands. As soon as her hands were free, she pushed him aside, pulled off the remainder of the ties, and got to her feet, slipping her trainers back on.

Tina didn't hesitate. Ignoring the pain in her hand and Mo's shouts to stay back as he followed her out, she ran over to the open roller door and out into the yard.

Mike wasn't moving and his eyes were closed. As she crouched down beside him, Tina could see the two entry wounds – one in his chest, one in his upper belly. There was no sign of The Wraith, but from the angle she'd fired from, and the fact that a high fence topped with barbed wire blocked off access to the railway track, there was only one way she could have gone.

Anger and a desire for vengeance coursed through Tina, eclipsing every other feeling. Yelling at Mo to help Mike, she picked up his discarded pistol with her good hand and sprinted through the yard, making for the end of the main building where a narrow lane ran round the other side.

As Tina rounded the corner, not even slowing down, she saw The Wraith twenty yards further on, making for the road, having discarded her mask. She gave chase, her footsteps crunching on the gravel, already lifting the pistol to fire, the bleeding hand down by her side. In the distance she could hear sirens drawing closer.

Hearing her approach, The Wraith swung round, and Tina saw her for the first time, unmasked. In that single second it struck her that the woman who'd murdered her neighbour, possibly her former lover, boss and friend, and who'd almost murdered Tina herself too, was strikingly attractive – not at all the sort of person you'd expect to cause so much grief and pain.

And then, still running, Tina pulled the trigger, three times in rapid succession. The recoil from the third shot made her stumble and fall to the ground, which may well have saved her life because The Wraith was already firing back into the space where Tina had been.

But, as Tina rolled onto her side, bringing the gun back up, she saw that The Wraith had been hit somewhere near the top of her right leg and was clutching the wound with one hand while staggering around in a tight circle, still holding the gun, lifting it up to aim – not at Tina, but someone behind her.

'Armed police!' she heard Mo call out, his voice faltering just a little. 'Drop your weapon!'

The sirens were loud now, but reinforcements still weren't quite here.

The Wraith straightened, her finger tensing on the trigger.

Tina squinted down the pistol's sights, her hand shaking slightly, looking for a body shot.

The Wraith didn't move.

A second passed.

Then she dropped the gun and raised her free hand. 'I surrender.'

'Step away from the gun!' shouted Mo.

The Wraith took a tentative step backwards, still clutching her leg.

Which was when Tina got back to her feet and strode towards her, still holding Mike's pistol out in front of her.

'Tina, get out of the way!' shouted Mo, but still she kept walking until she stood directly in front of the woman who'd almost killed her twice. Now making *her* stare down the barrel of the gun.

The Wraith stared back at her defiantly, although her face was contorted in pain. 'Do as your friend says,' she hissed through gritted teeth. 'I'm unarmed and I'm surrendering.'

'Move out of the way, Tina – now!' Mo's voice came from only feet behind her, angry and tense.

Tina ignored him. Her finger tightened on the trigger. 'This is for my neighbour, Mrs West,' she said. 'And for everyone else you've killed.'

The Wraith suddenly looked utterly terrified, her poise completely gone in that one second, and she seemed to visibly shrink. 'God please, no.'

'Don't do it, Tina!' shouted Mo.

Tina thought of Mrs West, of Mike, of the man she'd tortured to death on a live-stream feed to his wife ... of every person this woman had destroyed in her foul career.

She squeezed the trigger.

And stopped. Just at the last second.

'You can rot in prison, bitch,' she said, and turned away.

At that moment she heard movement behind her and Mo suddenly yelled a warning.

The noise of bullets filled the air, and Tina fell forward.

50

'I cannot tell you how saddened I am to hear about the deaths of two brave police officers, cut down in the line of duty like this,' said Alastair Sheridan solemnly as he conducted an interview with the BBC over his laptop via Skype.

He was pleased that the BBC had approached him faster than anyone else, bar the Prime Minister, who'd still yet to make an official statement on the killings. It showed how important he was, how high up the pecking order.

'People sometimes forget what an incredibly difficult job the police do, in often dangerous circumstances, as we've seen today, and with fewer and fewer resources. I've long said that the government needs to divert resources from other areas to give the police force the support it needs to maintain law and order. I also believe we are going to have to take a much tougher line on criminals in this country, because right now it really is beginning to look like they're taking over our streets, and that is a frankly intolerable situation. We cannot let it happen. It would be an insult to the memory of these two brave officers.'

Alastair knew you could never go far wrong on the law and order ticket. The voters never failed to lap it up. And at the moment it was an especially useful stick to beat the PM with.

'Do we have any more details about what actually happened in this particular incident?' he asked the interviewer, a boring middle-aged man who seemed to think that dyeing his hair the colour of turd would make him look younger. Four hours had passed since it had taken place but that was a lifetime these days.

Unfortunately, the interviewer didn't, or none that he could say on air anyway, and that was the problem with the BBC. It was always behind the curve.

Alastair wound up the interview with some thoughts and prayers for the victims' families then said a suitably sombre goodbye and got up to rejoin his family and the Buxton-Smythes on the veranda, where they'd been enjoying a Thai dinner personally prepared by one of Zagreb's top chefs, who'd been flown in especially. Alastair was in a particularly jovial mood, and he was just checking his Twitter feed to see how many people had liked his earlier post condemning the police killings (27,618 in less than two hours) when he saw the name Tina Boyd trending.

He clicked on one of the posts and saw that there was a rumour that the two police officers had been killed while rescuing Tina

Boyd from a disused garage where she was being held against her will, and that Tina herself had been killed.

Alastair grinned, and there was a real spring in his step as he went back out onto the veranda and sat down at the head of the table, picking up his glass and taking a big gulp of Cristal.

'Now, where we?'

51

Tina wasn't dead. She was in a hospital bed trying to come to terms with the events of the last few hours.

One second she'd been about to kill the woman known as The Wraith, but then, as she'd lowered the gun and turned her back, everything had happened so suddenly that it had all been over in a flash. Using Tina as cover, The Wraith had gone for her gun, only for Mo Khan to open fire on her as Tina dived to the ground.

Tina wasn't sure whether or not The Wraith was dead. The last she'd seen was Mo giving her first aid while she lay motionless on the gravel. But it didn't look good for her. Still, as far as Tina was concerned, it was nothing less than she deserved.

It was the shock of Mike's death that had been like a hammer blow to her. Tina had seen violent death too many times before but even so, she'd only rarely lost people close to her, and none of them had she actually seen die. Mike had died right in front of her. Big, strong, dependable Mike – a good cop, and one who'd faced extreme danger before and come out the other side unscathed, who'd been only months from retirement; the man she'd never have expected to succumb to the job. And now he was gone. Worse still, he'd only been there because Tina had phoned him and he'd been trying to save her. It made her feel doubly responsible for his death.

The police had already questioned her about what had happened, and she'd told them. The two detectives, both women, had been sympathetic rather than hostile, and had told her that the first officer she'd seen shot had also died of his wounds.

The detectives had gone now, leaving two armed officers outside her door for, as they put it, her protection, but Tina was pretty certain they were also there to stop her from leaving.

It was ten p.m. and she was lying in her hospital bed, staring up at the ceiling, knowing that she needed to borrow a phone to call her brother in Spain to let the family know what had happened before they heard about it on the news. They'd be horrified and would want to come home to see her. Her mum would insist on it. And Tina didn't want that. She felt guilty enough as it was, without ruining their holiday too, and putting them in needless danger. All she wanted was to be left alone to grieve for Mike in peace.

But it didn't look like that was going to be an option because, barely ten minutes after the departure of the detectives, there was a knock on the door and someone she was very much not expecting stepped inside, carrying a large bunch of flowers, and shut the door behind him.

'How are you feeling?' asked George Bannister, the Home Office minister and, as anyone who watched the news would know, Alastair Sheridan's permanent sidekick, his unofficial campaign manager for the job of Prime Minister.

Tina stiffened at the sight of him, and sat up in bed. 'Mr Bannister, isn't it? What are you doing here?'

'I need to talk to you,' he said, leaning the flowers against the wall and approaching the bed. 'Do you mind if I sit down?'

'Go ahead,' she said, watching him as he sat down warily on one of the plastic chairs. He was a small, fussy-looking man with thinning hair and tense body language. From what she knew, he was academically very bright and highly efficient in his governmental roles, but was missing any of the charisma that a leading politician needs, which made him the perfect foil for Sheridan.

Bannister leaned forward in the seat. 'I want to assure you that we're not being recorded,' he said, 'which means I can speak frankly, and I want you to speak frankly too.'

He paused there, and Tina felt the first flickering of contempt for him. His discomfort told her all she needed to know: he'd been sent here by Alastair Sheridan.

'First of all, I want to say that I'm very sorry to hear about what happened to you today. I understand that you were a friend of one of the officers who was killed.'

'Thank you, Mr Bannister, but I'd prefer it if you ditched the niceties,' she told him, 'and got on with what you came here to say.'

He nodded. 'All right. Would you mind putting your hands where I can see them so that I know you're not recording any of this?'

Tina put her hands over the covers. 'I haven't got my phone right now, Mr Bannister. It was left in my car when I was abducted. I'm still waiting for the police to give it back to me. Perhaps you could help on that.'

'I'll see what I can do.' He glanced back towards the door, then back at Tina, and specifically her hands, as if he still didn't quite trust her. He looked very, very nervous. 'I suspect', he said at last, 'that you know a lot about ...' He swallowed hard. 'The real Alastair Sheridan.'

'If you mean that he's a serial killer, yes, I do.'

'He's an incredibly dangerous man,' Bannister said quietly.

'Then why are you helping him?'

Bannister sighed. 'He has something on me. Something that he's been blackmailing me with for a long time.'

Tina didn't say anything.

'He has to be stopped, Miss Boyd. But I can't do that. Answer me a question. You have my word it goes no further than this room. Are you still in touch with Ray Mason?'

Tina suspected Bannister's word counted for next to nothing but he'd given her something so she decided to give him something in return. 'I may be able to get hold of him if I have to,' she answered carefully.

'I know he's not in the country,' said Bannister. 'And I also know that he was smuggled out, and by whom. A few hours ago, the French police raided a holiday home where it was believed

Mason was hiding. He wasn't there, but the police were of the opinion that he had been and that they'd only just missed him. Which they had.'

Tina frowned, thinking that Bannister was worryingly well informed. 'How do you know?'

'Because I phoned the house and warned him to get out.'

'Why?'

'Alastair is out of control, and has to be stopped. And I know Mason wants to kill him, just like he killed Cem Kalaman.'

'It was Sheridan who set Ray up on the Kalaman hit,' said Tina.

'I thought as much,' said Bannister. 'I'd been warning him for a long time that his association with Kalaman would come to haunt him if he wasn't careful. It looks like he took me at my word.'

'He uses contract killers to clean up his mess. One of them murdered my neighbour. She was eighty-five. That same woman was the one who tried to kill me today, and who killed the two officers.'

'I know,' said Bannister, 'and she's now dead, so she can do you no further harm. It was the murder of your neighbour which finally prompted me to contact you. I can't stand it any longer.' He paused. 'Alastair's got to go.'

'When you say "go" ...'

'I mean permanently.' He looked at her. 'He has to die, Miss Boyd.'

Even after everything he'd said, Tina was still shocked to hear the words come out of his mouth. She'd seen this guy, a Home

Office minister, so many times on TV, droning on about crime and asylum numbers, or standing next to Alastair Sheridan, his old school friend, the man he now wanted to have murdered.

'And you want Ray to do it?' She raised her eyebrows. 'Jesus, he must have something very, very big on you.'

Bannister cleared his throat. 'It's enough. However, I want to make it clear that it has nothing to do with the crimes he and Kalaman and whoever else are responsible for. I've never killed, or indeed hurt, anyone.'

'Maybe not, but like all politicians you like to get other people to do your dirty work.'

He ignored the barb. 'Alastair Sheridan is currently on holiday with his wife and family in Dubrovnik. They went there this morning. However, Alastair has a number of business interests in Bosnia-Herzegovina and he will be leaving his family and travelling by land to Sarajevo on Friday, where he'll be addressing a civic event in the City Hall. There'll be tight security there. Alastair's popular in Bosnia and he's being wooed by senior government figures who want him to invest some of his hedge fund money in their country. But while he's there, he won't be staying in Sarajevo. Two years ago, he and Kalaman used a shell company to buy an isolated property up in the mountains ten kilometres north of the city. I think they were planning to turn it into an eastern European version of the farm in Wales where they murdered the girls.'

'How do you know all this?' Tina asked him.

'I'm a Home Office minister, and I've also been close to Alastair for a long time. The combination puts me in a good position to unearth this kind of information. I don't know if they've already murdered any girls there, but a lone female hiker from Hungary went missing not far away last summer. The point is, Alastair can operate with a degree of impunity while he's there. He can't kill easily but he can certainly indulge in his sadistic tendencies far from anyone's gaze. Bosnia's a poor country and money has a very loud voice there.' He paused. 'Anyway, Alastair will be staying for several days at the house before returning to his family. I suspect in that time he'll want to indulge a little. He also won't have his British police escort with him. The house is protected only by private security.'

Tina thought about what Bannister was saying. It made sense. Men like Alastair Sheridan – sadistic, violent killers – could never stop their activities. They might be able to control them temporarily but, in the end, the urge to kill or injure would always come to the fore. One way or another they would continue until they were either caught, or got too old, and Alastair appeared to be a long way from either.

'How do I know this isn't some sort of trap you're setting up with Sheridan to catch or kill Ray?'

'We both know what Alastair's done, the depths to which he's sunk,' said Bannister, meeting her eye. 'I'm a lot of things, some of them not that good, but I'm not a monster. I promise you this is no trap.' He reached into the inside pocket of his suit jacket and took out a mobile phone. 'The address and location of the house in Bosnia are stored in this phone. It's unregistered. You have my word no one will try to trace it.' He placed it on the bed next to her.

Die Alone

Tina smiled coldly. 'You're a politician. Your word isn't worth shit.'

'But you've got things on me now. That should be enough.'

She thought about it. The Wraith was dead, but this wouldn't stop Alastair Sheridan: he'd only find another killer at a later date to silence her. Until he was in prison or dead, she wasn't entirely safe. 'I can't guarantee I'll be able to get hold of Ray. And I can't guarantee that he'll do what you want either.'

'I know that. But will you try?'

'Can you get the NCA off my back, and stop them from charging me with aiding an offender? And don't give me any of that bullshit about not interfering in the legal process, because I know you can do it.'

Bannister sighed. 'I'll see what I can do.'

'Then so will I,' said Tina. 'But I'll tell you this: if you try to betray either Ray or me, I'll make certain you live to regret it.'

52

Night had fallen when I finally made it into Paris.

The drive there had been long because I'd been forced to avoid the toll roads in case the camera picked up the rental car which, as the man on the phone had told me, needed changing fast. That man, I was now sure, was the Home Office minister George Bannister, Alastair Sheridan's close political colleague. I'd been following Sheridan's progress with a mixture of cynicism and alarm during my time in prison, and consequently had seen and heard plenty of Bannister.

Why Bannister was helping me was anyone's guess but he clearly was, because if it hadn't been for his call, I'd have been in custody or dead now. I also felt bad for the Brennans. Somehow the police had linked me to them, which meant they'd be trawling through all their records, and it wouldn't be hard for them to put a case together for assisting an offender.

According to the car's satnav, I was about a mile north of the Gare du Nord train station in one of the less salubrious areas of the city. Pulling up in a back street, I parked in the shadow of a graffiti-strewn train viaduct and removed the satnav, but kept the keys in the ignition to make it more attractive for any passing thief, then got out and started walking south.

I used to love walking. It was my means of relaxation, a chance to clear the head or to mull through a case while breathing in fresh air and exploring the world. Walking represented freedom. It was why I'd missed it so much in prison. And it was why it felt so good walking now. It was dark, and it was a shitty area, and those few people who were about stared menacingly, but I didn't care about any of that. I'd faced enough in my life to know not to be scared by street thugs, and because they couldn't sense fear, they left me alone.

The last time I'd been in Paris was seven years ago, with a woman called Jo for a long weekend in May.

Paris in the spring. It fulfilled all the clichés. The sun was shining, the food was superb, Edith Piaf played in the jazz cafés on the Left Bank close to Notre-Dame, and I recall it being one of the best weekends of my life, although to be fair there haven't been a huge number to choose from. Jo was the only other woman I've ever loved aside from Tina. We'd met after she'd come into our offices to demonstrate a new facial recognition software package, and I'd fallen for her pretty much on sight. We'd moved in together, along with her twin seven-year-old daughters Chloe and Louise, got engaged, then married. Everything had been great. We really were one big happy family and I'd genuinely thought we'd be together for ever.

In the end it had been two years, and it had finished abruptly when Jo found out that I'd taken the law into my own hands and broken into the home of a criminal whom I'd then beaten unconscious. It had been a stupid, insane thing to do, and once again my deep-seated anger at the perceived injustices of the world had got the better of me. The criminal in question, a violent thug called Kevin Wallcott, had definitely deserved what I'd done to him. He'd crippled a child for life while chasing someone else in his Range Rover during a road rage incident, and had somehow got off with a sentence of barely a year. He'd then carried on offending, even ramming another car in a similar road rage incident. The guy had needed to be taught a lesson. I'd done that.

But Jo hadn't seen it that way. She'd told me she didn't trust me round the children if I was capable of that degree of violence and had asked me to move out immediately. That was what had hurt the most. The fact that she thought I'd ever lay a finger on her daughters whom I'd doted on like they were my own.

And that had been that. The healthiest relationship of my life, my one chance of redemption and a life of peace, and I'd thrown it all away.

If I could go back in time, would I change things? Would I shake my head and curse Kevin Wallcott but then simply let it go, ignoring the fact that he hadn't paid enough for his crimes?

Jesus, yes. I'd never have touched him. I'd have done anything to get my old life back.

But it was way too late for that now. Because now here I was, a wanted man. I'd almost been killed twice in the last four days, almost been captured the same number of times. I'd shot four men, one in cold blood, and involved other people in my escape, and potentially put them right in the firing line as well. Some men crack under the pressure of being constantly on their guard while being flung from one violent and dangerous situation to another, while others become harder and stronger. They get used to this lifestyle, and begin to act on instinct, and without fear. Soldiers fighting on front lines in wars are typical examples; they develop a fatalistic cloak of protection. For the first time, I was conscious that this was happening to me. I was exhausted. I was certain I was headed towards my doom. But I was no longer scared.

The Boulevard de Magenta, which runs south of the Gare du Nord towards the River Seine and the tourist district, is a street of cheap fast-food takeaways, dodgy-looking phone shops, and not a tourist in sight. Even at this late hour quite a few of the places were still open, and I stopped at one of the phone shops and bought a relatively cheap Huawei with a pre-loaded sim card from a man who was clearly only interested in my money, which suited me fine. I also stopped at a tabac shop where I was able to buy pepper spray and two knives, one spring-loaded, the other small with a three-inch blade to hang on a chain round my neck.

Now I needed somewhere to stay. Clearly I'd have preferred a hotel in a more upmarket area, but for those kinds of places you need credit cards, so on an adjoining street I found a suitably scabrous guesthouse, with peeling paintwork and the O missing on the illuminated sign. There were even a couple of shifty-looking kids hanging about outside smoking skunk so powerful-smelling that the next stop for them was probably the psychiatric ward. They watched me vaguely through the cloud of toxic smoke as if I was some strange apparition as I walked past them to the entrance, holding my breath.

I had to ring a bell to get inside and the front desk was fortified as if they were expecting an imminent military assault. The man behind the mesh, a short, fat fellow with a thick moustache who I guessed was the owner, gave me the kind of suspicious look that told me he wasn't used to getting drop-in custom. There was a cheap portable TV on the wall next to him. It was showing the French news and I hoped that my escape wasn't a story here because if my new mugshot started appearing I was in big trouble.

I told the guy I wanted a room for two nights in my schoolboy French, and he was slightly more fastidious than I'd been expecting because he checked my passport before giving me a key and taking €100 in payment, plus a further €50 as a damage deposit, all paid in cash.

The room definitely wasn't worth the money. It was small, cramped and way too hot, with a view over to the back of the next building – a far cry from the boutique hotel opposite the Panthéon building in the Sorbonne where Jo and I had spent our weekend. But for now it suited my purpose.

I threw off the backpack and got on the bed, pulling out my new phone and using it to get on the internet and check the UK news.

The main headline was big, bold and shocking. Two police officers had been shot dead during the rescue of a kidnap victim in north London. A female suspect had also been shot dead, and two people arrested.

But it was when I read further down the article that I became more concerned because I saw that there were unconfirmed reports that one of the dead officers was none other than Mike Bolt, and that Tina Boyd was also involved. Apparently, she'd been taken to hospital with unspecified injuries.

Christ. What had I got her into? I had to find out what was going on.

I logged into our joint email account and saw that there was already a message in the drafts section. I opened it up and started reading.

Ray. You need to call me. It's urgent. I have a new number, 07727 918647. I am in hospital but have private room and should be able to talk.

It could have been a trick. If Tina was cooperating with the authorities, they could be using her to lure me in so they could track my phone.

But in the end I still trusted her, and I had to know she was all right. I looked at my watch. Just short of eleven p.m. UK time. I made the call.

She answered with a whisper: 'Is that you?'

It felt good to hear her voice again. 'Yeah, it's me. I've just seen a report you were kidnapped and Mike Bolt was killed in the rescue bid.'

'It's true,' she said quietly.

'Jesus, Tina, I'm so sorry.'

'The Kalamans snatched me. They brought in that bitch, the one you called The Wraith, to torture me into giving them your whereabouts. I didn't tell them, before you ask.'

I felt sick. 'Are you hurt?'

'A little, but I'll be out of here tomorrow.'

'And then?'

'I don't know. I'm under police guard at the moment. They're talking about moving me into witness protection, but I don't think it's going to come to that. I'm pretty sure the Kalamans won't try and get me again. It's not good for business.'

'You're still a threat to Sheridan.'

'Listen, I got a visit from none other than George Bannister, the Home Office minister and Alastair's supposed ally.'

'That's strange,' I said. 'I'm certain he was the person who phoned the Brennans' French landline today and told me to get out just before the house was raided.'

'He told me it was him when we spoke,' said Tina. 'He also told me where Sheridan is going to be this Friday, and that he's going to be unprotected and vulnerable. The thing is, the location is just outside Sarajevo in Bosnia.'

'Go on.'

'Not now,' she whispered. 'I'll put all the details in a draft in the account. It's up to you what you do with it. Don't feel obliged to go after him. I know it's hard enough for you as it is.'

The thing was, I did feel obliged. It was hard not to, given all I'd put Tina through. But it was more than that. Alastair Sheridan had played a big part in ruining my life. Even if I did manage to create a new life somewhere else – and right now, that was a big if – I'd always be looking over my shoulder. And I'd always know that he would continue to ruin lives, just as he'd done all his adult life. Maybe I should have learned my lesson from what happened with Kevin Wallcott, but one of the few things I'm truly proud of is the fact that I've ended the careers and the lives of a lot of very bad people over the years. In that respect, I've made the world a slightly better place. Whenever I think about that – which is not often enough – it makes me feel good. And the world would be a much better place without Alastair Sheridan in it.

'Are you still there?' asked Tina.

I took a deep breath. 'Yeah, I'm still here.'

'What are you going to do?'

This time I didn't hesitate. 'I'm going to kill him.'

'I wish I could be there with you. We make a good team.'

'Tina, you remember what I said in the car, just before we parted? I did mean it. Whatever happens, I'll always love you.'

I heard her swallow hard. That's the thing with emotional goodbyes. They're so difficult to do.

I cut the call and lay back on my bed, staring at the ceiling and trying in vain to calm the turmoil swirling around in my head.

53

The only thing that could have put Alastair in a better mood that night was if Tina Boyd had also been killed in the shootout back in London, which he'd now found out had resulted in the death of that psychotic hitwoman The Wraith, thereby saving Alastair both money and grief. Even so, Boyd alone was no real problem and he'd definitely find a way to deal with her later. Subtly, of course. But he'd get her.

He got everyone in the end.

It had been a wonderful evening with the Buxton-Smythes, sitting out on the veranda overlooking the wine-dark Adriatic Sea dotted with tiny islands, so characteristic of this end of the Croatian coast, while the nannies dealt with the offspring. The food had been sublime, which is usually the way when money is no object, and Ginny Buxton-Smythe had looked especially ravishing in a simple but elegant white dress that showed off her tan, and four-inch black heels. More than once Alastair had caught her giving him sneaky glances out of the corner of her eye. Naughty bitch. Clearly Piers wasn't giving her enough of the right attention.

But of course, Ginny was totally out of bounds. Alastair had a public reputation to keep up, and fucking his friend's wife wasn't going to do much to help it; and anyway, there was no way he'd be able to control himself with someone like Ginny. He would just *have* to be brutal. She needed a good, solid beating. She deserved it.

It had now been almost a year since he'd last given full vent to his urges. That had been in Bosnia when he and Cem had tortured, raped and killed a young hiker they'd bought to order from a local crime gang over the course of an entertaining three days. He felt a pang then when he thought of Cem. They'd had some fun together.

But life always has to move on, and move on Alastair already had. He'd been corresponding via email with a representative of the same gang they'd got the hiker from last year, about the possibility of procuring him another girl. Unlike Cem, who'd been able to take the edge off his urges simply through having rough sex with prostitutes, this had never worked for Alastair (although he'd obviously tried). He needed more. He needed, in truth, to kill. Because for him it was always about the power.

It was gone midnight now and he stood alone, hands resting on the veranda balustrade, looking out to sea. The Buxton-Smythes had left, and his wife and child were in bed, as was the nanny, a large Polish woman who was older than Alastair, whom Katherine had doubtless hired to make sure he avoided temptation. He closed his eyes, enjoying the warm breeze on his face, then felt the buzz of his unofficial phone – the one he religiously kept away from his wife – in the pocket of his Givenchy shorts.

Taking it out, he saw he had a WhatsApp message from an unidentified number. He knew exactly who it would be from though, and he was right.

We have something ready for you Friday. It does not need to be returned.

He smiled. Perfect.

The hunt was back on, and it would be held in honour of Cem Kalaman. It seemed a fitting tribute.

Part Six

54

I slept well that night, waking in my poky little hotel room at 8.15, feeling groggy but refreshed. The window was open and I'd kicked off the covers in the night but the room still felt hot.

It took me a couple of seconds to remember where I was and the situation I was in. Let's face it, my future still wasn't looking too bright, but at least I was free, and I was reminded of the words of an old army colleague of mine who'd lost a leg to an IED in Iraq, and then gone on to suffer two bouts of cancer afterwards, all by the age of forty-five. When I'd asked him once what was the best day of his life, he'd answered: 'Today.'

Every day you're above ground is a good day. I'd had that belief tested to extremes during my time in prison, and I hadn't believed it. But I believed it now.

Having said that, my new day didn't get off to a flying start. I had to remove a cockroach the size of a swollen thumb from the bath, and when I finally got the shower to work there was no hot water, and if the state of the shower head was anything to go by it was probably giving me Legionnaires' disease as well.

Afterwards, I got dressed in my last spare set of clean clothes, then checked the email address Tina and I shared. As she'd promised, the drafts section contained details of when Alastair Sheridan would be in Sarajevo, what he was doing, and the location of the house a few miles outside, bought apparently through a shell company, where he'd be staying. He was arriving there on Friday and would be staying for the weekend before heading back to Dubrovnik by car, a drive of approximately four hours. This gave me plenty of time.

During his time in Bosnia he would have no official British police guard, but as a politician and businessman who'd invested heavily in the country both through his hedge fund and with his own money, he was well respected enough to have a police escort both ways. He was going alone, ostensibly to hike in the hills surrounding the city, but the house he was in was isolated and far from prying eyes, and Bosnia, I knew from my own experience in organized crime, was a haven for people smuggling. If you wanted something, whatever that something was, you could probably get it there. Tina also mentioned that a twenty-five-year-old hiker from Budapest, travelling alone, had gone missing less than five miles away in August the previous year.

I memorized the woman's name, Lydia Molnar, and Googled her. She was a pretty auburn-haired girl with a big smile who'd initially come to Bosnia as part of a hiking group but, according to the most detailed report I read, had decided to stay on for a few days, having fallen in love with the natural beauty of the mountains and forests surrounding Sarajevo. I tried to find out whether Sheridan had been in the country at the time she'd disappeared, but couldn't see anything online.

But it wouldn't be a coincidence. These things never are.

I looked at her photo. Another life destroyed by a man who clearly thought he was invincible. But therein lay his Achilles' heel. If he was indulging in his savagery while in Bosnia then he would have to be doing it away from any police escort.

And that made him vulnerable.

My hotel (and I use the term loosely) didn't serve breakfast, but even if it had, I'd have declined. Instead, I took a walk in the direction of Notre-Dame, basking in the beautiful morning sunlight. I stopped en route at a pavement café and ate a huge breakfast of omelette, ham, cheese, French toast, and even half a dozen oysters. I followed that with muesli with yoghurt and fresh fruit, and washed it all down with plenty of coffee.

I was free, and it might have been temporary but by God it felt good.

However, there were still things that had to be done, and fast. One: I needed transport. Two: I needed to talk to Archie Barker.

I decided on sorting the transport first. It wasn't that hard. My French might have been basic but with the help of Google Translate I sat at my table shopping around online until I found a sales advert for a Citroën van for €4,000. The seller was based in the Montrouge district, a couple of miles south of where I was now. I still had close to €9,000 in cash so I could afford to make the purchase and, after a short, slightly awkward conversation (his English was about as good as my French), I agreed to go there at two o'clock that afternoon to take a look at it.

Now it was time to talk to Archie. I was taking a big risk, I knew that, which was why I'd been putting it off, but I wasn't going to get very far without him. Besides, the official reward on my head was fifty grand, and I didn't think he'd go to the authorities for that amount. As for the Kalaman money, I was just going to have to take the chance that he either hadn't heard about it, or if he had, wouldn't be tempted by that either. He was, after all, forever in my debt.

I called his old mobile phone number as I was walking along the banks of the Seine in the direction of the Eiffel Tower. This was my favourite part of Paris, with magnificent old buildings rising up on both sides, but without the noise and bustle of the thousands of tourists already thronging the streets on the other side of the high walls that lined the river.

The phone rang for a long time and I was thinking of giving up when a voice finally answered, 'Who's this?'

It was Archie. I recognized the accent immediately, even though it had lost a little of its cut-glass inflection.

The moment of truth. 'It's Ray Mason.'

Archie made a thin whistling sound. 'Now you are a man I definitely wasn't expecting to hear from. How did you get this number?'

'You gave it to me, remember? A long time ago. I memorized it.'

'I'm impressed. No one memorizes anything any more.'

'I don't want to go all *Godfather* on you, Archie, but you told me once that you were forever in my debt, and now the time's come to collect. I need your help.'

A pause. 'How exactly?'

I still had a choice here. I could simply ask Archie to put me in touch with a high-quality forger who could put together the documents I needed to open a bank account, and forget all about Alastair Sheridan. If I did that, I reckoned I had a 60 per cent chance of being able to start a new life somewhere else, maybe even more, because that would give me the access to the one thing all people on the run needed. Money.

It was the sensible choice. The rational one.

But the cowardly one too.

'I need you to put me in touch with someone who can supply me with a gun,' I said.

There was a long silence.

'I'm retired, Ray,' Archie said eventually. 'You know that. You encouraged me to make the move, and I'll always be thankful to you for that.'

'Just like you'll always be thankful I saved your life. I know you still know people. Help me.'

He made some noises of exasperation down the other end of the line, the kind a mechanic makes just before he tells you that the repair on your car's going to be a very big job.

'None of it will come back to you,' I told him. 'It's just a favour, then we're quits. Please.'

'Where are you?'

I thought about telling him I was in Paris but I didn't want to carry the gun across borders unless it was a last resort. 'I'm on the move. I'm going to be in Sarajevo in the next couple of days. You know anyone there?'

'Possibly. I'll make some phone calls and come back to you.'

'And if you know any good forgers down there, that would be a big help too.'

'I'll call you back. Are you going to be on this number?'

'Yeah, I will be. But don't be long.'

'I'll do what I can,' he said, not sounding remotely enthusiastic, and ended the call.

While I waited for him to call back, I meandered northwards, seeing the Eiffel Tower rise up to the left of me. Paris is a grand city. One that's proud of itself. You could see it in the majestic architecture; the palaces; the ornate bridges crossing the Seine, opening up to iconic landmarks and stunning wide boulevards, lined with trees in full leaf. Even the path by the river's edge was a boulevard in itself where cyclists, walkers, horse riders and numerous electric scooter riders mixed freely and easily, no one getting in each other's way, and I enjoyed the relative peace it gave me. It struck me then that I could walk like this every day, free as a bird, if I just let go of my pursuit of Alastair Sheridan.

I passed under a bridge where a homeless man sat, still wrapped in his sleeping bag, talking quietly to himself. He had a bowl in front of him but made no effort to ask me for any money. He didn't even look up, and I wondered what his story was and how he'd got to this point in his life. Someone once said that we're all the products of our own choices, but this, I thought, was only half true. A lot of choices are made for us, way back when we're young, and those are the ones that often set us on our paths, good or bad. Mine was made for me when I was seven years old and my father tried to kill me. That had lent a dark cloak to everything that followed. You can work to limit the damage. But you never repair it entirely.

And sometimes it can consume you.

Half an hour later, as I was passing under the Pont d'Iéna, my new phone rang.

'I've got a contact in Sarajevo who can help,' said Archie. 'As soon as you're in the city, let me know and I'll organize the intros. Then we're quits, Ray. All right?'

55

Buying a car is remarkably easy when it's second-hand, a private sale, and the man selling it just wants to see the money. My guy did, and his English improved remarkably as he gave me a rundown of everything to do with the car. I gave it a quick test-drive round the block with him in it, showed him my fake driving licence, which he wasn't very interested in, and gave him the cash, which he was very interested in.

Then I was off. I didn't bother spending a second night in my hotel but instead drove straight across eastern France, again avoiding the toll roads, and slept in the back of the van near the German border.

Die Alone

The following morning, having endured a pretty crap night's sleep, I started early, crossed the border without any checks at all (ah, the joy of the Schengen Agreement), and drove south-east across Germany, crossing the Austrian border near the beautiful medieval city of Salzburg where I managed to find a guesthouse with views down the hill to the cathedral and the river, whose owners not only gave me an excellent dinner, but also washed my clothes. I was finding that the further I got from the UK, the more relaxed I became. The owners of the guesthouse, a gay couple in their sixties, were interested in talking. Usually this would have made me wary, but I could see their interest was genuine, so I gave them a story of how I'd got divorced a few months earlier and had decided to take off on a trip round Europe. I'd shaved off my beard in Paris and my hair was slowly beginning to grow back, so I felt more confident that I wasn't likely to be recognized.

Setting off refreshed the following morning, I drove through Austria, Slovenia and Croatia in pretty much one go, and only had my passport checked for the first time when I arrived at Gradiška on the Bosnian border. It passed muster easily enough and I kept on going, finally pulling into Sarajevo at dawn on Friday morning, the day Alastair Sheridan was also due to arrive.

Let me tell you a few things about Sarajevo. One: considering it's fairly well known for a city on the far reaches of southern Europe, it's small, with a population of under four hundred thousand. Two: strategically speaking, it's probably the most badly placed city going, sitting in a valley surrounded by hills on three sides, making it very easy to besiege – a fact the Serbs took full advantage of during the war of 1992 to 1995. Three: considering it was under siege for pretty much the whole war, with daily artillery bombardment, it's in remarkably good shape, especially the old city which, bar the odd spray of shrapnel pockmarks on some of the buildings, looks completely intact.

According to Google, the main tourist area was round the old Turkish Baščaršija Square and bazaar, on the north bank of the river, so I found a small, basic hotel on a hill running down to it, where they had parking on a side road, and where they were happy to be paid in cash. I gave them enough for three nights, figuring I wasn't going to need to be in the city any longer given that that was how long Sheridan was supposedly staying in the area, and as soon as I was in my room (very small, but clean, with no cockroaches) I hit the sack and was asleep almost before I shut my eyes.

I didn't wake until early afternoon and, after a long shower, I called Archie Barker and told him I was in Sarajevo.

'I'll get my contact to call you. His name's Marco.'

'How do you know him?'

'Well, I suppose there's no harm in telling you,' said Archie. 'I met up with him several times in the early 2000s as the representative of some business people in London who wanted to open a reliable land-smuggling route into the EU for certain products.'

'What kind of products?'

'It's vulgar to ask those kinds of questions, Ray. Suffice it to say, Marco is well connected in Sarajevo and beyond. He can organize what you need, and he can be trusted. They're business people first and foremost in that area of the Balkans. As long as you've got the money. And you do have the money, don't you, Ray?'

'Yeah, I've got the money.'

'Then there'll be no problem. Good luck with everything. I won't ask what you're going to do with the gun.'

'That would be vulgar too,' I told him. 'I'll give you a warning though, Archie. Between friends. If anything goes wrong, I'll hold you responsible. And I know where to find you.'

'I wouldn't dream of it, dear boy,' he replied, sounding grievously wounded, but in my experience it's always best with criminals to appeal to their self-interest rather than their good nature, since without exception they tend to act with the former in mind.

'Good,' I said, and ended the call, wondering exactly what kind of products it was that Marco had been smuggling for Archie's so-called business people. Drugs? Women? Guns? Whatever it was, it wouldn't be harmless. And that was the thing with even the most genial of criminals (and Archie was by some distance the most genial I'd met): they were still always prepared to do the wrong thing for material gain, and not give much, if any, thought to the human cost involved.

That meant I couldn't entirely trust him, so I was feeling a little nervous as I waited for Marco's call. I was also hungry, so I headed out of the hotel and through Baščaršija Square, which was heaving with an unusual mix of Western, Chinese and Gulf Arab tourists, and with far more burkhas on display than I'd been expecting. The smell of spices and Middle Eastern cooking was in the air, and the tall, thin minarets of the mosques rose into the sky, giving the place a strongly Islamic feel.

However, as soon as you were through the bazaar, everything became Westernized again, with flashy-looking designer shops set between bars, nightclubs and restaurants. I found a place near to the old cathedral that had outside tables and, rather than go native, I ordered a large Sicilian pizza with a beer. I was halfway through the pizza and most of the way through the beer when the phone rang.

There was no one within immediate earshot so I took the call. 'Marco?'

'Yes, that is me,' answered a heavily accented voice. 'And you are Ray, yes? I understand you want to buy one or two things. It's best we meet, I think. Whereabouts are you?'

I wasn't going to give him the name of my hotel so I suggested we meet at the fountain in Baščaršija Square. 'I can be there in twenty minutes.'

'I'm out of the city at the moment,' Marco told me, 'but I can get you what you need. Why don't we meet there at nine p.m. tonight, and I'll take you to where we can pick up the item?'

I'd wanted to get the transaction over with well before night-fall but I didn't see I had much choice. 'OK. I want something good and reliable.'

'I can get you that. It will cost two thousand euros because of the nature of the transaction, and you will need to bring it with you.'

'I also need some papers in a certain name to help me set up a bank account.'

'I can organize that too,' he said, 'but first we'll deal with the other item. I'll see you at nine.'

I went back to my pizza, thinking that Marco had sounded very smooth on the phone. Too smooth.

Like anyone who's suffered a huge childhood trauma combined with a catastrophic loss of trust, I have a built-in antenna for danger, and in the back of my mind I could hear an alarm sounding.

I was going to have to be very careful.

56

Six hours later, I was standing at the fountain in the middle of the square. I'd spent the afternoon and evening wandering the city. It was surprisingly beautiful. I visited a mosque, a synagogue and the cathedral, marvelling at the way this city had united after coming close to being torn apart in that horrendous civil war. I'd also visited the genocide museum where I'd discovered that although Muslims made up the majority of the population, there were plenty of Serbs and Croats living there too, and everyone appeared to muddle along pretty well. What was nice was that there was no sign of animosity. The city had a laidback atmosphere.

The square was very busy, thronging with both tourists and locals. In the background, the call to prayer rang out, and I closed my eyes, taking in all the sounds. When I opened them, a man in a suit with an open-neck shirt and visible gold chain had appeared beside me. At first glance, in the near darkness, he looked pretty ordinary – if you excused the chain, which was as thick as an old-fashioned toilet pull. Short dark hair, early forties, medium height and build ... but straight away something felt wrong about him. It was as if he made the space he occupied slightly darker by his presence. His eyes were cold and his smile was both ingratiating and calculating.

'Marco, I'm guessing,' I said.

'Good to meet you, Ray,' said Marco, giving me what he thought was a subtle look up and down as we shook hands. 'Come with me.'

We started walking through the crowds in the direction of the main bazaar.

'Where are we going?' I asked.

'Obviously we cannot make the transaction here,' he said. 'The people we are buying from operate out of a building not far away. They have a variety of merchandise. You can pick what you need.'

I felt uneasy. I didn't like being unarmed and carrying a large amount of cash in a strange city where I was having to put my trust in the local criminals, but I told myself that Marco and the people he was putting me in touch with were business people, and business people like to do business.

Marco turned onto a narrow side street that quickly became a steep hill. After about fifty yards, during which we talked little, he stopped by an old Mercedes and got inside.

'We're going to a lot of trouble just to buy a pistol,' I said, getting in the passenger seat as he started the engine.

He lit a cigarette and puffed hard on it, blowing the smoke out of the window as he drove up the hill. 'Sarajevo isn't some cowboy town where guns are everywhere. It has a bad reputation but an unfair one, and it's all because of the war, which wasn't our fault in the first place.' He looked at me. 'Do you know, when I was a boy, this city was a cool place. We hosted the Winter Olympics; everyone lived together happily – Muslim, Serb, Croat. And now you people just think we're violent hicks.'

'I don't think that,' I said. 'Were you here during the siege?'

He nodded. 'It started when I was sixteen so I was old enough to fight. I was a volunteer in the Free Bosnian Army. It was hard to take the fight to the Serbs. They stayed up in the hills like cowards, relying on their heavy weaponry, but when they did try to break into the city, we hit them hard. And we showed no mercy. They didn't try very often.'

I had a renewed respect for him then. He'd seen danger and hardship in a way that we in the West have no concept of. I've always thought of myself as a tough man but, for all the bad things that have happened to me, I've at least grown up in a country of relative stability and peace.

'It must have been hard living like that.'

'It was. Especially seeing the city that was our home destroyed around us. But our enemies never broke our people and now peace reigns, my friend, and guns, I have to tell you, are in short supply.'

Die Alone

'OK, fair enough, you've convinced me,' I said, staring out of the window as we moved from the old city out into the suburbs where the roads were wider and modern residential tower blocks, some still under construction, lined both sides.

'You know the First World War started here back in 1914?' said Marco, who now seemed to have morphed into the local tour guide.

'I did,' I told him. 'I always enjoyed history at school. The assassination of Franz Ferdinand, right?'

'That's right, but that's not the whole story.' Marco's eyes gleamed with enthusiasm as he took a final drag on his cigarette and chucked it out of the window. 'The history books get it wrong. They say it was all pre-planned, and indeed there was an attempt to assassinate him earlier that morning with a bomb by a group of Serb nationalists which failed. Ah, but the actual shooting ...' He waved a finger at me. 'That was different. You see, Ferdinand's motorcade was travelling back from a function at the City Hall when his vehicle took an inexplicable wrong turning and immediately got stuck behind another vehicle. This was just outside a delicatessen where a man called Gavrilo Princip was queuing for a sandwich. Now Princip was also a Serb nationalist and didn't like Franz Ferdinand, but he hadn't been planning on killing him.' Marco shrugged. 'He was hungry. He just wanted his sandwich, but then he sees the hated Ferdinand in an open-top car right outside the front door of the delicatessen. So he pulls a pistol out of his pocket, strolls right up to the car and shoots him and his wife dead. Just like that. Can you imagine it? If there'd been no queue there, or they'd had more people behind the counter, or Princip just hadn't wanted a sandwich that day? There'd probably have been no First World War, and therefore no Second either.'

He pulled the Mercedes into a deserted car park in front of a single-storey warehouse building.

'Imagine that, Ray. Fifty million lives lost, all over a fucking sandwich. But that's the way of the world, my friend. Small choices can lead to some very big results.'

'Don't I know it,' I said, getting out of the car and following him up to the front door.

The door was opened from the inside before we even got there by a large, unshaven man in a loud lime-green tracksuit and very white trainers, who looked like he hadn't done any exercise in his life. He nodded at Marco, and it was clear that they knew each other well. They said a few words to each other in Serbo-Croat, and Tracksuit moved aside.

'Come on in,' said Marco.

I followed him into a small reception room, shutting the door behind me but making sure not to lock it in case I needed to make a quick escape.

'My friend here needs to search you in case you have a con-cealed weapon.'

'If I had a concealed weapon I wouldn't need to be here,' I told him, but I lifted my arms anyway, and let Tracksuit give me what I have to say was a pretty cursory search. He found the flick knife I'd bought in Paris in my back pocket and threw it down on the reception desk, before leading Marco and me down a long corridor to the back of the building and into a large storeroom, lined with boxes. On a table in the middle were three pistols side by side, all without their magazines.

Tracksuit went behind the table and made a gesture with his hand for me to take a look.

'It's just a matter of choosing the one you want,' said Marco. 'My friend here is reliable.'

I noticed that Marco's voice had risen a couple of decibels as he spoke – and then, as I heard movement behind me, I realized why. I just had time to glance over my shoulder and see a figure emerging from behind a curtain, but before I could react I felt a cable being looped round my neck and pulled tight.

My air supply was cut off instantly as I was pulled backwards, then a second later the pressure was eased just enough for me to take tiny breaths.

Marco smiled and took a phone from his pocket, while Tracksuit loaded one of the guns on the table with a magazine and pointed it at me.

'Apologies for this, my friend, but there is a very large reward on your head. Not only that, but a good friend and business partner of mine, who's invested a lot of money in the country, is also very keen to see you dead. His name's Alastair Sheridan and he says you two are acquainted with each other.'

I tried to speak but could barely manage a mangled squeak.

'There's no need to say anything, my friend,' said Marco, raising the phone in my direction. 'But Mr Sheridan would like me to record your death so he can view it later for his entertainment.'

He nodded to the man holding the cord round my neck, and the next second it tightened once again. My would-be assassin forced me backwards, pushing his knee into my back as he applied the pressure. Already I could feel my vision blurring. In a matter of seconds I was going be unconscious.

But I hadn't come entirely unprepared. The neck knife I'd bought in Paris – small, with a three-inch, razor-sharp blade – was still hanging from a cord round my neck, having not been picked up in the search. I grabbed at the cable throttling me with one hand, just to distract the people watching me die from what I was about to do, then shoved my other hand up beneath my shirt, acting like it was all part of a futile struggle, and yanked the blade free from its plastic holder. It was so small that even when my hand came back out with it I don't think anyone noticed. At least not until I reached round and shoved it hilt-deep into my attacker's thigh three times in rapid succession.

The attacker howled in pain and let go of the cable as, coughing and gasping for air, I shoved it in a fourth time and let go, rolling free of his grip.

'Shoot him!' yelled Marco at Tracksuit, at the same time shoving the phone in his pocket and making for the door.

Tracksuit squinted and took aim, and straight away I guessed he wasn't a good shot, but then he didn't need to be in a room this small with barely five yards between us.

The two most important things to do when someone's aiming a gun at you are to keep moving and to try to put obstacles between you and them. The guy who'd tried to kill me – burly, bearded and bald – was hobbling around, clutching at his bleeding leg while trying to remove the neck knife. Still coughing, but fuelled by the kind of adrenalin that comes when someone's trying to kill you, I jumped to my feet. Tracksuit immediately fired two shots, but I was already behind the other guy, and I grabbed him by the shirt and propelled him towards Tracksuit. As he fell into the table, knocking it backwards, Tracksuit jumped backwards too, stumbling into a couple of boxes.

He righted himself quickly but not quite quickly enough. As he raised his arm to fire, I careered into him, knocking his arm to one side, and driving my forehead into his nose.

This time he went straight over backwards into the boxes, his head smacking hard against a shelf, and dropped the gun. I landed on top of him and punched him hard in the face before jumping off him and scrambling on my hands and knees over to the gun.

I grabbed it and turned round, just as he was sitting up.

His eyes widened as I shot him once in the face. They then widened some more, and he toppled over on his side without a word or sound.

I stood up and, ignoring the other guy, whose trouser leg was now completely drenched in blood, suggesting that I must have severed an artery, took off after Marco. He was still running up the corridor, almost at the end now.

'Marco!' I yelled, my voice hoarse and painful. 'Stop or you're dead!'

If it had been me, I'd have taken my chances and continued running, given that he was only a couple of seconds away from safety, but I was beginning to work out that, for all his talk, Marco wasn't exactly a brave man. He stopped straight away and turned round with his hands up.

'Get over here,' I told him, pointing the gun at his head.

He walked towards me looking worried, as well he should have done. I wasn't feeling, or I suspect looking, especially merciful.

'Listen, man,' he said, stopping a few feet away, hands still firmly in the air, 'it was only business. I've got nothing against you personally.'

'That doesn't really make me feel any better,' I said, conscious that the act of speaking was really hurting my throat. 'You're going to have to atone.'

'Sure, man, sure. Whatever you say.'

His eyes darted towards a door to my left. Just a flicker. But it was enough for me to know that something else was going on.

Then I heard it. A high-pitched moan, partially muffled. It was coming from somewhere behind the door. It also sounded human.

'If you want Sheridan, I can give him to you,' said Marco quickly. 'I can take you to him right now.'

'Open the door,' I told him.

He acted confused. 'Which one?'

The muffled moan came again. Faint but audible to both of us.

'You know which one.'

I took a step back to give him room, keeping the gun pointed straight at his chest, and watched him turn the handle.

'It's locked,' he said.

'I know you have the key so open it or I'll do to you what I've just done to your friends.'

Die Alone

He looked at me, clearly decided it was best to comply, and fished out a key, turning it in the lock. 'It's not what you think,' he said, moving away as I looked inside.

I felt my insides clench. It wasn't what I thought. It was worse. Far worse.

57

As was often the case, Alastair Sheridan was pleased with himself. He'd just delivered a speech that was both measured and statesmanlike to an auditorium full of the great and the good of Bosnia-Herzegovina at Vijećnica, Sarajevo's historic City Hall, and was now in the back of a limousine supplied by the office of the Presidency, being driven to the house deep in the forested hills above the city which he and Cem had bought through a shell company a couple of years back.

The limousine had a police escort, again supplied by the Presidency, which was standard practice when Alastair was in town, given his importance as a British politician and an investor in the country, but it was especially needed tonight. Alastair's friend and occasional business partner Marco Kovich, whom he'd met the previous year through Cem, had warned him of the presence in the city of Ray Mason. How that cockroach had managed to track Alastair all the way here was anyone's guess, but the most important thing was that Marco stopped him, which he'd promised to do.

Alastair checked his phone. He was waiting for a message from Marco to tell him that Mason had been dealt with, permanently. Alastair needed to see proof that Mason was finally dead. Only then could he relax entirely.

There was no message. Alastair checked his watch. It was 10.30 p.m. He should have heard by now. Either way, however, Mason couldn't touch him. The house was covered by year-round private security, and when Alastair was in residence he made sure that he had two guards on the perimeter at all times. The guards were supplied by Marco, and were not the type of men to ask questions or be too curious, which was a good thing because tonight Alastair was expecting a special delivery.

He felt a shiver of excitement inside as he thought of the fun he was going to have later. It was just a pity that Cem couldn't be there to share it with him.

Still, he thought, at least it meant he'd have her all to himself.

58

The girl couldn't have been more than fifteen, and she was sat cramped in a wooden carry-cage only just about big enough to hold a large dog, a filthy gag covering her mouth. Her feet were bare and she was clothed in a dark T-shirt and white, patterned skirt that had become grubby and stained. Her eyes, pale blue, were wide with fear and desperation.

I turned to Marco. 'You piece of shit,' I said quietly. 'She's for Sheridan, isn't she?'

He tried to answer but no words came out. He was too busy staring at the gun, probably concluding that I was about to kill him. And anyway, how do you come up with an excuse for why you're keeping a young girl in a cage?

'Let her out now.'

He nodded rapidly and unlocked the cage, gesturing for the girl to get out. But she didn't move. She looked absolutely terrified.

I approached her slowly, still keeping my gun trained on Marco, trying to look as unthreatening to her as possible. 'It's going to be OK. Do you speak English?'

She shook her head.

I put out a hand but she wouldn't take it, and I noticed that she was wearing old-fashioned handcuffs. I turned to Marco. 'Uncuff her and help her out. And tell her she's going to be OK.'

As he approached her she flinched visibly, clearly having been on the wrong side of him before, but he said something in Serbo-Croat, his tone gentle, and she allowed him to remove her handcuffs and help her out. She was bent over like an old woman and she looked unsteady on her feet so I gestured for her to sit down in a chair in the corner, which she did.

'How long's she been in there for?' I said, taking the handcuffs and key from Marco.

'Just a few hours.'

'When's she going to Sheridan? And tell me the truth or I'll hurt you.'

'Tonight.'

'And you're delivering her, right?'

He nodded furtively.

'And you know he's planning to kill her?' I was finding it hard not to kill him myself, there and then. 'Of course you do. I bet you were going to make a lot of money out of it too.'

'We're not rich like you people. We have to take what work we can.'

'Well, you're going to work for me tonight to atone for what you've done. I assume Sheridan wants confirmation that you've killed me. How do you communicate?'

'Via email.'

'Get the address up on your phone now and show me the last message from him.'

He did as he was told, and handed me the phone. I glanced briefly at the conversation they'd been having about the girl. Alastair was indeed expecting her tonight. He was paying Marco €100,000 for her, on the basis that she wouldn't need to be returned. I felt sick and vengeful.

I told Marco to stand facing the opposite wall away from the girl and then used his phone to send back a message to Alastair saying that the deed was done and I was dead, but that I was having trouble uploading the video and would show it to him later when I delivered the girl. Then I pocketed the phone.

'OK, let's go. We're going to drop the girl off at the nearest good hospital.'

As Marco turned back from the wall, I launched a kick that caught him right between the legs, sending him collapsing to his knees. He looked up at me imploringly, his face white as a sheet, and I thought he was about to vomit.

'That's just so you don't get any ideas,' I told him, and turned towards the girl, who was sat hugging her feet to her chest, watching us raptly.

I smiled, wanting to reassure her that she was safe now, but she didn't smile back. Instead, she simply stared at me with wild animal fear, and I wondered what terrible journey she'd been on to get to this place where she'd become nothing more than a disposable product to be consumed by monsters.

When Marco had got back to his feet, I pushed him out of the door and gestured for the girl to follow, hoping she'd respond. She hesitated, then got to her feet and followed.

As I picked up the switchblade from the desk where Tracksuit had put it, Marco's phone buzzed in my pocket.

I ushered Marco into the front of the car and the girl and I got in the back. Then, as he started the engine, I took out the phone.

Good. When are you coming?? read Sheridan's text.

My text back was even shorter: *Soon.*

59

Half an hour later, Marco was driving his Mercedes up a long, winding hill through dense forest. Below us to the south I could see the lights of Sarajevo shimmering in the valley under a bright three-quarter moon. I'd made him drop the girl off at a private hospital in the city centre, and had given her a thousand euros of my own money to help pay for anything she needed. As soon as she knew she was free, she was out of the car and racing up the hospital steps in her bare feet and, watching her go, I truly hoped that she made it back home and managed to put the ordeal behind her.

Now it was just the two of us, and Marco wasn't going anywhere since I'd cuffed his right wrist to the steering wheel. As he drove, I emptied the magazine and checked the number of bullets. Nine. More than enough.

'You say Sheridan's got two guards on the property. Where will they be?' I asked him.

'He keeps them well away from the house,' said Marco. 'One is usually in the gatehouse at the entrance, where the camera screens are. The other is meant to be patrolling the grounds. Most of the time I expect they are both in the gatehouse.' He looked back over his shoulder. 'What are you planning to do?'

I knew exactly what I was going to do. Until I'd shot Cem Kalaman a week ago I'd had my doubts that I could ever kill the way an assassin kills. But I knew now for sure that I could, and that Alastair Sheridan could no longer be allowed to live. The thought that he would have raped and murdered the girl in the cage, and made her final hours, possibly days, a living hell, steeled my nerves.

'I'm going to kill him,' I said. 'And then you're going to drive me back to the city, unless you fancy dying in there with him.'

He shook his head energetically. 'No, I don't.'

'I didn't think so. You're a piece of shit, Marco, but my quarrel's with Sheridan, so if you do as you're told, you live. But the moment you try to double-cross me, you die.'

Marco looked at me in the rear-view mirror. 'I'm not going to do anything stupid, OK? But this is fucked up, my friend. You can't just kill Sheridan. He's going to be the next leader of your country.'

'Well, that's the thing,' I said. 'He isn't.'

Marco evidently decided that it was best just to shut up, because that's what he did. A couple of minutes later he took a turning down a narrow, newly tarmacked road and slowed the car.

'We're coming up to the gatehouse. If my man at the gate sees my handcuffs he'll know something's wrong.'

I passed the key over to him and slid down in the seat so I was out of sight. 'I've got the gun trained right on your back, Marco. One wrong move and I start shooting.'

'OK, OK,' he said, taking the cuffs off and chucking them down beside his seat.

A minute later, he came to a halt in front of a large, imposing gate lit by twin lamps, one on each gatepost, and pressed the button to let down the driver's side window.

I slid further down in the seat so I was almost lying down as a man approached and he and Marco had a quick conversation in Serbo-Croat. Then Marco brought the window up again and the gates opened.

We drove inside and I stayed down until, after about fifty yards, he brought the car to a halt. I sat up and saw that we'd parked in front of a large gothic-looking mansion with grey stone walls and swathes of ivy like jungle creepers running down them. There were lights on inside and the curtains were drawn.

'What now?' asked Marco.

'Does he have a camera watching the front door?'

'I'm not sure. I think so. Maybe.'

'Well, you'd better be the one who knocks on it then.'

I followed him out of the car. The night was still and peaceful, the moon bathing the house's neatly kept gardens in eerie light. No one appeared to be watching us from the gatehouse but, even so, I kept to the shadows and out of sight as Marco mounted the steps to the front door.

He knocked hard while I stayed round the corner, the gun already drawn, and then it was opened and I heard Alastair's voice, deep and cheery. 'Hello Marco, have you—'

He never finished the sentence. I was round the corner in an instant, and there he was. Alastair Sheridan. My nemesis. The man who'd murdered Dana Brennan and countless others. The man who'd destroyed my life.

His face didn't just fall, it collapsed as he saw me. But I didn't give him a chance to call out or shut the door. I gave Marco a hard shove and forced us both through the door and into a surprisingly narrow hallway.

'Marco,' I said as I shut the door behind me.

He turned round. Behind him, Sheridan was retreating with his hands raised.

'This is for the girl,' I said, and shot him right between the eyes.

Marco tottered, wearing an expression of surprise as a thin line of blood ran down the centre of his face and off the end of his nose. Then he collapsed straight to the floor.

The pistol was a .22 so the retort wasn't loud enough to be heard in the gatehouse, and I knew there wouldn't be a camera in here, not with the kind of thing Sheridan had been planning.

'Oh God,' said Sheridan, hands outstretched in supplication. 'Please. I'll give you money. Anything. Don't hurt me.' He continued his retreat into a large living room done out in dark woods and dominated by a huge, ornate stone fireplace until a large chaise longue blocked his passage. He stood against it, literally shaking with fear, tears running down his face.

I stopped ten feet from him. Raised the still-smoking pistol.

'Please, Mr Mason. Ray. Don't do this. I am rich. I can give you anything you want. I swear to God I will never hurt another soul. I will be a force for good. I'm sick. I need help.'

Fair play to him, he was trying every potential angle that might result in mercy. I let him continue, my face impassive, and I think he knew then that he had no chance. His knees began to shake uncontrollably and it looked like he might collapse.

'Did you enjoy killing Dana Brennan?' I asked him. 'A thirteen-year-old girl who was going shopping for her mother. Did it make you feel good ending her life?'

'It wasn't ... I didn't ... I didn't know what I was doing.' His face crumpled and he dissolved into loud sobs.

I thought of Dana. Of her parents. Hollowed-out versions of their former selves. A family utterly destroyed.

'I've got no mercy for you,' I told him, wanting to make him squirm in his last few seconds. It's a terrible thing to say, but I was actually enjoying watching another human being suffer.

And it was for that reason that I didn't hear the guards coming through the back of the house until it was almost too late.

I caught a brief glance of one of them through the open lounge doors as he crept through the dining room towards us. He was armed with a shotgun, and I could just make out a second figure behind him.

I swung round fast, firing immediately, but at least one of them fired too and I felt myself being blown backwards by an intense, unstoppable force. I went down hard, the gun flying away out of sight, and lay on the floor, my head down, suddenly finding it very hard to move.

I let out a low moan and rolled over. Both guards were lying injured on the floor, clearly out of action. But unfortunately so was I.

For a few moments I didn't move, the shock of my injury knocking me temporarily off-kilter. Then I looked down and saw blood seeping through my shirt in a rough circle, a few inches below my heart. It hurt. It hurt bad. I felt round my back, looking for the exit hole, and found a big hunk of flesh missing. It was hard to know how seriously I'd been wounded. There was plenty of blood, but I was still conscious.

From my prone position, I saw a pair of patent leather loafers coming towards me and then I was grabbed by the hair and yanked round so that I was staring up at Alastair Sheridan's face as he crouched down beside me, pushing the pistol into my face.

But this time his tears were gone and he was grinning intensely, his eyes alive with a dark, manic joy. 'Now I've got you, you fuck. Just you and me. I'm going to let you bleed for a bit then, when you're nice and weak, I'm going to cut you slowly into little pieces, and while I do it, I'm going to tell you all about how we killed your little friend Dana.' His grin grew wider. 'How we listened to her scream and scream until we'd snuffed out her worthless little life. Because that's what her life was to us. Worthless. Like all the others.' He pushed the gun into my face harder, barely able to suppress his intense excitement as he revelled in who he really was, free from the gaze of the outside world.

In this small space, deep in a forest, I too saw him as he truly was. A monster. And he saw me as just one more victim in a long, long line.

We stared at each other, my teeth clenched against the hot pain that was coursing through my body. I suddenly felt terribly tired.

'You failed, Mason,' he said, taking a deep breath, his smile calmer now. 'After all this time, and at the last hurdle, you failed. How does that feel?'

'It feels . . .' I said slowly, my voice little more than a croak. 'It feels . . .'

He leaned in closer, the smile widening. 'It feels what, Mason?'

'It feels . . . like success.' And as I spoke the words, I brought up the switchblade, flicked it open, and shoved it straight up through his rib cage and into his heart.

The gun went off close to my ear but then dropped from Sheridan's hand as he wavered in his crouch, an expression of utter shock on his face as if he couldn't believe that I'd had the audacity to harm him. He fell back onto his behind, staring down at the switchblade, buried to the hilt inside him. His fingers fluttered close to the handle, touching it almost daintily, but then the hand dropped to his side, his mouth formed a small, perfectly round O, and he rolled over onto his side.

Slowly, carefully, I forced myself to my feet, taking hold of the pistol, preparing to finish him off.

But he was already gone. It was over. The Bone Field killers were all finally dead. I'd won and, amid the pain, I felt a small but palpable sense of satisfaction.

I fired a single round into his head, just to make sure, then threw away the gun, before staggering through to the kitchen where I used two handtowels tied together to form a tourniquet for my wound. I felt faint and sick, but still very much alive.

With a sigh, I made my way back down the hallway, stopping by Marco's body to take the car keys out of his pocket, before opening the front door and walking unsteadily out into the silent, peaceful night, leaving my enemies dead behind me.

Epilogue
Eight months later

Tina Boyd lay back in the hammock and stared up at the perfect azure sky, thinking about all that had happened these past few months.

Alastair Sheridan's death in an isolated mansion in Bosnia was initially treated as a national tragedy in the UK. Here was a charismatic family man and self-made entrepreneur who, for a short time, had been seen by many as the possible saviour of the dysfunctional British political system, and as a result the words of praise bestowed on him by the great and the good were effusive and plentiful.

But then, just as had happened with the fallen icon Jimmy Savile, the rumours started to surface. The house his body had been found in was owned by a company with potential links to organized crime, and the fact that there were three other bodies in the house, all those of men linked to a local criminal gang, raised more questions. As the rumours proliferated, a picture began to emerge of a man with a very dark side.

And then, when the remains of a Hungarian hiker, missing since the previous summer, were found buried in the grounds of the house, the truth finally came out: Alastair Sheridan, like Cem Kalaman, was one of the infamous Bone Field killers.

The news had a cataclysmic effect on the nation's psyche, and trust in politicians, already at a low ebb, sank even further. Sheridan's wife and child went into hiding. His hedge fund collapsed. Even those who'd been close to him, like his parliamentary colleague George Bannister, were forced to resign, so great was the taint of Sheridan.

And what of the man suspected of killing him? On the night Sheridan was believed to have died, Ray Mason was captured on CCTV receiving treatment for a gunshot injury at the Bosanes Hospital in Sarajevo. As was procedure with gunshot injuries, the police were informed, but by the time they arrived at the hospital, Mason was gone, and he hadn't been seen since, despite a huge international manhunt.

And here was the thing. The Alastair Sheridan story had everything, and the public's appetite for all the grisly details was insatiable, which was why the media were so keen to talk to Tina Boyd. Tina had been a part of the story and, although she never ended up facing any charges in relation to Ray Mason's escape, the rumours that she'd played a role refused to die away, so the big-money offers for her story came flooding in.

Usually, Tina would have turned them down flat. She was a private person who gained no joy from having her name splashed all over the news. But this time she didn't. With her business suffering, and because she had a hankering to do something different, she'd sold her story for £100,000, and given a series of interviews on the Bone Field case, and her part in it, as well as her life with the fugitive killer Ray Mason. The media were also especially interested in the part played by the assassin, The Wraith, who'd tortured Tina in a futile effort to find out her former lover's whereabouts.

In the end, Tina had become something of a hero. Brave, loyal and resilient. But being a hero didn't sit so easily with her either. She just wanted to be left alone, so, after a couple of operations on the damaged tendons in her left hand, she'd rented out her cottage and had gone travelling overseas.

She'd been gone two months now, crisscrossing first Europe, then Asia, and now the South Pacific where, for the past week, she'd been relaxing on a beach in the Cook Islands, thousands of miles from civilization. It was another gloriously sunny afternoon, with a gentle breeze coming in from a perfectly blue sea, as she got up from the hammock in front of her beach hut and strolled along the wet sand in the direction of the headland half a mile away.

In the distance, a tiny figure walked towards her, the only other person on the whole beach, and as he drew closer and lifted an arm in greeting, she smiled in recognition and waved back, thinking that however dark things became, it was still a beautiful world out there.

You just had to make the decision to leave the crap behind and go and find it.

About the Author

Simon Kernick is one of Britain's most exciting thriller writers. He arrived on the crime writing scene with his highly acclaimed debut novel *The Business of Dying*, the story of a corrupt cop moonlighting as a hitman. Simon's big breakthrough came with his novel *Relentless* which was the biggest selling thriller of 2007. His most recent crime thrillers include *Siege*, *Ultimatum*, *Stay Alive* and *The Final Minute*. He is also the author of the bestselling three-part serial thrillers *Dead Man's Gift* and *One By One*.

Simon talks both on and off the record to members of the Counter Terrorism Command and the Serious and Organised Crime Agency, so he gets to hear first hand what actually happens in the dark and murky underbelly of UK crime.

Find out more about Simon and his books online at

www.simonkernick.com

/SimonKernick

@simonkernick

ALSO BY SIMON KERNICK

WE CAN SEE YOU

You have it all. Success. A beautiful home. A happy family.

AND THEN IN A HEARTBEAT, IT'S ALL GONE.

Your daughter has been taken. The people who have her will kill her if you involve the police. You can't really rely on anyone, not even your husband. Because it seems you have enemies, too.

But remember, they can see you. And they know everything about you. Including secrets you'd hoped were buried in the distant past.

As your nightmare begins, you can be cerain of only two things: that you will do anything to get your daughter back alive.

And that time is running out...

'It will keep you breathlessly on the edge of your seat.'
Sarah Pinborough

arrow books